# DAISY ROBERTS IS DEAD

*A story of love, friendship and hope*

BY

Claire Gallagher

Copyright © Claire Gallagher 2023
This book is sold subject to the condition that it shall not, by way of trade or otherwise, be lent, resold, hired out, or otherwise circulated without the publisher's prior consent in any form of binding or cover other than that in which it is published and without a similar condition including this condition being imposed on the subsequent publisher.
The moral right of Claire Gallagher has been asserted.

This is a work of fiction. Names, characters, businesses, organisations, places, events and incidents either are the product of the author's imagination or are used fictitiously. Any resemblance to actual persons, living or dead, events, or locales is entirely coincidental.

*To mom and dad, with love.*

Thank you to my wonderful CBC friends,
without whom this novel wouldn't be what it is.

# CONTENTS

| | |
|---|---|
| Chapter One | 1 |
| Chapter Two | 6 |
| Chapter Three | 13 |
| Chapter Four | 20 |
| Chapter Five | 26 |
| Chapter Six | 33 |
| Chapter Seven | 40 |
| Chapter Eight | 46 |
| Chapter Nine | 54 |
| Chapter Ten | 59 |
| Chapter Eleven | 66 |
| Chapter Twelve | 74 |
| Chapter Thirteen | 81 |
| Chapter Fourteen | 87 |
| Chapter Fifteen | 93 |
| Chapter Sixteen | 97 |
| Chapter Seventeen | 103 |
| Chapter Eighteen | 110 |
| Chapter Nineteen | 117 |
| Chapter Twenty | 124 |
| Chapter Twenty-One | 130 |
| Chapter Twenty-Two | 135 |
| Chapter Twenty-Three | 141 |
| Chapter Twenty-Four | 149 |
| Chapter Twenty-Five | 154 |
| Chapter Twenty-Six | 159 |
| Chapter Twenty-Seven | 166 |
| Chapter Twenty-Eight | 170 |
| Chapter Twenty-Nine | 178 |
| Chapter Thirty | 184 |
| Chapter Thirty-One | 190 |
| Chapter Thirty-Two | 195 |
| Chapter Thirty-Three | 200 |

*Chapter Thirty-Four*..................................................................*206*
*Chapter Thirty-Five*..................................................................*211*
*Chapter Thirty-Six*...................................................................*216*
*Chapter Thirty-Seven*...............................................................*221*
*Chapter Thirty-Eight*................................................................*228*
*Chapter Thirty-Nine*.................................................................*234*
*Chapter Forty*..........................................................................*241*
*Chapter Forty-One*..................................................................*246*
*Chapter Forty-Two*..................................................................*253*
*Chapter Forty-Three*................................................................*260*
*Chapter Forty-Four*.................................................................*267*
*Chapter Forty-Five*..................................................................*274*
*Chapter Forty-Six*....................................................................*280*
*Chapter Forty-Seven*................................................................*286*
*Chapter Forty-Eight*................................................................*292*
*Chapter Forty-Nine*.................................................................*300*
*Chapter Fifty*...........................................................................*306*
*Chapter Fifty-One*...................................................................*312*
*Chapter Fifty-Two*...................................................................*317*
*Chapter Fifty-Three*.................................................................*323*
*Chapter Fifty-Four*..................................................................*329*
*Chapter Fifty-Five*...................................................................*336*

## Chapter One

I don't remember much about my death. A moment of panic. The screeching of tyres. An ear-shattering *bang*.

Then… nothing.

No bright light, no tunnel, no loved ones waiting to greet me, their faces smiling benevolently as they welcomed me to the afterlife. Just the high-pitched beeping of the traffic lights as they changed, signalling to pedestrians that it was now their turn to cross the junction, oblivious to the carnage before them.

Later, I would think a lot about those traffic lights. The merciless way that they had continued on with their mundane task, unwilling to pause in their relentless routine as they systematically sequenced from red to green and back again.

*They should have turned black,* I thought. *Black for mourning, black for death. Black for the colour my heart turned as the realisation hit me that I was no longer alive.*

But back then, I found myself standing next to my smashed-up VW, watching the aftermath of the crash in stunned disbelief. My body was slumped over in the driver's seat, unmoving. Sack-like. My head rested limply on the steering wheel. The mass of curly hair on top of it was darkly crimson. Blood-slick. Rain drummed on the shattered windscreen, incessantly, just inches away from my face, as if it was trying to wake me up. But it was a fruitless task; my body remained limp, unresponsive. Dead.

I took all this in almost instantly, a snapshot of a cataclysm.

The shrill scream of a young woman pierced the air, almost seeming to slice its thick, metallic weight in two. It was replaced by a deep, inhuman groaning as she stood, just feet away from the site of the impact, staring at the gruesome scene before her.

She'd been waiting to cross the road, hunched under her umbrella, a flash of colour against a sepia backdrop. She'd been minding her own business. Perhaps planning her morning, or day dreaming about the man, or woman, that she'd spent the night with. Then, in an instant, her peaceful reverie was shattered.

Her free hand was pressed tightly over her mouth, her eyes inhumanly wide, her breaths rapid. She reminded me of a frightened horse, ready to bolt.

Much later, I would wonder if she ever had flashbacks to the sight of my lifeless body hunched over the wheel, or if she suffered recurrent nightmares where my caved-in head suddenly turned and looked at her, the eyes bloodshot and staring.

But at the time, seeing the young woman's reaction, a creeping sense of horror enveloped me.

"Help me!" I screamed at her, finding my voice at last.

As if he'd heard me, the lorry driver's door flung open, bouncing back on him so that he had to catch it before it rebounded fully and hit him, trapping him against the cab. The middle-aged man, ashen and shaking, blood pouring down his face from a nasty gash on his head, which soon mixed with the rain as it ran in rivulets down his face, rushed through the downpour to my car.

*"Oh, God. Oh, Jesus. Oh, God. Oh, Jesus."* He repeated it again and again as he leaned against the vehicle after checking my neck for a pulse, as if needing its support to remain upright.

Too late. Too damn late. His futile prayer went unanswered.

Gradually, a small crowd gathered around the crumpled car, their pale, wet faces under their dripping hoods reflecting shared horror and sorrow. Two men pulled out their phones and turned away, talking into the handsets in low, urgent voices, before standing around with the rest, solemnly. Helplessly. A few people approached the stricken lorry driver, quietly, awkwardly offering comfort, and avoiding looking at the young woman resting, motionless, nearby, perhaps secretly relieved that the face was turned away from them.

Soon, the wailing sound of a siren could be heard in the distance, growing louder, louder, drowning out the ability of the bystanders to hear each other speak, until the ambulance was suddenly upon us, and the blaring cut off abruptly.

Everything seemed to pause in the quiet that followed.

Then all hell broke loose.

I attempted to talk to the paramedics when they climbed out of the emergency vehicle. I pleaded with them to help me, to save me, my panicked voice loud amongst the ensuing chaos of a dozen onlookers all trying to talk to them at once, but they couldn't see or hear me; they just rushed right through me. The sensation was unpleasant, an icy *sucking* feeling that made me feel so nauseated that I stumbled beneath the unpleasant wave that washed over me.

Numb, I stood back and watched them do their checks, a tall man and a short, stocky woman, working calmly and efficiently, their faces sombre, almost, but not quite, expressionless. Just another day at the office.

Would they return home later that day, once their shift had ended, and perhaps look at their loved ones and think about the poor young woman who'd died so tragically that morning? Would they pray? Would they thank their God that it wasn't one of them?

*They would,* I thought. *Of course they would. How could they not?*

The police arrived next, blue lights flashing, and the two uniformed men brought order to the scene as they began making the area safe and started questioning the lorry driver and witnesses. I was too distracted to pay any attention to what they said.

I followed my poor, battered body as it was placed onto a stretcher and lifted into the ambulance. Not knowing what else to do, I climbed inside and sat in a daze beside my covered corpse as it was transported to the local hospital, surrounded by sterile medical equipment, the hum of the engine the only sound.

No sirens for the already-deceased.

I was twenty-six years of age, and my life was over. I

thought of my parents' grief, and my fiancé's devastation. We had been childhood sweethearts. Bitter tears burned in my eyes, sharp and stinging, as I realised I'd never get to see the children we would have created together. They would have had my dark hair, I decided tremulously, and Ben's green eyes. Light brown skin from their mixed heritage. They would have wanted for nothing.

I wept then. For Ben, for me, for the unborn children who would have been the physical manifestation of our love. I wept beside my cooling body, as the ambulance rumbled along, wanting more than anything to be wrapped in the comforting arms of the man I had adored for more than a decade.

As I thought of Ben, the yearning that grew inside of me became so strong that I screamed a silent scream, my nails digging into my open-mouthed face. I doubled over, clutching at my chest; it was as if a hole had opened up where my heart was and I needed to seal it. Suddenly, I felt a *pop* in that exact spot, a sensation as if my body was about to turn itself inside out, and the interior of the ambulance vanished.

## *Chapter Two*

Yelling an expletive, I collapsed onto a familiar tiled floor, landing painlessly on my knees. Momentarily disorientated, and more than a little startled by the intensity of the sensation of being physically moved from one location to another, it took me a second to realise that I had somehow been transported back home. I looked around my black-and-white tiled kitchen in wide-eyed disbelief.

It was a Saturday, and Ben was supposed to be working on a report while I did the food shopping. Just a normal day. His laptop was on the breakfast bar, waiting to be utilised, but it was closed. Instead of typing out the latest market analysis of God-knows-what, he was using wooden spoons to vigorously bang pots and pans, which he'd arranged into a drum kit, while rock music blasted through the wall-mounted speakers. I recognised the band as one of his favourites.

Ben looked so incredibly vibrant, so wonderfully alive, his strong hands flashing rhythmically, his light brown hair flopping endearingly over his forehead, his pale-green eyes relaxed and carefree. I wanted to freeze the moment in time, forever, but I couldn't – the seconds ticked on, remorselessly.

As I stood watching him, I choked back a sob.

He stopped what he was doing to grab a piece of half-eaten toast off a plate, and passed wind loudly, the way that you feel entitled to do when you're on your own. Normally, I would snigger; instead, I burst into tears again.

He continued munching and banging, oblivious to my presence as I attempted to talk to him, my voice thick and almost incoherent.

*"Ben, something terrible has happened… Ben, help me… Ben, I need you… Ben, I'm sorry… Oh, my darling, I'm so sorry…"*

Gradually, my sobs subsided, and I hung around watching him for a while, my face contorted, my heart aching, as he finally turned off the music and settled down to work, a look of studious focus replacing the zealous expression that he'd worn just moments before.

*These are your last moments of living the life you've grown accustomed to,* I thought at him, shaking, as I waited with dread for the inevitable knock.

When it finally came, time seemed to slow down as Ben made his way obliviously through the bright yellow hallway with its slightly worn but still beautiful parquet flooring and opened the front door.

With a rushing sound in my ears, I watched him as if he was wading through water: his first realisation that there were two police officers standing on the doorstep; the tense set of his shoulders as he led them through to the living room; the change in his demeanour as they sombrely revealed their devastating news; the way the light in his eyes extinguished before they slowly closed, clouds blocking the sunlight. He stretched one arm out to steady himself against the frame of the doorway, where he'd remained as if knowing that he'd soon be desirous of an escape route. His head lowered as his body seemed to cave in on itself.

It was his mouth which drew my attention then, the way it twisted unnaturally, the way it was pulled tightly into a grimace but trembling slightly at the same time. It was a beautiful mouth, warm and firm, a mouth which I had loved to kiss. His lips would soften under mine, expressing all the tenderness I could ever ask for.

I never knew that lips that were capable of so much love could express such agony.

Eventually, Ben let out the breath that he'd been holding and this seemed to flip a switch so that time suddenly sped up again and sound came rushing back to me.

After the first sob, I couldn't take any more. I turned away, my eyes closing. I desperately wanted to be somewhere, anywhere other than where I was, see anything other than what I was witnessing – a good man, a strong man, the love of my life, being destroyed by the news of my death. I felt that strange inside-out sensation, my body turning in on itself, and with a *pop*, I vanished.

Stumbling, but managing somehow to stay on my feet this time, I reappeared in what appeared to be the morgue of the local hospital. I looked around as realisation dawned. The stark white space with its covered trolleys and refrigerated drawers instantly gave me the creeps, and it wasn't like I was particularly keen to see my mangled corpse, so I started wandering around the corridors, aimlessly, trying not to think too much. To feel too much.

What else could I do?

The first time I got to a closed door, I tentatively reached my hand out and *pressed* into it, thinking that I would simply attempt to pass straight through it. However, an unpleasant stream of icy cold flooded up my arm as it disappeared up to my wrist and I yanked my hand back sharply.

Feeling stupid, and more than a little sorry for myself, I stood in the empty corridor for some minutes, waiting for someone to come along and open the door so that I could sneak through, preferably while avoiding walking into them. However, it appeared that I'd found myself in the one section of the hospital that was used infrequently. Not a single person came through. I resisted the temptation to burst into self-pitying tears again.

Oh, I could see plenty of people in the adjoining corridor through the door's narrow window – doctors hurrying between patients, their expressions intense, distracted; nurses multi-tasking as they walked briskly between wards, looking tired as they presumably approached the end of their shift; and a lone cleaner wiping methodically around door handles, heading away from me, the harsh lights above reflecting off his bald head. But not one of them approached the door behind which I was waiting.

I shouted out to the cleaner, "Hey!" I don't know why – by now I had all the proof that I needed that no one could see or hear me. Oblivious, he continued on with his rhythmical chore, repeating each practised manoeuvre of his hand to sanitise the metal at each stop along the corridor, before eventually disappearing around the corner. A choreographed routine which was almost hypnotising to watch.

I thought about how I'd transported between my body and home and back again, seemingly just by the power of thought. Could I use this new power to get myself to the other side of this damn door?

I scrunched my eyes up tightly, willing myself to feel that *pop* and magically find myself where I wanted to be, but when I reopened them, nothing had changed.

*Fuck.*

Resigned, I sat down next to the wall and crossed my legs, ready to jump up the second the door began to open. I could have headed back the way I came, I suppose, but that would return me to the basement, and the dreaded morgue. I grimaced at the thought of it.

I sat there for several minutes. As the shock of my death began to wear off, I started to wonder about the afterlife. I frowned. Wasn't I supposed to be beamed off to some other place – Heaven, Hell or somewhere in between? Where were all the other ghosts? (Yes, I was actually a *ghost* now. *Jesus!*). And importantly, would I now be stuck in the jeans, hoodie and sneakers that I'd been wearing when I died for all eternity? *Thank Goodness I made the effort to shave my legs this morning,* I thought, incongruously.

Then I chided myself for my shallowness. One of the – many – weird things about being a new ghost is that you're both devastated and disbelieving at the same time, so your thoughts fluctuate between the deep and the mundane.

Deep – everything that I've ever known is over, my hopes, my dreams, my ability to receive and share love.

Mundane – did I remember to pay that bill that was overdue?

Finally, a face appeared in the narrow window of the door, and I lurched to my feet. The door swung open and a doctor began to walk through, blonde hair arranged into an elegant chignon, smart black heels clacking loudly on the hard floor. The second she was out of the way, and just before it closed automatically behind her, I twisted myself sideways and slid through the gap. The door shut with a *click* behind me. I'd made it to the other side. I felt my shoulders relax as a sense of relief washed over me.

After a couple more near-misses with closed doors, I found myself in the Accident and Emergency department and decided to sit down in an empty chair. It was fairly busy, and I had always been a people-watcher. There was an eclectic mixture of sick and injured individuals waiting to be seen by the medical staff and, in an attempt to take my mind off my melancholy predicament, I sat speculating about what their complaints were.

I felt oddly detached by this point, like everything that had taken place that morning had happened to someone else. It was as if my brain had decided to protect me by shutting down the part of it that dealt with grief.

Perhaps I was in shock.

Some of the patients' complaints were obvious – a blood-stained rag held to a cut head; a leg propped up on a chair; a child crying as he clutched at his tummy. Others were less so. I looked away from a man who was sat alone in the corner, tears intermittently dripping from his chin as he stared, expressionless, at the floor before him. He made no attempt to wipe the tears away. Eventually, he was collected by a member of staff who talked to him gently, reassuringly as he was led away.

I was just diagnosing the little boy with appendicitis when a voice at the side of me made me jump.

"Miserable day, isn't it?"

## *Chapter Three*

The accent was Jamaican. I turned to see a portly old lady looking right at me. She was wearing a purple coat and a black hat with an artificial red flower on it. I glanced around the waiting area in confusion. No one was paying us the slightest bit of attention.

"Are you talking to me?" I asked, my voice an octave higher than normal.

"Of course I'm talking to you," she frowned.

I looked out of the window, towards the busy car park. It was mid-February, and although it wasn't particularly cold that day, the sky was an ominous grey. It was still raining, as it had been persistently since the early hours of the morning. Before the crash, I vaguely remembered seeing sunlight glinting on the wet tarmac as it sneaked through a rare gap between the darkened clouds.

I opened my mouth to answer and then snapped it shut. There were more important things to discuss than the bloody weather.

"Are you…dead…too?" I questioned, looking at her uncertainly.

She snorted. "How else would I be speaking to you?"

"How did you know that *I* was?" I examined her more closely – there were no obvious signs that she was any different from the rest of the people in the waiting area.

She patted my hand. It felt completely normal – warm and soft. The human contact was comforting. "You get to be able to tell after a while," she assured me.

"Oh."

"Is it your first day?"

"Yes."

"Poor thing. So young too," she tutted. I nodded sadly.

"How long has it been for you?"

"Three years," she sighed, shifting her large rear in her seat as if trying to get more comfortable.

"Aren't we supposed to go to Heaven or somewhere?" I wondered.

She shrugged. "I'm waiting for my husband."

"Is he in the hospital?"

She nodded. "Second heart attack. I think this might be it."

"I'm... sorry?" Was that the right thing to say in such a circumstance?

She waved this away.

"What will happen when he…passes? Will you go to Heaven together? Is that how it works?" I asked, suddenly desperate to know that I wouldn't be stuck in this limbo for the rest of time.

"I guess so," she shrugged.

I looked around the room, my gaze landing on people randomly. Everyone appeared completely normal, if there is such a thing. "Where are all the other ghosts? Can you see any now?"

She glanced around then shook her head. "Most of them 'go' straight away from my experience. Only a few of us stay here for however long it takes."

"'However long it takes?' – you mean, until your partner also passes away?" I thought of my beautiful Ben – he was only twenty-seven. It looked like I had a long wait in store for me. The old lady just shrugged.

We sat in thoughtful silence for a while. I was still mixed between disbelief and acceptance. I could feel the sense of grief bubbling just under the surface of my skin but I quashed it before I allowed panic to take over.

"Shouldn't you be with your husband?" I asked eventually, hesitant.

"I'll head back to his room in a minute. I'm just taking a break. It gets depressing sitting by his bed with nothing to do but look at him lying there with all those tubes coming in and out of him, bless his heart."

I nodded in sympathy. What must it be like to see your loved one on the brink of death, unable to touch them, to comfort them? I couldn't imagine.

"What's your name, lovey?" she asked then.

"Daisy."

"I'm Leticia." She offered me her hand, and I shook it.

"You'll be wanting to know the rules I suppose," she said next, her eyebrows arched, a knowing look in her dark brown eyes.

"Rules?" I frowned.

"How all this works." She twirled her hand in the air, encompassing everything I could and couldn't see. Perhaps the whole universe.

"Well, I did try to pass through a closed door, unsuccessfully," I informed her dryly.

Leticia winced. "It's horrible, isn't it dear? You're much better off *thinking* yourself to places."

I shrugged. "I tried. It didn't work."

"You'll get used to it. You have to really *feel*, as well as think."

I thought back to my unplanned transportations, remembering the intense emotions I was experiencing at the time, and nodded my head. It made sense.

Leticia got me to practise, coaching me through the best way to channel my emotions, using visualisation techniques and memories.

"Just let the *need* and the *want* flood into your chest," she said at one point. "Picture the place you want to be and stop overthinking."

It was difficult at first, but Leticia's relaxed patience paid off. Eventually, I was zipping back and forth across the A & E department, and even went as far as a quick trip back to the morgue when I had gained enough confidence.

We sat then for a while, watching the people coming and going as they were called through the double doors by the doctors and nurses. I wondered for how many of them this trip to the hospital was to be a turning point in their lives, one they would look back on and say, "That. That was the day when everything changed." Or perhaps it would just be a blip, a small, insignificant memory, with no after-effect. An anecdote to be shared over a meal, unimportant. I pondered this for a while, then Leticia sighed, and heaved herself out of the chair. "Be seeing you, dear. Good luck."

"Bye," I murmured, and watched her vanish into thin air with a *pop*.

Suddenly, I felt very alone.

I contemplated attempting to return to the house to check on Ben, or to my parents' house to see how they were dealing with the news of my death, but I just couldn't face up to their grief in that moment. Remembering Ben's reaction, the thought of it was too overwhelming, too heart-wrenching.

I suddenly wanted to be somewhere peaceful, somewhere that didn't have the taint of death hanging over it. I yearned for space, for somewhere I could get perspective, and thought of the tranquillity of my local park. I closed my eyes and pictured it in my mind, feeling a calmness settle over my chest. I let the feeling wash over me, and tried not to panic when that inside-out sensation began to spread outward from my heart, and I folded in on myself.

When I opened my eyes, I found myself standing steadily on the bank of the park's large pond. I felt a small moment of satisfaction at my success and started walking its perimeter, replaying everything that had happened in my mind, trying to organise my crowded thoughts and emotions. I couldn't feel the rain; it passed right through me. My hair stayed dry, which is a plus to being a ghost – no more frizz.

Oblivious to my surroundings, I walked and walked, circling the moss-green water several times without getting out of breath. In fact, I wasn't sure I really needed to breathe at all – I was just doing it out of habit. I experimented with this a couple of times, and while it did indeed seem that breathing was no longer a necessity, the sensation of not doing so was uncomfortable and I just couldn't get used to it.

After some time, the rain stopped, and once I'd completed a few more laps, I got fed up of walking and decided to sit down on a bench and watch the ducks and swans for a while. There was a dark-haired man of around thirty already sitting at one end of the wooden seat when I made my way over to it. He was dressed for jogging, and I concluded that he was taking a break from exercising. I shuddered. I'd always hated running.

It was peaceful sitting by the pond, watching the birds bobbing their heads into the water as they searched for food, creating circles of ripples that reduced to nothing as they spread further away from the source of disruption, the surface gradually becoming smooth and still once again. *Those ripples will be like the memory of my existence,* I thought, *gradually fading away over time, eventually non-existent, as if I'd never been here.*

I suddenly felt very small.

I sat for a while longer, brooding, until a few people who must have been waiting for the rain to stop showed up – dog walkers with eager canines pulling desperately at their leads;

parents and children who'd come to feed the ducks, chattering happily; an elderly couple strolling hand-in-hand in their wellies, content to meander in silent companionship; and a middle-aged man who stopped to photograph the wildlife, his shoulders hunched as he held the camera up before him and positioned it for the best shot. I wondered how everything could seem so normal, when my whole world had been turned upside down.

The photographer turned and made his way over to the bench, and I quickly jumped up and moved out of his way. I didn't want him sitting on (in? through?) me. He took my place, and I lingered for a moment, watching as he pulled a sandwich out of his bag and started munching on it, ignoring the man in the joggers as he in turn ignored him.

It's funny how we do this. We willingly share the same moment in time and space with another person, an unusual and precious experience when you consider that there are over seven billion people living on the planet, and that billions more have gone before us, but for some reason we refuse to engage with them. *This moment in time will soon pass,* I thought, *and they'll each go their separate ways, perhaps never to cross paths again. And yet they make nothing of this encounter.* I brooded over this for a few moments and then decided with a deep breath that it was time to face the music.

## *Chapter Four*

Back at the house, after another successful transportation, which I had achieved by drawing on the intensity of my love for Ben, I discovered my parents sitting on the sofa, holding hands. The sofa was a cheerful shade of orange, and it seemed out of place in the heavy atmosphere of sorrow which now smothered the house like a fire blanket, extinguishing all possibility of hope and joy.

The sight of my parents made my heart ache. I wanted to throw myself into my dad's arms, and for Mum to tell me soothingly that everything was alright. That this was all just a bad dream. Instead, I just stood there in the middle of the living room, which was vibrantly alive with all of the potted plants that I had so lovingly nurtured, another sharp contrast to the pall of death which hung over the house. My breath hitched.

My mum had a sodden tissue crumpled in her hand, and she intermittently wiped at her eyes as fresh tears spilled over, smudging her mascara. Her chin-length blonde hair was dishevelled, and she had a stunned expression on her face. My dad's eyes were bloodshot, and his dark brown skin had a sickly pallor to it. He sat staring into space. They didn't talk.

The sound of a spoon rattling in a mug emanated from the kitchen, and a minute later Ben came through carrying three cups of tea. He always needed to do something with his hands when he was experiencing a strong emotion. He put the cups down on the coffee table, and sat down heavily on the armchair. He looked older, ill. His light brown hair was tousled, as if he'd been repeatedly running his hands through it. The flesh around his eyes was puffy and his face was pale, his lips dry and cracked.

"I'm so sorry," I told them softly as I stood before them, shaking with the force of my grief, but of course, they couldn't hear me. I felt a sudden burst of frustrated anger and kicked out at the coffee table, hard. My foot passed straight through it and that unpleasant cold sensation spread up to my calf. Afterwards, I stood there breathing heavily, almost gasping. It was the only sound in the silent room, but I was the only one who could hear it.

They remained in that frozen tableau for an indeterminate amount of time, while the tea grew cold and the clock ticked its way steadily into the next hour. The only change was when Ben put his head in his hands, and his shoulders started shaking. He was strangely silent during this episode. I watched him, helplessly, blinking back tears while wringing my hands and pacing back and forth across the small space while Mum rubbed his back and leaned her head against his.

It took the door bell ringing to galvanise them into action. Ben jumped up like he'd been electrocuted and stumbled through to the hallway, and Mum took a shaky breath and began dabbing more vigorously at her eyes. Dad wiped his hand down his face and sat up straighter.

We heard the door opening and then my best friend, Vicky, was rushing into the room, her straight black hair wildly tangled, her long red coat flapping. My parents stood up and they all clutched at each other, and the sound of fresh sobbing filled the air. Ben joined the group and Vicky opened her arms for him. I couldn't take any more, and schooled myself to transport back to the now-desperately-appealing anonymity of the hospital. Anything to get away from the weight of their grief, which pressed down on me, almost suffocating in its intensity and threatening to consume me.

\*

I hung out at the hospital for a while. It was evening by now, and the A & E department was starting to get busier. A few drunks were already making their presence felt, their voices loud and obnoxious, their unpredictability unsettling some of the other patients, who sat eyeing them warily out of the corner of their eyes, their bodies tense as if they were prey animals preparing to flee from a predator.

I sat in on a few consultations, like a voyeur, and they were a welcome distraction from envisioning what was happening back at my house. Guilt gnawed at me for not being there, like maggots feasting on a corpse, but there was nothing I could do for them now. Selfishly, I couldn't face being a witness to their suffering.

I've always had a tendency to avoid difficult times.

To allow more time to pass, I decided to visit Leticia. As soon as I thought of her, allowing emotion to flood my chest – this time the strong need that I had for human interaction – I found myself at her side. We were in a private room, and her husband was exactly as she'd described him – lying on the bed, motionless, with tubes sticking out all over him.

"Hello, dear," Leticia said, with little surprise evident in her voice.

"Hello," I whispered.

She tutted. "You don't need to whisper – you can't disturb him."

"Oh yes." I blushed, or at least I would have, if I could. "How is he?"

"The same." She patted his hand.

"What's his name?"

"He's Derek." His name was like a caress on her lips. I felt a warmth radiate from where my heart should have been beating.

"You've been married a long time?" I asked.

"Fifty-two years."

"Wow." No wonder she was waiting for him.

We sat in companionable silence for a while. The only sounds were the beeping of the heart monitor and the hissing of the respirator which was keeping Derek alive, forcing his chest to rise up and down, up and down.

"Can I ask what you've been doing with yourself for the past three years?" I asked her eventually, in a tentative voice. I wasn't sure of the etiquette in these circumstances.

She looked at me in surprise. "Keeping Derek company."

I frowned in confusion. "But he can't see or hear you, can he?"

She sucked her teeth. "Of course not, but that doesn't mean that *I* can't see and hear *him*. He talks to me all the time."

"Oh." I paused. "What…what does he say?"

"Oh, he talks about all sorts of things – the weather, what's on the television, what he's going to cook for dinner, who he saw at the bookies." She chuckled. "In fact, I think he enjoys being able to talk to me without being interrupted."

I smiled, and she looked at me closely, her eyes knowing. "What about *your* family, dear? Shouldn't you be with *them* now?"

I hesitated. "I can't face their grief."

She nodded and patted my hand, and the feel of the momentary contact lingered, awakening the skin and leaving a pleasant echo of sensation that lasted for several seconds. I hadn't realised how much I needed the human contact. "It's hard at first," she told me. "It does get easier though."

We lapsed into silence again.

When a nurse bustled into the room to tend to Derek, I decided that it was time to go. I said goodbye to Leticia and she smiled and told me to come visit again, assuming they would still be there. Smiling gratefully, I promised that I would.

I meandered around the hospital for another hour or so, and witnessed my first death. It was an old lady, her skin almost translucent, her body emaciated, her cheeks sunken with age, mummy-like, and she couldn't be resuscitated. I can't describe the moment of her passing, only that the poignancy of seeing a life ending touched me in the same way that witnessing a birth would. It felt special, like a privilege. A lump formed in my throat as she took her last breath.

Moved beyond words, I waited for the old lady's ghost-form to appear at her bedside, but it never did. She must have gone wherever it is that we end up immediately, like Leticia said happens to most people when they die. I wondered why this hadn't happened to Leticia, or myself. Most people had a partner to wait for when they passed, yet most people apparently 'went' straight away. What was so different about us?

Just before midnight, I returned to the house. My parents and Vicky had gone, and Ben was lying on our bed, fully dressed, with the light on. His hand was stretched out to rest on my pillow, where a single hair remained. I lay down beside him, so that my head was below his arm, and gazed up into his handsome face. His eyes were glazed over as he stared at my smiling photograph which was angled towards him on his bedside table; he was completely expressionless as he looked at it.

We lay like that all night. He didn't sleep a wink.

## *Chapter Five*

The next morning, Ben didn't get up until someone knocked on the door for the third time. Like a robot, he sat up and turned slowly to put his feet on the floor, before rising stiffly and crossing the room. The machine-like effect was ruined as he tripped and caught hold of the door frame though. He took a second to steady himself and then carried on through the house and down the stairs to the front door. I closed my eyes against the painful evidence of the effect of my passing.

I heard my brother, Charles's, voice, so I made my way down to the entrance hall. I found them clasped in a tight embrace, my sister-in-law, Beth, behind them with one hand resting on Charles's shoulder and the other dabbing at her blue eyes with a tissue. They must have got up early to make the three-hour drive from the town where they lived, I realised, feeling intensely grateful. Tears pricked at my eyes as I watched my loved ones comforting each other, the bond between them unmistakeable.

Eventually, Ben and Charles pulled apart, and Ben led them into the living room. I debated with myself about whether I could face staying to witness another round of grieving, but although it appeared that I didn't need sleep anymore, the night had worn me out emotionally. I needed a break. With barely any consideration, I channelled my emotions and transported myself back to the park. It got easier every time.

It wasn't raining that day, but the sky remained a palette of soft greys. I stood watching the gossiping ducks and geese, safe and secure in their micro-world and oblivious to human suffering. I tried not to think about the scene that must be taking place back at my house – the retelling of the events of the previous morning, the expressions of shock and sorrow. The tears. The 'if onlys'. Then, out of habit more than any need to sit down, I turned to make my way over to the bench. To my surprise, the same jogger was sat in exactly the same place as yesterday. *Blimey, he's dedicated,* I thought, as I took a seat at the opposite end to him.

Knowing that he couldn't see me, I studied his profile. He had thick, heavy eyebrows, a straight nose with slightly flared nostrils and dark stubble lining his jaw. He was rather good-looking, I realised now that I was examining him more closely.

"Why are you staring at me?" he suddenly burst out in an Irish accent. I jumped.

"Shit! You scared me!" I put my hand over where my heart should have been pounding. He turned to face me.

"You again." He frowned and pursed his lips as if he'd eaten something sour. He turned back to face the pond.

"Are…are you a ghost?" I asked foolishly. He rolled his eyes and didn't answer. "Why didn't you speak to me when I was here yesterday?"

"Why would I?"

"I don't know – isn't there a form of ghost etiquette or something?"

He sighed.

"How long have you -"

"This is *my* bench."

My eyebrows shot up. "*Your* bench?"

"*Mine*. And I don't like sharing."

I stared at him in amazement. "But this is a public park!"

He didn't answer, but his jaw clenched subtly.

"What happened to y-"

"Look. I want you to go, alright? I don't like talking to people."

I sat gazing at him in disbelief and he suddenly turned to face me again. "*Buzz! Off!*" he shouted, his face contorted with rage, and I decided to make like a tree, asap.

I returned to the house.

Ben had made more tea, and the three of them were sat around, talking quietly. At least, Charles and Beth were; Ben was staring into space, nodding occasionally to what they were saying, but each time he did, it was slightly too late. I noticed Charles look at Beth in concern, his brown eyes pinched behind his black-rimmed glasses.

"Why don't we all go for a walk? Get some fresh air?" Charles suggested, putting his cup down on the coffee table with a gentle clank. Ben didn't move.

"I'll get your coat, love," Beth said, brushing her dark hair back off her face before standing up and heading out into the hallway. Charles patted Ben's knee.

When she returned with his jacket, Ben stood up automatically and allowed Beth to hold it open for him so that he could put his arms through the sleeves, like a child. The sight made my heart clench.

"Have you got your keys, mate?" Charles asked gently. A look of confusion crossed Ben's face, and then he was patting his pockets, before nodding jerkily.

I followed them out of the house, slipping my hand into Ben's as we walked. He didn't react, and I couldn't feel anything, but the gesture gave me comfort. I thought of other days, other walks, when we would stroll these streets, usually in the evenings after dinner if the weather was fine. We would chat about our day with no distractions, touching, always touching.

Charles and Beth made small talk as we headed down the quiet street, their breaths frosting like wispy apparitions in the cold air, but if you asked me now, I couldn't remember a single thing that they said. I was too busy looking at Ben's face, while my heart broke into tiny pieces.

As you can imagine, I wasn't paying any attention to which direction we were headed in, and when I finally realised that I was back at the park, it was too late. Grumpy Irishman had spotted me and was glaring at me from his perch on the bench. For a split second, I contemplated disappearing, but I didn't want to leave Ben like this. Stubbornly, I stuck my chin out and stared back in defiance, and he snorted in disgust and turned back to face the pond. Triumphantly, I carried on walking with my family.

We skirted the perimeter of the pond a couple of times, and all the while Grumpy Irishman studiously ignored us as he scowled fiercely at the murky water.

After a while, I forgot about his presence; I was too engrossed in spotting the early signs of spring that were emerging. Crocuses and snowdrops were sprouting out of the grass in patches of multi-coloured chaos, and daffodil blades were already pointing at the pale grey sky. This was usually my favourite time of year. I loved this season of re-birth after the long winter – the new leaves unfurling on the skeletal trees; the pink-white blossoms that would soon drift lazily in the breeze; the tulips that would burst open like elegant crinoline skirts. How ironic that my death would coincide with the emergence of so much new life.

If only I had known that the previous spring would be my last. That I'd experienced my final summer of feeling the sun kiss my skin. My last Bonfire Night inhaling the pungent smoke and the acrid scent of gunpowder as my breath fogged in the frosty air and the crisp leaves crunched under my boots. My last Christmas dinner. My last Valentine's Day, only two days before. What would I have done differently?

Would I have appreciated these special times more? Would I have lived in the moment to a greater extent, seeing, hearing, smelling, feeling the world around me, absorbing the wonderful *aliveness* of everything?

*I would,* I thought. *Of course I would.*

My wistful musing was interrupted by Charles urging everyone to take a break. He led us over to a bench which was positioned diagonally opposite to Grumpy Irishman's, on the other side of the pond. I stood awkwardly as the three of them filled the available space.

They sat in silence for a few moments, and then Ben put his head in his hands and started sobbing. It was quiet at first, hardly noticeable, but it gradually grew louder. He was sat between Charles and Beth, and they put their arms across his shoulders, which were heaving.

I knelt down before him, and put my hands on his jean-covered thighs as I stared up into his beloved face, feeling my own contorted with reflected pain. Beth pulled out a wad of tissues from her coat pocket, keeping one for herself before passing the rest along. The three of them sat wiping their faces, but the tears they removed were only replaced with fresh ones. *Like their grief is dying and being reborn,* I thought, *reincarnating over and over again, unceasing in its hold on them.*

I felt a hand on my shoulder, and I turned in surprise to see Grumpy Irishman behind me. We made brief eye contact before Ben made a strangled noise, and I turned back to him without otherwise acknowledging the other ghost. The five of us remained frozen like that for what seemed like hours, but in reality, it could only have been a few minutes. Gradually, the crying subsided, and I felt the hand on my shoulder disappear.

They must have been starting to get cold then, because Charles suggested that they'd best be heading back. I put my hand in Ben's again as we started walking, wishing I could feel the brush of his jacketed arm against mine; such a simple thing, but already so sorely missed.

When I looked across the pond, Grumpy Irishman was back to scowling at the water. He didn't acknowledge our departure.

## Chapter Six

Back at the house, Beth made Ben a sandwich, which he attempted to eat, but it was clear that he had difficulty swallowing it and he left most of it untouched. He looked exhausted, his eyes shadowed and strained, his face pale, and Charles, who was observing him closely, encouraged him to return to bed.

"Get some rest, mate," he told him, and Ben nodded gratefully, then saw them out. I watched him climb the stairs heavily and listened as the bedroom door shut softly.

Restless, I contemplated going to my mum and dad's, which is where Charles and Beth were almost certainly heading, but I decided to check in with Leticia first. To be honest, I needed to see a friendly face, to interact with someone instead of being a mere passive observer of grief, lonesome in my isolated state of existence.

She was sitting at Derek's bedside, exactly where I'd left her, and I wondered if she'd had a break since I'd first met her in A & E. She looked so tired – her shoulders were slumped, her eyes strained. After greeting her quietly and asking how Derek was ("No change"), I suggested we go for a walk around the hospital.

"No thank you, dear," she said in a kind voice but with a melancholy undertone. "The doctor's coming soon. It's nearly time."

I nodded and put my hand on her shoulder briefly, before murmuring goodbye, and vanishing.

*

I arrived at my parents' house just before Charles and Beth. I found my mum and dad looking up local funeral directors on the internet and talking quietly to each other about coffins and flowers, music and eulogies. I glanced over their shoulders, but to be honest I wasn't really interested in the different types of eco-coffin that my body could be burned in. It wasn't something that I wanted to think about. Who would?

The doorbell rang then and my dad got up to let my brother and his wife in. They all hugged and cried again and I was hit by a feeling of guilt so intense that it took my breath away. I was left feeling sick and shaky, and I think I would have vomited if I was able to.

The ever-present tea was produced and they all sat around quietly discussing the administration of death – registering the passing, the funeral arrangements, notifying the rest of my family and friends and my work colleagues, sorting my finances out. The list was seemingly endless. Surprisingly, they seemed relieved to have all of these things to organise; I guess it was a distraction from thinking about the reason why it was necessary. Having never grieved for someone, it wasn't something that I was expecting.

Eventually, I left them to it. I found myself thinking back to the site of the crash, feeling curious about the place of my death now that the immediate panic had passed, and instantly I was there. I looked around. They had cleared up well – whoever 'they' were – there was no sign of any detritus remaining from the accident.

*What a job,* I thought. *What a terrible job, to have to clean up a death-scene.*

I stood on the pavement under the wide grey sky, watching the traffic flow past me in both directions, oblivious to the event that had taken place there only the day before. The only evidence that something had happened was a few bunches of fresh flowers tied to a nearby lamppost – their pretty pastel colours loud against the dull background of the junction, their beauty contrasting with the ugliness of the scene that they memorialised – and a police sign that asked for any witnesses to contact them. *How quickly time moves on* I thought then, my eyes watering.

I sat down on the grass verge and crossed my legs, unable to feel the cold dampness of the lingering frost which still glistened crisply on the green blades. I suppose I could have sat in the middle of the road – it wouldn't have made any difference – but I still had that ingrained sense of avoiding danger, even when I knew logically that there was none. I thought back to the accident, trying to remember exactly how it had come about, but it was all a vague blur. Oh, the aftermath was sharp in my memory. I could re-play it in my head, film-like, but the minutes and seconds leading up to it were faded into the mists of time.

*This is the last place I was alive,* I thought, and my heart felt like a stone in my chest. I felt tears pool once again in my eyes.

*Enough now!* I told myself angrily, dashing my hand over my wet cheeks. *What's done is done and there's no changing it back. Stop feeling sorry for yourself! Pull yourself together! People die every day. It's time to accept the fact that it was your time. That's all. It was just your time.*

I stayed there for a few hours longer, becoming hypnotised by the traffic, before returning to the house. Ben was still in bed, but wide awake, and I wondered if he had managed to get any sleep at all. I lay down beside him, and the night passed slowly as I stroked his face and whispered to him of how much I loved him.

\*

On Monday, my parents collected Ben and drove to the funeral home. I hung around, bored, meandering around the large room and absorbing the sight of the floral displays and other attempts that the staff had made to make the purpose of the building seem less depressing than the reality, while they met with the funeral director and discussed their requirements.

My mum and dad took the lead; Ben stayed mostly silent. He nodded along with their suggestions whenever they asked for his opinion, but it was unclear whether he was actually aware of what he was agreeing to. Ben was an only child. His parents lived in Spain, and I was glad to hear that they were flying over the next day. He was starting to seriously worry me.

To my relief, Mum and Dad practically ordered Ben to return to their house when the appointment was over and he went along compliantly, following them through the car park like a lost puppy. Meanwhile, I was drawn back to the hospital to see how Derek was doing.

I thought myself back to his room, half-expecting the two of them to be gone and a new patient to be in Derek's place in the bed, but I found him to be exactly the same as I'd left him the day before. Leticia's chair, however, was empty. I watched Derek's chest lifting up and down for a while, listening to the heart monitor's regular high-pitched beeps to reassure myself that he was still alive, before heading down to the A & E department.

Leticia was sat in a different chair, but I spotted her distinctive hat through the crowd. There was an empty seat next to her, so I made my way over to it and plonked myself down.

"Hi, Leticia."

"Hello, deary," she smiled, her eyes twinkling tiredly.

"Still no change?"

"No. He's a stubborn one. Always has been."

"He's a man," I said knowingly.

"Hmm mmm," she nodded, rolling her eyes at me. I giggled. "You're waiting for your gentleman too, aren't you?" she added more seriously after a pause.

I sighed. "He's not doing too well."

"No. It's hard for them at first. It will get easier." She patted my hand as she said this. The grandmotherly gesture was like hot chicken soup for my soul. "How are *you* doing, dear?" she asked, looking at me closely, kindly.

I shrugged, trying to remain stoic. "It's easier for me. I still get to see everyone." She nodded in understanding. "I met another ghost yesterday," I added, after a pause.

"Oh? Yes, you see them around now and again."

"He wasn't as nice as you. He told me to 'buzz off'."

"Poor soul," she tutted.

"'Poor soul'?" I repeated in amazement. "I think he might have been the rudest man I've ever met."

"There's always more to the story when people behave like that. Things are never black and white," she told me, with a wise look.

I thought back to when Grumpy Irishman had put his hand on my shoulder when I was crying, and felt bad. What *was* his story, anyway?

I decided to change the subject. "How did you and Derek meet?"

She smiled nostalgically, her eyes softening. "It was at a dance hall. When I first laid eyes on him, he was dancing with another girl. I thought he was the most elegant man I'd ever seen."

"And then he saw you?" I smiled.

She nodded. "And that, as they say, was that."

I sighed. I thought back to the day when I'd started Sixth Form College and had first encountered Ben. It had been like that for us too – an instant connection, a spark, immediate knowledge that *this* was the one.

*How lucky I was,* I thought. *So very, very lucky.*

We continued to chat, comfortable in each other's company, and I heard anecdotes about their life together that made me alternately chuckle and sigh: the time he'd won the pools and had run out into the street shirtless, waving the paper slip around and whooping in delight; when she'd got jealous of him flirting with the lady who worked the counter at the bookies and had locked him out of the house; the birth of their first child.

All too soon, Leticia decided it was time to return to Derek's bedside. I joined her for a while, and we sat in quiet companionship watching his chest rise up and down, up and down.

One thing that being a ghost certainly teaches you is patience.

## Chapter Seven

When I returned to the house, I discovered that Ben was back home. He was sitting on the sofa. The TV was on, but I could tell that he wasn't really watching it. He looked so lost and alone, it broke my heart.

Just as I was getting settled in for an evening of joining him in staring at the television, a knock sounded at the front door. Ben heaved himself up out of the chair and sluggishly made his way through to the entrance hall. I peered around the living room doorway and saw Vicky standing on the threshold clutching two bottles of wine, her scarlet coat bright against the darkness of the street.

"Come on – let's get pissed," she told him in a firm voice.

He opened the door wider and she stepped into the house. He was silent as he led her through to the kitchen and she poured the pinot into two glasses as she prattled on about her day – she'd spent the whole day in bed looking through old photo albums and crying copiously before deciding that alcohol and a friend to weep with was what was needed. She eventually got a chuckle out of him when she reminded him of the photo of a group of us re-enacting The Beatles' Abbey Road album cover during a trip to London. It made me smile too.

They headed through to the living room, and Ben gradually became more talkative as the alcohol took effect and Vicky reminisced about the past. He joined in with some of the stories, and added his own. The time we were on holiday in Corfu and I was mortified when my bikini top fell down in front of a group of teenaged boys, who had cheered and clapped. When I'd performed karaoke for the first and only time, my voice off-key and shaky with nerves. When I had my first job interview after I'd qualified as a teacher and I threw up over the Headteacher's meticulously organised desk. We were all soon laughing. Seeing Ben's face light up was like a ray of hope in the darkness, and for the first time I knew that he was going to be alright.

I don't know if it was the effect of the alcohol or if the conversation had been therapeutic for him, or if he was just plain exhausted by this time, but Ben slept that night. I lay beside him again, listening to him snore and feeling nostalgic for the new memories that we'd never create together. Happy memories, funny memories. I braced myself for the years to come – years of watching his recollections of me gradually fade, as he had new experiences, made new memories, without me.

*

Ben's parents arrived the next day. I hung around while they consoled him and talked quietly about the funeral arrangements, but when his mum noticed that there was hardly any food in the house and she announced that they should all go to the supermarket, I decided to take a break. I could only handle his mum in small doses at the best of times.

I checked in with Leticia and Derek, then, restless, I

headed to see what was happening at work. I was an English teacher at the local Comprehensive school and I was curious to see how the news of my death had been received and who was covering my classes.

I thought myself into my third-period year-eight class. A supply teacher was covering the lesson, but she looked more than a little frazzled. She was trying to explain the past perfect tense, but the kids weren't paying her a blind bit of notice. Instead, they sat chatting and throwing things at each other. I frowned as I noticed a girl whose behaviour was usually exemplary launch a pencil at a boy on the other side of the room. The supply teacher pretended not to see it.

Unable to watch any more, I vanished, and reappeared in the staff room. It was quiet. There were only a few members of staff sat marking books during their free period, including one of my friends, Amy. The two of us had been Newly Qualified Teachers together and had bonded immediately over first-day nerves.

When I looked more closely, however, I noticed that although she had a pen in her hand and an exercise book open in front of her, the page covered in the looping handwriting of an adolescent girl, the i's dotted with hearts, Amy wasn't really looking at it. She was sat staring down at the table, her wavy auburn hair forming a private curtain around her pale face.

I sat by her side until the lunch bell rang and more staff started flooding into the room. The noise of their chatter filled the air, together with the hum and regular *ping* of the microwave and the repeated boiling of the kettle, but Amy remained unchanged. Eventually, one of our colleagues, Bal, took a cup of coffee over to her and sat down on the other side of her. He talked to her softly, and she started wiping her eyes. They hugged, and he said something I didn't catch that made her chuckle.

I smiled. I'd always liked Bal – I'd also suspected for a long time that he had a crush on Amy, but she was too shy to give him any encouragement and so he'd never made a move. *Go on, guys,* I thought. *Life's too short. Let my death be the thing that finally breaks down that barrier between you.*

I watched them for a while and then took a walk around the school. After wandering around the nearly empty corridors, I decided to take a look behind the tennis courts. The staff had long held suspicions that the kids were getting up to something back there, but we'd never been able to catch them. I thought myself there, and found myself in the middle of a large group of year ten and elevens. A cloud of cigarette smoke curled into the air, dissipating above their heads, and I'd have been coughing violently if I was alive. On the side lines of the group, two couples were snogging without seeming to need to come up for oxygen, and there was some kind of exchange happening in the corner, of what I couldn't make out.

Suddenly, there was a whistle from one of the boys and the group scattered. A minute later, the Assistant Head, Dan, appeared around the side of the tennis court, his eyes scanning like search lights. But he was too late. I couldn't help a small chuckle at the kids' organisational skills, and hoped that they would one day put them to better use. Who didn't break the rules a few times when they were teenagers? I thought back to my own youth, and some of the antics I'd got up to with my friends. *Keep running, kids,* I willed them. *I hope they never catch you.*

\*

I checked in on Ben and his parents (his mum had roped him into giving the house a spring clean in what I *think* was her way of trying to distract him, but I may be being generous) then returned to school to sit in on a few of the afternoon lessons. Amy's teaching style was calm and methodical; Bal was lively and entertaining; some staff were surprisingly lax, while others seemed overly strict; very few lessons were boring however, and I was rather proud of my team of colleagues by the time the bell rang to signal the end of the day. I watched the students pour out of the exits, like ants out of an ant hill, chattering loudly and relishing their long-awaited freedom from another full day of being expected to sustain high concentration levels and follow stringent rules.

I'd been debating with myself as to what to do next all day, but finally I decided to bite the bullet. Deciding that I needed as many friends as I could get, I braced myself for a return to the park.

Surprise, surprise, Grumpy Irishman was sat on the bench, scowling down at the darkly-green water. He didn't look up as I made my way over to him.

"May I sit down?"

He shrugged, and I took that as permission.

We sat watching the birds feed and fight among themselves. The geese were particularly aggressive. A few dog walkers strolled past, but none of them stopped. The day was too blustery for them to want to sit down and take-in the scenery.

"I wanted to thank you, for yesterday," I finally uttered.

"You're welcome," he answered stiffly after a pause.

"Why… why do you sit here day after day?" I mustered the courage to ask.

"That's my business," he snapped.

"Fair enough."

We sat for a while longer without speaking, then I vanished.

## Chapter Eight

I returned home to find Deirdre, Ben's mum, cooking a roast dinner, her face pinkening in the steam as she opened the oven door to check on the sizzling meat that I was unable to smell, while his dad, Phil, droned on at him about the rental market in Benalmádena. At least they were distracting him and making sure that he ate.

I stayed with them for the rest of the evening, while they ate quietly and watched a game show, then retired to bed with Ben. He was back to not sleeping again though, and he shifted about restlessly before finally getting up again at around one a.m. and plodding down to the lounge. He left the light off and turned the TV on, muting it before switching to the 24-hour news channel and putting the subtitles on. Then he lay on the sofa staring at it until he finally nodded off for half an hour at around three o'clock. After which, he woke with a jerk and looked around in disorientation.

*My poor darling,* I thought sadly, my heart crumbling as I watched him. *What have I done to you?*

He didn't move until his mum came downstairs at seven-thirty and started fussing about how he'd spent the night on the sofa. She bustled him off to have a shower and he went without argument. I hung around for a few hours while they went through their morning routines. My parents arrived at ten and they sat drinking tea and discussing the funeral arrangements with Deirdre and Phil while Ben sat in silence.

When Mum and Dad left after lunch, Ben announced quietly that he needed a nap. I followed him up the stairs and was pleased when he nodded off almost as soon as his head hit the pillow. I smiled to see his face softened in sleep, the lines of grief relaxing in slumber, and wished that I could tuck the bed cover around him more securely.

While he slept, I decided to go and see how Derek was doing.

When I arrived in his room, I discovered a small group clustered around his bed. There was a middle-aged couple and two teenagers. Leticia was sat in a chair in the corner.

"Your family?" I asked softly.

She nodded. "He had another attack early this morning."

"I'm sorry."

"It's hard to see him suffer so, but he will soon be released from this mortal coil."

I nodded and put my hand on hers, then sat down on the floor with my legs crossed and leaned back against the wall. We sat listening to the family murmur to each other.

"What do you think Heaven's like?" I finally uttered quietly.

"'He will wipe away every tear from their eyes, and death shall be no more, neither shall there be mourning, nor crying, nor pain anymore, for the former things have passed away'," she answered fervently.

"The Bible?"

She nodded. "Revelation."

"That's beautiful."

"'There will be no more night,' she continued. 'They will not need the light of a lamp or the light of the sun, for the Lord God will give them light. And they will reign forever and ever.'"

We were quiet then. I'd never been particularly religious, but the words were comforting. Or maybe it was just Leticia's calm presence that soothed me.

I stayed for a couple of hours, watching as the family took their leave, taking turns to rest their hand on Derek or lean down to tenderly kiss his slack cheek, and then headed back home. Vicky was there again, and she was trying to persuade Ben to go to the pub with her. He was reluctant, but eventually he agreed. Vicky waited while he changed out of the baggy sweatpants and stained t-shirt that he'd been wearing.

I followed them down the road to our local. It was already dark, the crescent moon hanging like a silver ornament in the sky, and the wind blew hard enough for them to pull their coats more tightly around themselves, but I felt nothing.

It was a Wednesday, and fairly quiet in the pub. It was the sort of place that had daily regulars – usually older men who liked to drink on their own while reading the newspaper or watching sport on the big TV. I spotted a few of them as I hung back while Ben and Vicky ordered their drinks at the bar.

"Alright, love?" one of the men suddenly said while looking right at me. He was perched on one of the stools that lined the bar. He had a bald head and a beer belly, a pleasant face with ruddy cheeks, and bright blue eyes.

"Hello," I answered cautiously. *Should I expect another kind soul like Leticia, or another miserable sod like Grumpy Irishman?* I wondered.

"I'm Dean." He held out his hand. I shook it, it was dry and firm, and said "Daisy" in return.

"New?" he asked.

I nodded.

"That's tough. It gets easier."

"So I've been told."

"Ah, you've met another one of us, have you?"

"At the hospital."

"Waiting for a loved one?"

"Yes."

"Me too." He cast a yearning look at the middle-aged barmaid who was serving Ben. She had bleached blonde hair and she was wearing a low-cut top which revealed her ample cleavage. Her face was made up immaculately, and her lip-sticked smile lit up the room.

"Your wife?" I asked, looking at her curiously.

He shook his head sadly. "No, but I always wanted her to be."

"It didn't happen?"

He sighed. "Came here for years, and never told her how I felt. Then I had my heart attack and here we are."

"That's a shame," I said sympathetically. At least Ben and I'd had our ten years together. Ten years in the knowledge of our mutual love. What would it be like to die never having experienced the beauty of sharing your feelings and your life with the one you desired more than any other?

While I was pondering this, an unassuming man appeared at our side and made to sit on Dean's stool.

"Not that seat!" the barmaid snapped, and the man hurried timidly to another.

"Can she see you?" I asked incredulously, my eyes wide.

He chuckled. "No, but I always sat on this stool and she won't let anyone else have it."

"Wow," I said in awe.

He nodded proudly, then asked, "So what's your story?"

"I'm waiting for my fiancé." I gestured over to where Ben was now sat down at a table with Vicky. They were talking in low voices between sips of their drinks.

He looked over at him and frowned. "Don't take this the wrong way, love, but I hope you have a long wait."

"Me too," I said, grimacing.

He sighed. "Eight years I've been waiting, but it's been an honour to witness her living her life to the full."

"Do…do you get bored sometimes?" I asked hesitantly. Don't get me wrong, I loved Ben, but it's not like every moment of his life was riveting. Whose was?

"I do, love. That's when I go travelling."

"Travelling?" I frowned.

"Oh, aye. I've seen it all – the Eiffel Tower, the Leaning Tower of Pisa, the Statue of Liberty, the Sydney Opera House. There's a big world out there."

"I-I hadn't thought of that."

"And the beauty of it is that you can be there in an instant." He snapped his fingers. "No long-haul flights. And," he winked, "it's completely free."

I bit my lip. I didn't want to leave Ben for too long at the moment, but fifty (fingers crossed) years was a long time. Perhaps one day I would get to see all the places I had dreamed of seeing? Albeit on my own, and not with my husband as I'd always planned.

"The world'll still be there when you're ready," Dean told me, patting my hand as if he'd heard my thoughts. I nodded, and told him that I'd better re-join my friends. He smiled and told me to come and visit him again, and, as I had with Leticia, I promised that I would. He turned back to watch the rugby on the large screen as I made my way over to Ben and Vicky's table.

I listened to them talking about our college days, days when our gang of friends would gather on the sofas in the common room between lessons and drink mediocre coffee from an ancient machine, and once again Ben opened up under the influence of alcohol and Vicky's chatty manner. I was grateful to my friend for everything she was doing for him, though I sensed that she needed this as much as he did. Vicky was a force of nature, but she had a tender side that only a few select people got to witness.

We stayed for a few hours, before they decided to call it a night. I waved to Dean as we left.

\*

Ben slept again that night. I lay next to him listening to him snore. I usually found it annoying, but it was a sound I welcomed now.

At around three a.m. I began to grow restless, so I checked in with Leticia and Derek at the hospital and then curiosity drove me back to the moonlit park. I appeared some distance behind the bench. Lo and behold, I could see Grumpy Irishman's silhouette perched in exactly the same spot as usual, framed by the inky blackness of the pond. I watched him for a while, and he never moved. I wondered what he did in the daytime when someone wanted to sit in his place, and suspected that he didn't budge then either. A shiver ran down my spine.

I returned to the pub, and found myself in the darkened lounge. The chairs were all flipped upside down on the tables, the silhouetted beer taps lined up evenly behind the bar, waiting patiently for the sun to rise high in the sky, when the door would reopen and the patrons would return and they would serve their thirst-quenching purpose once again. Dean was nowhere to be seen. Perhaps he spent the nights with the barmaid, watching her sleep as I watched Ben?

Thinking of my fiancé, I decided to return home.

I found him wide awake and staring up at the ceiling. I was just settling into bed beside him when he spoke.

"I'm so *angry* with you, you know," he burst out.

I froze, and stared at him closely. He was still looking up at the ceiling. I waited to see if he would speak again.

Minutes passed, but he didn't utter another word; he just

sighed and lay his arm across his forehead. I lowered myself down until I was in my usual position next to him, and spent the rest of the night staring up at the ceiling with him, trying to remember the different stages of grief.

## *Chapter Nine*

I settled into a bit of a routine over the next couple of days. I would hang out with Ben for a few hours in the morning, and then visit the hospital to see how Derek was doing, before visiting my parents then spending the afternoon watching lessons at school, like an Ofsted inspector. After school, I would check in with Ben and then hang out for an hour or two with Dean, who I discovered to be laid back and funny, and more than a little wise.

In the evening, I would return to Leticia and Derek at the hospital. The family visited between seven and eight every night, and I got to know them and like them. Their son, Raymond, was very serious and had a scholarly air about him, but he would hold Derek's hand tenderly for the duration of their stay. Their daughter, Judith, was more overtly emotional; I liked the way that she wore her heart on her sleeve and fussed about ensuring that Derek's pillow and sheets were straight. To my surprise, the teenagers, Maisie and Luke, would sit talking quietly with the adults and watching over their grandfather respectfully; not once did I see them hunched over a screen.

At night, I lay with Ben. His mum had persuaded him to

get some sleeping pills off our GP, so he was now sleeping through until about five a.m. consistently, to my relief. The bags under his eyes were still present, but they weren't anywhere near as bad as they had been a few days earlier. I would lie beside him, watching him, listening to him breathe, and thinking over the events of the day. I was unable to sleep, but the rest seemed to do me good, emotionally if not physically.

At around three a.m., like clockwork, I would get the urge to return to the park. I would stand on the grass in the moonlight, about ten metres back from the bench, and watch Grumpy Irishman's unmoving silhouette. If he suspected my presence, he never turned to check, and I would remain there for around half an hour, silent and staring, before returning home.

*

Saturday was the one-week anniversary of my death. I still couldn't remember the details of the crash. Had I been at fault? I remembered the lorry driver – especially his repeated prayer, which echoed around my head whenever I flashed back to that fatal morning – he'd had a nasty gash on his forehead, but otherwise he'd seemed okay, at least physically. I felt an immense amount of relief about this. After a short debate with myself, I decided to pay him a visit.

As soon as I thought about him, remembered emotion from the aftermath flooding my chest as I pictured him, I was by his side. He was sitting on a garden chair behind a tired-looking, ex-council house, smoking and staring into space. An ashtray was overflowing on a small table beside him. I was glad that I couldn't smell its stale odour. The gash was now a scab with stitches still visible along its length. His eyes were sunken and his jaw and cheeks were covered with grey stubble. I was pretty sure that he'd been clean-shaven a week earlier.

"What happened?" I said to him softly, but of course, he didn't answer. From out of nowhere, I felt the sudden urge to cry.

After a minute or two, the back door opened and a middle-aged woman wearing worn slippers and an apron over her floral dress appeared with a cup of tea. Grey roots merged into brownish-red bobbed hair which hung around a worn face. She placed the cup on the table and rested her hand on his shoulder, keeping one arm across her thin chest as she shivered in the pervading chill of February.

"Why don't you come inside now, love? It's cold out here," she said quietly.

The lorry driver just shook his head, and took another drag of his cigarette without looking at her, and she frowned worriedly and opened her mouth as if to remonstrate, but decided against it. She turned and slapped back into the house, shutting the door softly behind her.

I sat down on a cracked step that led up to an untidy grassed area surrounded by tall hedges, and began playing with a loose thread that was hanging from the hem of my hoodie. It was quiet – even the birds seemed subdued. Within a few minutes, the lorry driver had finished his fag and was lighting another one.

"Those things'll kill you, you know," I told him darkly, breaking the silence.

I sat there for over an hour, while he smoked and drank

his cooling tea.

"It's my funeral on Monday," I informed him at one point. I don't know why. Perhaps I needed him to know, as if it would somehow help him to move on.

And another time: "Ben's struggling as well. But he'll be alright. And you will too. It just takes time." It occurred to me then that he might be facing a criminal prosecution, and I yanked on the thread, hard, and it broke. I watched it fall to the ground. *A ghost thread,* I thought incongruously. *Never to be carried by the wind. A permanent reminder that I was here.*

I thought about the chain of events that had to have happened to lead us both to be at that one point in space and time. We were like two skittles, positioned perfectly for the bowling ball to strike us and send our lives careering off in different directions, never to be the same again.

"If only one of us had left a few seconds earlier, or later," I murmured to him sadly. "This never would have happened." *But it did,* I thought, *and here we are.*

A sudden sense of panic filled my chest. I had a flash of Ben's face close to mine, full of concern and telling me to "Breathe, Daisy. Breathe!" and I felt an overwhelming need to escape.

Within an instant, I had vanished.

\*

Derek died that day. I turned up in his room in what had become an almost routine visit, with no expectation of any change, to find it completely empty. Even the heart monitor and respirator were gone. Momentarily surprised, I stared at the stripped-down bed. Then, just to make sure, I tried thinking myself to Leticia, but nothing happened. I remained exactly where I was. They had gone to wherever it is that we end up.

I touched the bed. "Hopefully see you again one day," I murmured, knowing how much I would miss my wise new friend. Then, feeling unsettled, as if the sun had suddenly been extinguished, leaving me in an icy darkness, I returned home to the comforting presence of my Ben.

\*

I spent most of Sunday at my parents' house. Charles and Beth were still there; they were planning to stay until the day after the funeral. Mum and Dad were holding up well, and I was less worried about them than Ben. After all, they had each other and he now had no one. I was hoping that the funeral would give him some sort of closure, and then he could gradually start to move on with his life. I told myself that it was for the best.

## Chapter Ten

Monday was an overcast day, and quite blustery – the kind of day when rain constantly threatened, but never fell. It was the perfect weather for a funeral.

I rode in the sombre black car with my family and Ben. They didn't talk. Their hands were clasped, their faces strained, as if their skin was suddenly too tight. We followed behind the hearse which carried my coffin slowly through the streets. Alongside the casket, flowers arranged into the shapes of letters spelled out the word 'DAUGHTER'. Ben had selected a pink wreath in the shape of a heart.

A sea of black greeted us at the crematorium, and I was touched to see that so many familiar faces had made the effort to attend. The school had closed for the day and most of my colleagues and more than a few of my students had made an appearance, some of whom were already wiping tears from their reddened eyes. They hung around outside in the wind, their dark jackets and long overcoats flapping like the wings of a flock of giant crows, and Ben and my parents made their way over to them and started shaking hands and accepting condolences, their faces pale and drawn, their voices low, before everyone headed inside.

A vicar whom I didn't know presided over the ceremony, but my mum and dad must have spent time with her beforehand because she talked knowledgeably about my life. I was described as a 'beautiful and loving daughter, sister, fiancé and friend, gone too soon' and I felt my eyes burn.

My favourite hymn was sung, *Make Me a Channel of Your Peace*, and the voices of over a hundred mourners joined in harmony filling the large atrium soothed my soul somewhat. Ben didn't join in with the singing, and when the minister read a passage from the Bible and fervently discussed its meaning, I was almost certain that he didn't hear it. He sat, shoulders slumped, staring at the floor expressionlessly throughout.

Vicky and my Head gave eloquent eulogies then, and Charles got up to say a few words too. Vicky called me 'the one person you could tell anything to, and never feel judged, the kind of person that everyone needs in their life', and her voice cracked. My Head, Norah, said that I was 'an inspirational teacher, dedicated and passionate, loved by staff and students alike'. Charles choked as he described me as 'a sister who was also a best friend'. Everyone was in tears by the end of it all, including Ben, whose dam of emotion finally burst.

Trembling, I watched the red curtains slowly creep closed on my coffin as sobs echoed around the room. I flinched at the finality of it when the two sides finally met. It was like the book of my life closing with the softest of kisses.

My ashes were going to be buried in the crematorium's rose garden on another day, and a small headstone would be erected for me. Then it would all be done.

I held Ben's hand as he walked back outside like a zombie behind his parents, his best mate's arm across his shoulders. They stopped to thank the vicar then walked down the drive towards the car park. The next stop was the wake, where I hoped that they would all get pissed and shake off the gloom.

My parents had hired a room in an upmarket pub, and I watched as people climbed into their cars and began heading off. My attention was caught by a mourner at one of the graves which lined the sides of the long drive however. There was something different about her, something I couldn't quite put my finger on. Curious, I left Ben with his parents as they clambered into the car, and walked over to her slowly.

She was in her mid-to-late thirties. She was knelt down in front of a large headstone, one of many which appeared to me like the gapped teeth of a giant. Her blonde head was bowed. She didn't acknowledge me as I rounded the grave and read what was inscribed on it.

*Florence Hadley*

*Beloved wife and mother*

*Always in our hearts*

The death date was written underneath. She had died some ten years earlier.

"You?" I queried quietly.

She jerked and looked up at me, stunned. Her face was pretty, pixie-like, with wide blue eyes and a slightly upturned nose.

"You can see me?"

I nodded. "I'm Daisy." I held out my hand. She looked at

it warily, then shook it. Her hand was delicate, her grasp gentle.

"Kate." She gestured to the headstone. "This is my mother. I was…I was hoping to see her."

"Are you new?" I asked gently. She nodded.

"When did you pass?"

"This morning."

"I'm sorry," I said sadly.

"It was expected," she shrugged, then added matter-of-factly, "Breast cancer."

"Oh," I responded, then pointed at my chest. "Car accident."

She grimaced in sympathy. "Where would she be?" she asked next, gesturing in bewilderment to the grave. It was a neat grave, well-tended. Her mum had been loved; her memory was still treasured after all these years.

"Is your father still alive?"

"No."

"Then they must be together – wherever it is that we end up." I explained what Leticia had told me.

"So, I'm waiting for my husband?"

"I guess so."

She thought about this for a minute, then smiled. "I'll get to see my children grow up."

I felt a lump in my throat at this, and I nodded, unable to speak. She clapped her hands and stood up. "I'd better be getting back to them. Thank you, Daisy." She hesitated, then held out her hand again. I shook it. "Can I – can I visit you sometimes?"

"I'd like that," I managed to say. I told her to just think of me, and she'd find me. She smiled, then stood there expectantly for a few seconds, before a sheepish expression crept over her face.

"I don't know how to get back," she admitted.

I smiled at her reassuringly. "It's hard at first."

Patiently, I coached her into drawing on her love for her family, her strong desire to be with them. She was a quick learner. Within a few minutes, she had vanished.

I thought myself to the pub then. The mourners were just arriving. I stayed by Ben while people got the drinks in and found themselves a table. A quiet hum of conversation soon filled the wood-panelled room. I looked around, admiring the elegant space. It had Art Deco lights and Art Deco mirrors in which I couldn't see myself reflected.

Ben's friends pulled a few of the tables together and he ended up in a group with them and Vicky and a couple of our college friends, Jules and Asia. At first, all of the guests talked softly, their manner stiff and formal, but over the next hour, they began to relax, and eventually the sound of laughter could be heard above the general hubbub that had increased in the room. *This is more like it,* I thought.

I looked over at my mum and dad, and they were engaged in conversation with my auntie and uncle; Charles and Beth sat chatting with Bal and Amy; and a group of my colleagues had a table to themselves and they were talking earnestly about the curriculum.

Some things never change.

The pub staff brought the buffet food out then, and I watched as people collected plates and queued up at the long table which had been pushed against the wall. Vicky returned with a heaped plate for Ben, and I smiled gratefully at her as she encouraged him to eat, admonishing him gently when he only took a small bite.

The wake lasted for hours, and more than a few people ended up tipsy. As they gradually took their leave, they approached my family and Ben to say goodbye.

"She's one of the stars in the sky now," my dad's brother, uncle Trevor, slurred at Ben, grasping his hand in both of his. It was unusually poetic for him, and I was touched by the simple words.

"She'll be missed," Bal told Ben, clapping gently him on the back. Amy hugged him, and wiped her eyes as she pulled away.

Finally, there was just Ben, our parents and Charles and Beth left. My dad thanked the staff and left a tip, and then they all climbed tiredly into a cab. It was over.

*

That night, when I performed my nocturnal visit to the park, I found my feet moving forward as if of their own volition until I was stood in front of the bench. In the moonlight, I saw Grumpy Irishman look up at me in surprise. Whatever he saw on my face made him hesitate, then pat the space on the bench next to him, and I sank down into it.

We sat in silence for over an hour, watching the clouds

drift lazily across the face of the nearly full Moon, then I spoke softly.

"It was my funeral today." I kept looking forwards, towards the pond.

He sighed. "I'm sorry."

"Me too."

He shifted in his seat as if it was possible for him to be uncomfortable. "How did it happen?" he asked reluctantly.

"Car crash. I don't remember the details."

"Probably for the best."

"Hmmm," I agreed. Finally, I looked at him. "What… what about you?"

"Brain aneurysm," he answered after a pause. "I think."

"You think?"

"I haven't left the park since it happened."

I stared at him in shock. "What about your family?"

He shrugged, his face like marble.

I decided to drop the subject. I watched the breeze blow the reeds at the edge of the pond. *They bend but they never break* I thought, and the idea brought me a sense of peace.

After a while, I sighed and stood up.

"Come again," he said without looking at me. I nodded, then vanished.

## Chapter Eleven

I watched Charles and Beth say their goodbyes to Mum and Dad the next day, then checked back in with Ben before heading to school, which was back to business as usual. I watched an English lesson on Romeo and Juliet; a Science lesson on reproduction; a History lesson on the industrial revolution; and an Art lesson exploring impressionism. I stayed away from my old classes and the frazzled supply teacher.

Later, I sat with Ben as he watched TV while his mum prepared the evening meal and his dad read the newspaper, then I headed to see Dean at our local while they ate.

I sat on the empty stool next to his and asked him where I should go first when I was ready to travel.

He shrugged. "Depends what you're into. I like cities. My favourite to visit is Rome – there's always something to see there."

"I prefer nature," I told him.

"Then there's the Amazon, the Serengeti, the Himalayas…the list is endless."

I widened my eyes in awe; I hadn't even thought about being able to get to such places in the blink of an eye.

"And you won't be bothered by the heat, or the cold, or the altitude," Dean continued. "You could go and visit the penguins in Antarctica during a blizzard and not feel a thing. Heck, you could visit the sea bed!"

"What about Space?" I wondered.

His eyes bugged. "I hadn't even thought of Space!"

We stared at each other for a moment, before bursting into laughter. My laughter turned into quiet sobs.

"What's wrong?" Dean asked, panicking and looking around for help. Of course, there was none.

I shook my head. "I was hoping to do all of these things with Ben."

He patted my knee. "I know, love, I know." He looked over at the barmaid, Susie, and sighed.

Wiping my face, I decided to change the subject. "I met another ghost after my funeral. She was new."

"Did you explain things to her?"

I nodded.

"That's good. It's always confusing at first."

I bit my lip. "She had young kids."

He tutted, and shook his head, before saying, "That's the worst."

"What about when it's the child itself that dies?"

He frowned. "I've never seen a child ghost."

"Maybe they 'go' straight away," I suggested.

He nodded thoughtfully. We contemplated this for several

moments.

"Why don't ghosts get together more often?" I eventually wondered out loud.

"Why do you think?"

"I guess they're too busy watching over their loved ones."

He nodded. "We're always drawn back to them."

"Speaking of which, I'd best be getting back to Ben," I said, climbing off the stool. I held my hand up for a high-five, and vanished once he'd given it. The human contact was nice, albeit brief.

I spent the evening staring at the TV with Ben and his parents, then watched as he got ready for bed and took his sleeping pill.

Since he'd started on the tablets, I'd noticed that he didn't move at all in his sleep. He would lay there like a log, heavy and still. I listened to him breathing deeply for a few hours, thinking mournfully of the years stretched out ahead of me, then made my nightly visit to the park.

This time, I thought myself straight onto the bench and made Grumpy Irishman jump.

"Jesus!" he exclaimed, staring at me accusingly.

"Sorry," I replied sheepishly.

He tutted and looked away. "Don't do that again, Beautiful Nosy Girl."

I gazed at him in astonishment. "Is that what you call me?"

"Well, I don't know your name," he answered defensively.

"You could have asked," I told him dryly.

"Well?"

"Well, what?"

"What is it?"

"Daisy."

"Oh."

"And you are…?"

"Patrick," he answered reluctantly.

"Are we friends now?"

He sighed. "I suppose."

"Don't sound so happy about it, Grumpy Irishman."

He barked a laugh, his eyes sliding to mine. They shone in the moonlight. "I guess I deserve that."

"You do."

We sat in companionable silence for a while. I watched the ghost-like clouds drift slowly through the sky. A couple of stars were visible, twinkling as if attempting to outshine each other.

"How long has it been since you… passed?" I asked eventually.

"A few months."

"And you've been here every day?"

He nodded.

"Have you seen any other ghosts?"

"Occasionally. They don't stay for long."

I rolled my eyes at him. "I'm not surprised."

He chuckled darkly. "You were the exception."

"I'm stubborn."

"You're certainly that, Beautiful Nosy Girl."

"Why…why won't you visit your family?" I braced myself for his reaction to my prying question, but he just remained obstinately silent. I sighed and changed the subject. "*I've* met a few other ghosts."

"Oh?" he asked, but he didn't sound particularly interested to be honest. I ignored his lack of enthusiasm and started telling him all about Leticia, Dean and Kate.

Despite himself, I could tell that his interest gradually grew the more I talked. He even looked over at me incredulously when I told him about Dean's travels.

"He's been all the way to Australia?" he burst out.

I nodded, and he lapsed into a thoughtful silence. I could almost see the cogs turning. *Perhaps I've opened his mind and he'll re-think this stubborn vigil over his death-place,* I thought, surreptitiously crossing my fingers.

I stayed a little longer, telling him more about my ghost friends and discussing the places we'd travelled to in life, before I said goodbye and returned to Ben.

*

The next day, I was drawn inexorably back to the crash site. *Christ!* I thought. *I hope I'm not turning into Patrick.* It was one thing haunting a beautiful park, but quite another thing to haunt a road junction.

The flowers on the lamppost were past their best. The

petals and leaves drooped and their tips were turning brown. It was like some kind of metaphor for something, but I couldn't think what. Life? Love? Memory? Mourning? *Whatever starts off fresh and wilts or fades over time,* I thought. Some English teacher I was.

I watched the traffic at the crossroads for a while. The cars in their lines were like orderly ants, stopping and starting correctly at the traffic signals. What had gone wrong on that terrible day to change this calm orderliness into fatal chaos? I inevitably thought of the lorry driver then, and transported myself straight to him. He was sat on the toilet, his jeans around his ankles, his hands clasped before him, and I quickly thought myself outside of the small room.

I heard pots and pans banging and followed the noise downstairs and through a hallway filled with ornaments and miscellaneous bric-a-brac until I reached the kitchen. The same woman as last time, I presumed she was his wife, was making what looked like vegetable soup, the pan bubbling away as she used a knife to scrape carrots, onion and celery into it from a scarred chopping board. A television was on in the living room and I walked through and discovered a scruffy teenaged boy on the couch watching a late-morning chat show, the voices of the panellists raised in opinionated self-importance. Then the toilet flushed and the sound of running water could be heard through the pipes, and a minute later the lorry driver was coming down the stairs.

I met him in the hallway and followed him as he walked through the kitchen and out the back door without saying a word. He sat down in the same garden chair as before and picked a cigarette out of the box which was lying on the table, before lighting it and inhaling deeply. Then he sat staring into space.

"Anyone would have thought *you'd* died," I told him disapprovingly. "Anyway, the way you're going with those fags, it won't be long. Haven't you heard of vaping?"

He inhaled again and started coughing violently. I cocked my eyebrow. "Told you so."

The back door opened, and I got déjà vu as his wife brought out a cup of tea and placed it on the table. This time, however, she sighed and sat down beside him, the chair scraping loudly as she pulled it back.

"Al, you can't go on like this."

"Leave it, Pam."

"It wasn't your fault," she insisted. My ears perked up at this.

He shook his head. "You don't know that."

"What could you have done differently?"

His jaw clenched, but he didn't speak.

"Will you tell Olly that he needs to go to college tomorrow? It's the third day he's had off since the accident. You're setting a bad example."

Al didn't respond; he just took another pull on his cigarette. The tip glowed briefly, a bright orange-red, and bits of ash dropped onto his shirt, which he brushed away absently. His wife, Pam, sighed, then eased herself out of the chair and headed back inside, shutting the door softly.

"Well that went well," I told him.

"Why did you do it, damnit!" he suddenly burst out. I froze. He ground out his cigarette violently and stormed into the house. The door banged shut behind him. Within a few seconds, I heard him shouting at the boy.

I vanished to the comfort of home.

## Chapter Twelve

That night, I lay next to Ben thinking about what Pam had said and racking my brain about the events leading up to the accident. Had I run a red light or something? I nibbled on my bottom lip, before shaking my head – I remembered the signal changing in the aftermath. Perhaps I'd been speeding, or I'd cut him up? I was usually such a careful driver though. A wave of guilt hit me, and I shuddered. At least I'd only killed myself, and no one else. *But there's more than one way to ruin a life,* I thought, as images of Ben's drawn face and my parents' bloodshot eyes entered my mind. Not to mention Al and his family. I scrubbed my hands over my face, then headed for my nightly visit to the park.

\*

"What do you miss most about being alive?" I asked Patrick when we'd been sitting together for a while.

"Everything."

"But if you had to choose one thing?"

He quirked an eyebrow at me. "Sex."

I rolled my eyes. "You're so predictable."

"What do *you* miss?"

"Feeling the breeze, and the sun." I closed my eyes and recalled the sensations of wind and heat brushing against my skin.

He grunted.

"Is there anything you *don't* miss?"

He shook his head.

"What – nothing at all?" I asked incredulously, my eyes opening to stare at him in wonder.

"You don't understand. I had it all – the job, the money, the girl, the lifestyle. I was living the good life. Then, like that," he clicked his fingers, "it was all taken from me." His lip curled in resentment.

"I'm sorry," I said, softening. "Is…is that why you stay here?"

"I can't face seeing what I had before it was all taken away," he answered bitterly.

I thought about my own life: a successful career as a teacher; engaged to my childhood sweetheart; a loving family; close friends. I'd had it all too.

"Do you believe that things happen for a reason?"

He snorted. "What, like fate?"

"I guess so."

"No. It's all just random shite."

"Leticia believed in God."

"He's got a lot to answer for."

"You're so *angry*."

"You should be too! Look at the two of us, in our prime years, living our best lives and minding our own business, and then," he clicked his fingers again, "within a split second it's all over."

"Or maybe it's the beginning of something new?" I suggested hopefully.

"What, *Heaven*?" he responded, his voice dripping with sarcasm as he looked around at the moonlit park. There was a homeless man asleep on the bench opposite and we'd witnessed a drug deal taking place earlier in the night.

"Well," I said defensively, "there's obviously an afterlife, or we wouldn't be here, would we?"

"And where, exactly, do you think 'here' is?"

"Waiting for our loved ones on Earth before we go to wherever it is that we go. Like Leticia did."

"Purgatory more like it."

"You don't *have* to sit on this bench day after day," I answered, starting to grow angry.

"No, I could hang out at the hospital, and the school, and the pub with you," he said mockingly.

Hurt, I stood up and glared down at him. "Well, it's better than this *nothing* existence that *you've* consigned yourself to! It's about time you stopped feeling sorry for yourself and got a life!"

Before I vanished, I heard him bark a laugh.

\*

Kate turned up the next morning while Ben was taking a shower and I was sat watching his mum rearranging my kitchen drawers.

"Daisy!" she said urgently, her face contorted in distress.

"What's the matter?" I asked quickly, standing up and putting my hand on her arm.

"It's my youngest, Sam, he's been taken into hospital. Suspected meningitis. I don't know what to do. I feel so helpless." She was wringing her hands and her right leg was jittering restlessly.

I felt a pang in my chest at the disturbing news.

"Do you want me to come to the hospital to be with you?"

She nodded gratefully, her shoulders relaxing with relief, and within seconds we were on the children's ward.

"As if my family hasn't had enough crap to deal with lately," she said despairingly as we stood next to a hospital bed looking down at a small blonde boy of about three – a child emerging from the toddler years, the baby chubbiness mostly gone, the head still slightly large in proportion to the body. His face was flushed and a red rash was visible on his torso and arms. A tube connected a drip to the back of his hand. I swallowed at the sight of such a young child lying limp and suffering.

"He's in the best place," I reassured her. It was all I could think of to say.

She sat on the edge of the bed and put her hand over his, a helpless mother desperate to comfort her little boy. I watched until a movement in my peripheral vision caught my eye. A large, darkly-bearded man was sitting in a chair. He stirred and rubbed his face as if he'd just woken up.

"Poor John," Kate murmured as he made his way over to the bed and brushed back Sam's hair. The touch was so gentle, so loving, yet the hands were big and strong.

The child didn't stir.

I thought about what Patrick had said last night, about everything being random. Perhaps he was right – what other reason could there be for a man to lose his wife in the same week that his son became seriously ill? *What are you up to, God?* I thought. I felt a flash of anger at the cruelty of a world that could do this to a happy family.

I stayed with Kate for the rest of the day, while Sam slept and she told me stories about their family life in a soft voice. She painted a picture of contentment and fun, and recounted memories of their summer holidays in a pretty cottage by the sea. It was a good life with a little bit of chaos thrown in, as would be expected with two young children, and I giggled and sighed with her as she talked of John's first attempt to change a nappy, how she had dealt with Poppy's epic toddler tantrums in the supermarket, and the day that they had visited Monkey Forest and one of the cheeky blighters had stolen little Sam's snack.

"And then I discovered the lump," she ended sadly. "And within a few months it was all over."

I put my hand on her shoulder and we stared soberly down at Sam. "Please don't let it be over for my precious boy," she whispered, clutching his hand. His fingers twitched and curled around hers. I inhaled sharply, and Kate let out a sob.

I stayed with her until darkness had long fallen.

\*

I returned to Ben for the night. I sat up next to him while he lay there like a stone and thought about life and death and everything in between. I didn't visit Patrick.

\*

I spent most of the next few days at the hospital. I could tell that Kate found my presence comforting, a much-needed distraction from her constant anxiety. We would sit talking quietly while watching over the slumbering child, sharing confidences: the uneasy time when she was struggling with having two children under the age of three and had felt that she was going insane; the brief period of time when I had wondered, guiltily, if Ben and I had settled down too soon, before we could experience another kind of life. The result was that a strong bond developed between us during our uneasy vigil, and she thanked me more than once for being there, her face earnest, her eyes sincere.

"I don't know how I'd be coping if you weren't here," she told me one time, her voice low. She was staring down at Sam, a small wrinkle between her eyebrows, her eyes shining with unshed tears.

"There's nowhere else I'd rather be," I told her quietly, and it was true. There was no way I could have let Kate go through this uneasy vigil alone.

Kate's immense love for her young son shone through during those dark, difficult days, the force of it nearly overwhelming me. I watched in awe as she sat, day after day, never moving from his side, willing him with all that she had to fight the invasive bacteria, to recover, to thrive. Watching her, I thought to myself that she was the kind of mother that I'd always hoped to be one day – attentive, protective, fierce in her unconditional love for her children.

But I guess, now, we'd never know.

*

Eventually, the intravenous antibiotics started to take effect and the doctors began to express cautious optimism about Sam's recovery. To our inordinate relief, he slowly began to sit up and talk, and the joy on Kate and John's faces when he asked for pizza could have melted a snowman's heart (*or Patrick's*, I thought snidely).

Seeing Sam's health and energy returning was like watching a miracle unfold before my eyes. From the brink of death, he had returned unscathed. I silently thanked God, and felt at peace with the world.

## Chapter Thirteen

On Monday, I decided I'd neglected Ben for long enough. Other than popping to the hospital once in the morning and again in the afternoon, I remained at home. Deirdre and Phil were still there and weren't showing any signs of planning to leave any time soon, and I was glad of that. I wouldn't have felt as comfortable being away from him so regularly if he was all alone in the house.

My mum and dad visited in the afternoon and spent time trying to help Ben sort out my finances, then Vicky came in the evening. She was a breath of fresh air as she sat telling them about her work day. As she rabbited on about the awkward customers she'd had to deal with, Ben sat quietly, but I could tell that he was listening because he gave a small smile now and then at some of her more colourful descriptions. She was a welcome distraction in the usually gloom-laden house.

\*

I settled back into a routine over the rest of the week: Ben for a couple of hours in the morning; hospital twice per day; school for a few hours; back to Ben; check-in on Mum and Dad; then a chat with Dean at the pub before returning home to Ben. I stayed away from the park.

*

Saturday was the three-week anniversary of my death. After visiting the hospital, where I was delighted to hear that Sam was now well enough to be released, I returned to the crash site. *What is it about this place that keeps drawing me back?* I wondered as I again sat cross-legged on the grass verge and watched the steady traffic, unbothered by the stench of exhaust fumes. The flowers were completely dead by this time, the brittle brown petals crumbling like burnt paper in the breeze.

I stayed there for over an hour, thinking about what might have been and becoming lulled by the traffic, before I rose and decided to check on Al.

I found him digging in the garden, sweat glistening on his crusty scar as he put all his weight behind the spade so that he could turn the clay-like soil over before systematically chopping at it with the tool's edge.

"Well this is much better than sitting in that bloody chair, chain-smoking all day," I declared as I stood watching him with my hands on my hips. He must have been at it for a while, because his face was red and he was breathing heavily.

I spoke too soon though, because within a minute he threw down his spade and made his way over to the table, where he helped himself to a cigarette. I sighed and sloped over to my usual place on the step. The thread was still where I'd left it. I picked it up and ran it through my fingers for something to do, while we sat in silence.

"Are you back at work now?" I eventually asked him. He took a pull of his fag, releasing the smoke into the crisp air on a heavy exhalation. "I hope it hasn't put you off driving." He shifted his weight in his chair. "I think Ben should go back to work, at least when his mum and dad return to Spain. It would take his mind off things."

I twirled the thread around my finger. He sighed loudly.

The back door opened, and Pam brought a cup of tea out for him. "Thanks, love," he said quietly, and she rested her hand on his shoulder as she bent down and kissed his cheek before heading back inside.

"Progress," I told him, pleased. I watched him finish his cigarette and start on his tea. "I miss coffee," I sighed. "And chocolate." The thread was tight around my finger now. Normally, this would turn the tip a different colour as the circulation was cut off, but it remained unchanged. No blood flow, I guessed. He finished his tea and heaved himself out of the chair. He started walking back to the spade.

"What happened, Al?"

For a split second, I thought he hesitated, but he continued to the churned-up bed and started attacking the truculent ground with a vengeance. I watched him for a while, as a cloud passed in front of the sun, darkening the sky like a memory and causing an overwhelming feeling of sorrow to envelop me, until I felt that I was on the verge of drowning in it.

I took a deep breath to steady myself, bit my lip and returned home.

*

After a few hours of watching Ben trying to read a book, I began to grow restless. There was something I'd been thinking of doing, but I wasn't sure I could face it. Eventually, I gave myself a stern talking-to and thought myself to the park before I could change my mind.

I appeared across the pond from Patrick's bench, so he would have plenty of notice that I was coming. He watched me as I rounded the water and made my way over to him.

"About fecking time," he snapped, when I stopped in front of him. My eyebrows shot up.

"Excuse me?"

"Where have you been? You can't just turn up in a man's life and flip it upside down then disappear on him."

"Well, you can't just be rude to people and expect them to be eager to share your company again," I retorted.

He grunted at this.

"Besides, *you* could have come to *me* at any time."

"You know I don't move from this bench."

"You did once."

Another grunt.

"Haven't you got anything to say to me?"

He looked at me askance. I waited, my arms crossed and my foot tapping.

"Fine," I said, when it was clear that I wasn't going to get what I wanted, and prepared myself to disappear.

"I'm sorry," he growled quietly.

"Thank you. There – that wasn't so hard, was it?"

He sighed. "Are you going to sit down now?"

I smiled and made my way over, then sat watching the birds. They were gliding around the pond serenely, leaving ripples in their wake. Occasionally they would dip their heads into the water in their search for food. It was very restful.

"Well?" Patrick demanded after a while. I suddenly realised that he'd been staring at me for the last few minutes.

"Well, what?"

"Aren't you going to prattle on at me about what you've been up to?"

"'Prattle on'?"

He waved my outrage away. "Come on, tell me. You know you're my only source of entertainment."

"What – the ducks don't sing and dance for you?" I asked sardonically. He waited expectantly. I sighed and gave in. I told him about Kate's appearance on the morning after our tiff, and poor Sam's illness and our relief at his recovery. The routine I'd got into. My visit to Al that morning. Patrick listened without interrupting, and I wondered if I was the ghost equivalent of a soap opera for him.

"You've been busy," he told me when I finished. "I'm glad the boy's better."

I nodded, and we sat companionably for a while before it was time for me to return to Ben.

\*

I started going to the cinema. At first, it felt weird to sit watching a film without having paid, but I soon got used to it. I'd see a different movie every day, until I'd viewed all of them, and then I'd watch my favourite ones, usually romantic comedies, again. In between this, my visits to the school, and my catch-ups with Dean, Kate and Patrick, not to mention the occasional check-in with Al, I was rather busy. When I wasn't going about my day, I was at home with Ben, who was becoming more and more himself as time moved on.

*

My ashes were buried on a Wednesday near the end of March. Only Vicky, Ben and our parents were in attendance this time. I stood in the sunshine that I couldn't feel stoically studying the brief details of my life on the little headstone, while birdsong created an incongruously cheerful backing track to the sombre scene.

*Daisy Anne Roberts*

*Gone but Not Forgotten*

The years of my birth and death were underneath. This was all that would be left of my existence one day. For now, there were still photos, my clothes hung in the wardrobe, the memories of my friends and family. But one day all of these would be gone, and this headstone would be the only thing left to tell people that I once was here.

I felt like a tiny dot in the universe, here for a microsecond of its existence, like a bubble blown out of gum, which popped almost immediately. And yet, to us, our lives are so significant and have so much meaning. There's so much richness of feeling and complexity in our relationships. So much vitality in the way we love and laugh. Maybe bubble gum isn't the best analogy – maybe I should have used a firework instead.

More tears were shed in the rose garden, but they were calmer tears than before. I'd been dead for nearly six weeks.

## Chapter Fourteen

Ben's parents flew back to Spain the following day. I rode in the car as he drove them to the airport and watched them hug goodbye. He promised to call them if he felt that he needed to. I broke my routine and stuck closer to him for a few days, until I was sure that he was coping. He returned to work on the following Monday.

I sat in the passenger seat as he drove to the office in the rush hour traffic. I had never been there before and I was curious about exactly what he did all day. I needn't have bothered. After he was greeted by his colleagues and they quietly shared their condolences, which he accepted stoically, he sat catching up with emails and reading reports for the rest of the day.

I went to work with him for the rest of the week, but it was more of the same with a few spreadsheets and graphs thrown in for good measure. I knew he loved his job, but my God, it was dull as ditch water to watch.

I returned to my old routine during his work hours and spent the evenings and the nights with him, just like when I was alive and working. The weekends were different – I'd hang around with him for most of Saturday and Sunday, while he went about doing the housework and the food shopping, and meeting up with his friends and Vicky in the evening. I was glad he was getting out and about, although he wasn't quite back to being his old, lively self. At least he was *living* though. I don't mean at least he was alive. Living is more than that.

\*

When I'd seen all of the films at the cinema at least twice, I started going to matinee performances at the theatre. Kate joined me sometimes. We watched whatever play or musical was showing. We also made the occasional evening visit to the opera or ballet, and often wept together at the tragedies. Dean came with me to a couple of comedy clubs; it felt good to have a friend to laugh with. I tried to persuade Patrick to attend some of these events, but he always refused, and I'd roll my eyes at his stubbornness.

During the day, I'd break up school visits with sitting in on lectures at the university. The Psychology department was particularly interesting. I learned all about Freudian theory and Behaviourism, Cognitive psychology and Brain Science. I was fascinated by the human mind, and drank in the knowledge imparted by the lecturers thirstily.

Sometimes, I'd stroll around the zoo. It was peaceful there, an oasis of calm on the edge of the bustling city. I was fascinated by the simple lives of the animals, their behaviours and relationships, the hierarchies and family dynamics. The monkeys were my favourites; I could watch their antics for hours.

\*

By the time May arrived, with its warmer, longer days and fresh lushness, I had acclimatised to my new existence rather well. In fact, I began to grow complacent, assuming that things would always be like this. I should have known better.

It was a Saturday night, and I'd been dead for three months. I was in a bar in the centre of town with Ben and his friends. Vicky wasn't there – she had some family thing to go to. Ben was knocking back the shots, and the group was particularly lively that night. The bar was rammed, and more than once I couldn't avoid someone passing *through* me as they made their way to order a fresh drink, or to the toilets. I shuddered every time it happened. Feeling fed up, I was just contemplating getting out of there when I noticed a pretty blonde woman strike up a conversation with Ben at the bar.

I watched as he smiled and returned her flirtation, my heart sinking. Like a masochist, I stayed to see where this was heading. He led her back to the table, and his mates made space for her and her friends. Ben ended up sat next to the pretty blonde, their heads close together in order to hear each other above the rowdy chatter around them. The group got even livelier.

After an hour or so, they all decided to head to a nightclub and I trailed along with a lump in my throat. The music in the club was above the level where people could hear each other talking, the bass pounding, so after a trip to the bar, most of the group ended up on the dance floor. Within minutes, Ben and the blonde girl were dancing closely. I stood in the flickering darkness, looking down on them from a vacant podium, feeling like my world was crashing down around me. When they started kissing, I think I'd have thrown up if I was able to.

I couldn't look away for the next half an hour as they danced and smooched under the pulsing lights. And then she said something in his ear and he nodded and let her lead him off the dance floor, hand in hand. Icy cold, I watched them collect their coats from the cloakroom and walk out of the club.

I stood like a statue on the podium, debating with myself as to whether I should follow them, but the thought sickened me. Instead, I found myself vanishing and reappearing on the bench in the park.

"Feck!" Patrick exclaimed. "I told you not to do that!" But one look at my face had him opening his arms to me. I fell into them and started sobbing out the story. My breath came in gasps.

"Oh, shit. Oh, Jesus," he murmured as I poured out what I'd seen and he stroked my hair soothingly.

"And they're probably shagging right now!" I finished with a wail and a fresh round of sobbing.

"Shh," he soothed. "He's drunk, and sad, and she's just a one-night stand. He still loves you."

I shook my head against his chest and he patted my back. "He does," he said. "Who could get over someone like you in just three short months?"

I sighed shakily, and we stayed like that for some time as my tears dried and my breaths became calmer.

Just before dawn, I thanked him quietly and returned home. Our bed was empty.

\*

I avoided going out on Saturday nights with Ben after that,

unless Vicky was going to be there. Her presence kept him on the straight and narrow, and he drank less than when it was just him and his friends. When our bed remained empty, I tried to tell myself that it was just a form of release, that it didn't mean that he'd forgotten me. He was only twenty-seven after all; it was unfair to expect him to live like a monk. At least he never brought them back to our house, where my photo was still on his bedside table and my clothes still hung in the wardrobe.

That would have been soul-destroying.

After a month or so of this though, it was beginning to feel like a form of torture. I started going further afield in my travels to distract myself. First, I would visit places of local interest in the surrounding counties – castles, stately homes, gardens and the like. I would stroll around examining the ornate rooms and immaculate flower beds, reading every plaque and information poster, desperate to take my mind off the situation.

Soon I was visiting other cities and seaside resorts. I went to Bath and Brighton, York and St. Ives. I explored all the places of interest and tourist shops in the historic towns and walked sedately along the beaches in the seaside towns, observing the people enjoying the sunshine and wishing I could smell the salty air and feel the sea breeze.

I spent a few weeks exploring London until I knew it like the back of my hand. I toured the British Museum, home to the Rosetta Stone and Elgin Marbles; the Tower of London, with its Beefeater guards and ravens protecting the Crown Jewels; took a cruise along the River Thames, from Westminster to Greenwich; rode on the London Eye, viewing the Houses of Parliament and Buckingham Palace from high on the big wheel; and took the spooky Jack the Ripper tour at night. I was restless and unhappy, and there was nowhere I wouldn't venture to distract myself. Occasionally, I would see another ghost, but I avoided engaging with them.

Each night, with the exception of too many Saturdays to count, I'd return to Ben, and lay beside him as he slept, but soon I couldn't even face this. I told Kate, Dean and Patrick that I was going to go away for a while, explaining my reasons, and they hugged me and told me that they'd miss me. Patrick asked why I couldn't come back each day, after all I could go back and forth anywhere in the world in the blink of an eye, but I shook my head and told him that I needed a complete break. Grudgingly, he wished me well. I asked Dean and Kate to visit him from time to time and they promised that they would. My heart swelled with gratitude for my ghost friends.

*Chapter Fifteen*

The day before I left, I spent the morning with my parents. It was a Sunday, and they were pottering about doing the gardening and giving the bedrooms a spring clean, chatting and laughing. It was the first time I'd seen them being light-hearted since my death and I was glad that I'd have this memory of them to take with me on my travels. I hung out watching them, smiling at their close bond, and talking to them in the quiet gaps, explaining why I wouldn't be around for a while. Even though they couldn't see or hear me, it gave me comfort to express myself and say goodbye in the only way I could.

I visited Al in the afternoon. He was watching horse racing on the TV, the sound of the commentator's rapid monologue filling the room with its characteristic sense of urgency. I sat beside him for a while before speaking.

"I'm going away, Al," I told him quietly during a lull between races. "And I don't know how long I'll be gone."

He didn't react.

"Sometimes I wonder if you can hear me. Or at least sense my presence."

Was that a slight tensing of his jaw?

"You need to get over this, Al. You're getting there slowly, but I'm pretty certain you haven't driven since the accident."

He sighed and shifted his weight on the couch.

"You need to get back in the saddle, mate. What are you going to do about work? You've got a family to provide for."

He wiped a hand down his face.

"Maybe me going away will be good for you?" I said sadly.

He closed his eyes briefly, and I vanished.

\*

My last evening in England was spent with Ben. He was working on a report at the breakfast bar. It reminded me of when I had first returned home after the accident, before he knew that I was dead. No pots and pans arranged into a drum kit this time while he listened to rock music at full volume. Instead, he sat in silence, alternately working and staring off into space. Not for the first time, I wondered what he was thinking about.

"I understand why you do what you do," I told him softly. "I just can't bear to be around to witness it."

I watched him for a while longer, wishing, fruitlessly, that things were different, that he had no need to look for comfort in the arms of other women because he still had me, Daisy, his childhood sweetheart. Then he shut down the laptop and started getting ready for bed. As he lay drifting off to sleep, I murmured, "I love you." But of course, I didn't get a response.

I spent the night lying on my side staring at his face; I memorised every line and shadow so that I could recall it when I was far away. The shallow frown line between his eyebrows, the grooves at the sides of his mouth, the little pointy bit on one of his ears, the way his hairline curved into a heart shape. All the things that made him uniquely Ben, I explored and filed away to be cherished when I was on the other side of the world, trying not to think about whom he was with on a Saturday night.

\*

I didn't know how long I would be gone for, but I knew that I needed space, and time away. Dean had said that it was an honour to watch Susie go about her life, but I wasn't there yet. And anyway, I wondered if he'd have felt the same if she'd found a partner. Would he have accepted the situation, or tried to escape from the pain of it as I was doing?

Maybe I'd gain the long-term perspective needed by taking myself away from the situation for a while. Maybe I'd learn to see these liaisons as just transitory interludes in his life, as time brought him ever closer to the day when we would finally be reunited. I could learn to see the women as mere shooting stars to my stable, omnipresent Polaris.

Maybe.

\*

At dawn, I kissed a still-slumbering Ben goodbye, and vanished. I had one last stop to make before heading off on my travels. I reappeared at the road junction where the crash had occurred. The flowers were completely gone by now – there was just a dirty piece of ragged string still attached to the lamppost to mark where they'd once been. *It's just like me,* I thought. *I'm the flowers that disappear from this place, and all that's left is the thread which connects Ben's heart to mine.*

I watched the sparse traffic for a while as the sun crested the horizon. The cars appeared less like ants when there were fewer of them. They still followed the coloured signals of the traffic lights, but the more random timing of their appearance made them seem less orderly, and therefore less predictable. It unsettled me, and I began to grow restless.

Soon, I was gone.

## Chapter Sixteen

If you had a lifetime ahead of you, and you could go anywhere in the universe, where would you go first? I had decided on Egypt. I appeared in front of the Great Pyramid at Giza, under a baking hot sun that I couldn't feel. The stone structure towered above me by well over a hundred metres and the suburban sprawl of Cairo could be seen not too far away through the haze. I walked across the sandy floor, leaving no footprints, and explored the area. Three large pyramids dominated the surroundings, tombs to bygone pharaohs, but there were other structures dotted around too, including an ancient graveyard.

I stood in awe looking up at the colossal Sphinx, its eroded limestone face and reclining lion's body facing the urban spread of the city as if watching over it benevolently. I sat on top of it for a while watching the flow of tourists, camels and horses, even quad bikes, traversing the area, their loud engines cutting through the tranquillity of the scene, as wispy clouds progressed dreamily across the wide blue sky. Then, curious, I joined a tour group and ventured inside the Great Pyramid.

We descended a wooden walkway through a stone tunnel

cut into the rock and entered a series of plain-walled chambers as the guide recited facts at the group. I mooched about in some of the blocked off areas, but there wasn't really much to see, and I felt a sense of disappointment. One of the members of the group asked the guide about the more elaborate decoration of the tombs at the Valley of the Kings then however, and I decided to take a look.

Within an instant, I was in Luxor, inside the tomb of Ramses III according to yet another tour guide. This time, an abundance of neat hieroglyphics adorned the walls, as well as intricate reliefs of pharaohs and gods – the falcon-headed Horus and the jackal-headed Anubis especially captured my attention. Time seemed to stand still as I explored the pillared hall and breath-taking chambers. I couldn't have asked for a better distraction.

The tour ended, but I stayed for a while longer, watching the tourists come and go and observing their varied reactions to the scenes before them – gasps, smiles and intense fascination. It was late afternoon before I emerged into the bright sunlight and spent some time exploring the sandy valley. I ended up at the Temple of Hatshepsut a few kilometres away, studying the stone effigies of the Kings along its colonnaded façade, before ducking inside and exploring the inner reliefs, paintings and inscriptions of the temple.

Mentally weary from a full day of exploring, I joined a Nile cruise then. I sat on the roof of a traditional wooden sailboat called a felucca, watching the sun sink in the burnt orange sky as laughing children played along the banks of the river and women chatted and washed clothes nearby. The dark water rippled in the breeze and reflected the golden light of the sunset.

It was a relaxing way to end the day, and I was disappointed when it was all over and the boat docked for the night.

I lay down and stared up at the Moon as the people around me drank and talked to each other under the dim lights, before they finally settled down to sleep on the communal mattress. The boat rocked gently under the starlit sky and I contemplated the enormity of history.

My life was a microsecond, less, in the lifespan of the universe. Unimportant. The blink of an eye. Yet to me it held so much significance, so much that was precious: the remembered warmth of my parents' arms; my first kiss, when I was fifteen; the magical day I swam with dolphins in the Caribbean; the first lesson I taught which I knew had been truly inspiring to my students; and that special day when I met Ben. Now they were just memories, fragile, like a spider's web. I had to hold on to them, or they would float away on the winds of time.

The years ahead weighed heavily on me, and I lay there trying to distract myself by attempting to identify the constellations in the night sky. I contemplated a trip to the other side of the world, where it was now day time, but I needed a break after the stimulation of the day. The night passed slowly but peacefully.

In the morning, I watched the sun rise and the world come slowly to life around me. When the vibrant streaks of warm colour had faded from the sky, I ventured into Cairo and paid a visit to the Museum of Egyptian Antiquities. There were over a hundred thousand artefacts on display, including the famous Tutankhamun collection with its beautiful gold death mask and sarcophagus, and I spent the whole day exploring.

At one point in the afternoon, I noticed an older man trailing behind a woman in a wheelchair as she slowly made her way around the exhibits with a female friend. There was something different about him, something I couldn't quite put my finger on, and when he nodded at me as he passed by, I had the confirmation that he too was a ghost. I smiled and nodded back, and we continued on our way, heading in opposite directions, never to cross paths again. Not for the first time, I wondered why some of us remained here with our loved ones while so many others passed on immediately to whatever it was that awaited us. The answer eluded me.

I stayed in Egypt for several more days, spending each night on the roof of a different felucca, contemplating the meaning of life, and death, and by the end of them I was ready for a change. I was eager to explore nature, to be somewhere less crowded, so I transported myself down to the Serengeti National Park in Tanzania.

For weeks I explored the vast wildlife sanctuary: the savannahs of the south, which stretched endlessly to the horizon, broken only by the acacias which dotted the landscape like lonely sentinels; the western corridor of more-dense bush and forest, where the swollen Grumeti river flowed; and the north, where it bordered the Masai Mara Reserve.

I joined tour group after tour group, absorbing the knowledge of the guides like a sponge and observing with wide-eyed wonder the Great Migration of hundreds of thousands of wildebeest and zebra; the epic fights between hungry predators and terrified prey; the graceful elephants and elegant giraffes sedately feeding their young. I saw crocodiles and hippos, cheetahs and lions, and hundreds of other species all fighting for survival as they battled their way through the circle of life.

I saw a lot of the world after that, but the Serengeti stuck in my mind as one of the most memorable places I visited – second only to one other.

At night, I would rest with the elephants. Something about their calm presence soothed me. I got to know one herd particularly well, and I even named them as I grew to differentiate their personalities. My favourite was a calf I named Lucky, because I'd twice witnessed him narrowly escape being taken down by a ravenous lion. I would rest against him as he slept, and I'd stare up at my silver friend, the Moon.

One evening, I was trying to distract myself from thinking about the fact that it was a Saturday night by trying to make out the craters on its surface, when I suddenly remembered the conversation I'd had with Dean about how it was now possible to go *anywhere*. Without giving myself chance to chicken out, I took a deep breath and thought myself straight onto the dusty satellite.

I found myself gazing open-mouthed at the Earth, now hundreds of thousands of miles away. It hung just over the horizon like a jewelled orb with wispy white clouds swirling over brown and green patches of land and vast blue oceans. When I could finally tear my eyes away, I turned in a circle and absorbed the rest of the incredible view. A blanket of stars glittered against the inky vacuum of Space, the largest and brightest being the sun. *It's like an impressionist's painting,* I thought, thinking of Van Gogh's *Starry Night Over the Rhone*.

I looked down at the lunar surface – it was covered in a fine, dark-grey, talcum-powder-like dust with pebbles, rocks and boulders scattered across it. I started walking, exploring the craters and the highlands and lowlands, unaffected by the lower gravity and leaving no trace of footprints behind. If it was taking too long to get to a feature I wanted to examine more closely, I would just think myself to it and I'd be there in an instant.

I'd been on the Moon for a couple of hours before I remembered the Apollo landing of 1969 and the subsequent missions which had brought astronauts on such an awe-inspiring journey. I thought myself to the flag which I knew they'd left behind. The Stars and Stripes was ragged and had been bleached by the sun, but the aluminium pole was still in pretty good condition. Heavy, ridged footprints were still visible in the grey dust. I mooched around and discovered an unbelievable amount of debris scattered about – including what appeared to be a lunar module.

I found the plaque left behind by Armstrong and Aldrin, proclaiming that they came in peace for all mankind, and felt humbled to be one of the few people to have lain their eyes on it.

In all the months I spent exploring on Earth, from then on I spent every single night on the Moon. I discovered six landing sites in total and never got over the amount of junk that had been left behind. There was no wind on the Moon, so everything lay exactly where it had been placed by the men who'd come and gone before me. I wondered how the landscape would change in future, if humans returned, and hoped they'd bloody well clean up a bit.

## Chapter Seventeen

After my time in the Serengeti, I left Africa and decided to return to civilisation for a while. I headed to New York and did the full tourist thing. There, I befriended another ghost, named Kim, whom I met on top of the Empire State building. We hit it off straight away after she accidentally walked into me, surprising us both and then making us laugh at the unexpectedness of it. She had passed when she was fifty, but it had been seventy years since her birth, and she was waiting for her husband, Ray. He'd proposed to her on top of the iconic landmark and she told me that she often returned there out of nostalgia. I sighed when she related the romantic story, and Kim's eyes moistened.

Kim was a short, plump brunette and a native New Yorker; she knew the place like the back of her hand. She spent days showing me around all the well-known hotspots, and quite a few of the lesser-known. From admiring the view across New York Harbour from the top of the Statue of Liberty to strolling around the lush oasis of Central Park, exploring the exhibits at the Museum of Modern Art to dancing in a basement nightclub to an incredible live band – you name it, we did it. I'd say I made a friend for life in Kim, but perhaps a friend in death would be more appropriate.

At the end of the week, I asked her if she wanted to come with me to my next destination – the Amazon – but she shook her head regretfully and told me that she couldn't be away from her husband for too long. I understood. He was nearly eighty by this time and not in the best of health. Promising to stay in touch, we hugged goodbye, both of us with tears in our eyes, knowing how special it was to form a connection with another ghost when there were so few of us around, and then I headed to Brazil.

The Amazon rainforest was another highlight of my travels. I joined a canoeing tour, feeling relaxed as we drifted along the river, watched by a thousand eyes in the secretive jungle which surrounded us; sat bird-watching high in the canopy of the trees, admiring the vibrant colours of what looked like large pieces of flying candy; witnessed creatures like anacondas, jaguars, sloths and howler monkeys in their natural habitats. I even ventured under the water to get up-close and personal with the piranhas and pink river dolphins, smiling as they darted around me, shuddering when they passed through me.

The noise of the forest was incredible – a concert of buzzing and chirping, with the loudest animals being the frogs, cicadas, birds and howlers. Occasionally, a piercing noise would startle me. I never quite got used to it.

One tour group I tagged along with visited the Bora Community, a tribe which maintained many of their traditional beliefs and customs. I listened as the well-rehearsed guide recited a few facts about the indigenous people, their language, history and culture, and gazed around curiously at the men, women and children in their exotic skirts, necklaces, feathers and body paint, as they walked at a leisurely pace between their thatched wooden houses. We were led to the Maloca, their ceremonial lodge, where we sat and watched a performance of a traditional dance, then I strolled around the village while the tourists succumbed to the pressure to buy souvenirs.

The guide had mentioned that there were estimated to be nearly one hundred uncontacted tribes in the Amazon, and I quickly decided that I'd like to find one of them.

It took weeks of research, including eavesdropping on tour guides and studying maps over people's shoulders in tourist information centres, and randomly zipping around the Amazon basin, before I thought to tag along on a few helicopter rides and finally encountered a group living deep in the jungle. They wore elaborate red body paint on their almost-naked bodies, lived in thatched huts surrounded by plots of corn, manioc and bananas, and used bows and arrows to hunt animals for meat.

I encountered an older male ghost here, who was wary of me at first. But as the days passed and I did nothing but smile at him reassuringly and observe the people going about their business (as if I was capable of doing anything else), he came to relax around me and even to smile back at me.

One day, I was watching some children playing when he came over to me and started speaking. I wasn't sure what he was doing at first, but it soon became clear from his pointing and the repetition of certain sounds that he was trying to teach me some words in his language. I listened carefully, and was soon repeating back to him what I believed to be the words for 'children', 'house' and 'banana', my mouth struggling to make the shapes of the unfamiliar sounds. He was very patient with me and over the next few days we had several sessions where he would teach me a handful of new words each time. His name was difficult to pronounce, but it sounded something like Huipi. He was a small, gentle man, and I grew to like him very much.

From the way Huipi watched one of the women, I could tell that she was the one he was waiting for. She too was small, with kind eyes and high cheekbones. I would point between them and smile, and he would nod and smile back.

I stayed with the tribe for nearly a month and grew very attached to them, but inevitably I began to grow restless. I didn't know the word for goodbye, but I tried my best to convey the meaning of it to Huipi on my last day. From the sad expression on his face, I think he understood.

"I'll try to visit again one day," I promised him, as I'd promised Kim, but he just looked at me quizzically. I took his hand and squeezed it, then I vanished.

My stay with the tribe had been eye-opening, an insight into a completely different, more simple way of life, but I was once again in need of a little civilisation. I arrived in Rio de Janeiro, and perched atop the statue of Christ the Redeemer, looking over the city and shoreline and allowing myself a few moments to think about Ben. I was tempted to pop back to check on him, but in the end, I decided I still wasn't quite ready to face up to the new reality of his life without me. Running away in order to protect my heart had seemed to be the only solution, and it still felt incredibly fragile.

I spent the day exploring the sprawling city, including

tagging along in a cable car to pay a visit to Sugarloaf Mountain, where I enjoyed the panoramic views of Rio – its famous beaches, historical centre, modern skyscrapers, National Park and large harbour, before once again heading to the Moon for the night.

I stayed in Rio for a few days. Watching the sun set each evening from Ipanema beach was magical, and although I was regretful to be experiencing it alone, I wouldn't have missed it for the world. I encountered a few ghosts in the city, but none with whom I became close. We were like ships that passed in the night – a flash of a smile or a nod of acknowledgement, and then we continued to head off in our own directions, each coping in our own way with the pleasure-pain of watching our loved ones living their lives without us.

After Brazil, I travelled to Nepal, where I explored the historic capital, Kathmandu, and discovered beautiful Hindu temples and ancient Buddhist monasteries, my eyes wide as they took in the fascinating sights of a culture so very different from my own. Then, inevitably, I joined a group of trekkers who were heading to Everest base camp.

For eight days, I tagged along as the group wound its way through lush lowlands and alpine forest, past Sherpa villages which clung to the sheer mountain slopes, and yet more Buddhist monasteries perched high amongst the clouds. We used suspension bridges strung with colourful prayer flags to cross rivers, and once we had to move out of the way of an on-coming caravan of yaks. The landscape was dotted with rhododendron, magnolias and juniper, and we spotted golden eagles and snow pigeons soaring through the air. The vast views of the Himalayan valleys were truly breath-taking. It was almost impossible to take in the scale of it all.

When we finally reached base camp – after lots of rests for acclimatisation, which I'd spend exploring the scenic mountain villages with their little teahouses – I decided to go ahead to the summit. I appeared amongst a brightly-coloured collection of national flags high above the fluffy white clouds and gazed out at the jagged, snow-covered peaks which seemed to stretch for miles before disappearing into a haze beneath the vast blue sky. I stayed up there for hours, feeling smaller than I've ever felt in my life.

Egypt had taught me my own insignificance in time, and now Everest was teaching me a lesson of scale.

*How small I am,* I thought. *I'm as a raindrop compared to an ocean. My presence on the Earth created barely a ripple, and yet my micro-world was so very vast to me. It encompassed everyone I loved, and everywhere I went, everything I did and everything I ever hoped and dreamed. And now the ripples are fading, and the surface will soon be smooth again, as if I never existed.*

I thought of my family and Ben then, and hoped that I would remain significant at least to them, if to no one else. But then they too would be gone, and then so would *their* ripples, and then the ripples of those who remembered *them* would fade, and so on and so on. My mind started to spin, and I began to feel sick. *This is what altitude sickness must feel like* I thought, and I decided that I'd stayed on Everest's summit for long enough.

I visited China after that, and walked a section of the Great Wall which cut through the northern part of the country, marvelling at the ingenuity of the ancient ones who had built it. Then to India, where I hopped on and off trains exploring the country like a back-packer, losing myself in the vibrantly bustling cities where there seemed to be few traffic laws and cows roamed freely. In Australia, I stared in wonder at the abundance of colourful life darting around the Great Barrier Reef as I sat amongst the coral and experienced a few close encounters with several different species of shark. I headed to Italy after that, and took in the antiquity of Rome, the beauty of Florence and the pristine elegance of the Leaning Tower of Pisa.

It was approaching Christmas by this point, and I was beginning to feel the tug of home. Perhaps it was the thread which attached my heart to Ben's? Who knows. I made one final stop in Antarctica, where I walked among a colony of Emperor penguins for a day. I admired the huddled males patiently incubating their eggs against the harsh conditions while they waited for the females to return from their feeding trip to the sea, before I steeled myself and thought myself back home.

## Chapter Eighteen

I reappeared in my living room, where Ben was sat watching the TV. It was a Sunday evening, and I had been away for over six months.

"I'm back, sweetheart," I murmured to him. I made my way over to the couch and sat down beside him, leaning in to kiss him on the cheek before resting my head against his shoulder. He didn't react, but I was used to this by now. We remained like that until he decided to turn in for the night.

I watched him get ready for bed, pleased to note that he no longer appeared to need sleeping pills to get a good night's rest. I lay beside him until dawn crept into the room, watching his features relaxed in sleep. It was the first night I'd spent away from my friend the Moon in months, but I was exactly where I wanted to be.

*

Christmas was a quiet affair that first year after my death. Ben's parents flew over again and they all joined my mum and dad and Charles and Beth for dinner. Everyone was subdued as they ate, and often the only sound that could be heard was the clicking and scraping of knives and forks against the plates, the atmosphere far from merry. Ben finished less than half of his meal and then removed himself from the table and started drinking quite heavily as he sat watching TV. I sighed. I used to love Christmas.

I remembered holidays of the past – unwrapping presents with the excitement of small children; chatting as we cooked dinner together, then raising a toast over plates of steaming turkey surrounded by all the trimmings; snuggling up on the sofa watching a festive movie, feeling full and sleepy; then, later, going for a bracing walk, holding hands and smiling at strangers as we wished them a Merry Christmas.

Vicky popped by in the late afternoon, and the cold air wafted into the hallway with her, making my mum hurry to bustle her inside and close the front door. Her chatty exuberance perked everyone up somewhat. I could almost see the mental effort that she was making to stop everyone from wallowing in the doldrums. I could almost hear her say: "Come on, guys! This isn't what Daisy would've wanted! It's *Christmas* for Heaven's sake!"

She roped everyone into playing a few games, and it became more like the Christmases I remembered. A lump formed in my throat. Once again, I was filled with so much gratitude for my best friend.

When it was all over and Ben and his parents were saying goodbye, looking full and sleepy and much less tense than they had at the start of the day, I popped to wish my ghost friends a Merry Christmas. Kate was watching her children playing with their new toys in the cosy living room while their grandparents talked quietly with John in the kitchen.

"He's found it hard," Kate told me when we could hear the sound of subdued sobbing coming from the other room. I squeezed her hand and she went through to be with him. I stayed watching the children for a while. *You have your whole lives ahead of you,* I thought. *You have so much to look forward to. You can do anything, go anywhere, be anyone you want to be. Don't waste a single opportunity. Live. Really live.*

When Kate came back through to the living room, we chatted quietly for a while, smiling occasionally at the children's excited immersion in their role-playing games, and then I decided it was time to say goodbye. We hugged, promising to catch up again soon.

The pub was fairly busy when I visited Dean. I guess lots of people like to celebrate Christmas with a drink in the company of a few locals. Susie was serving behind the bar, and after wishing Dean a 'Happy Christmas' with a peck on the cheek, I asked him if she ever took a day off.

He chuckled. "This pub's her life."

"You're telling me." But a part of me wondered if she was drawn to Dean's presence like he was drawn to hers. I saw the love in his eyes whenever he looked at her, and I would often see her gaze with a faraway, wistful look in her eyes at the stool that he occupied. I wondered what it would be like when they were finally reunited. The thought made me smile.

After visiting with Dean for a while, I popped to New York to wish Kim Season's Greetings. She wasn't having a great Christmas. I discovered her in a hospital in a flood of tears. Her husband, Ray, had pneumonia and wasn't expected to survive the night.

I sat by his bedside with her, offering a hand to hold and quiet words of comfort, which she clung on to with a look of relieved gratitude on her drawn face now she knew that she wouldn't have to complete this most difficult of vigils alone.

Ray took his last rattling breath just before midnight. With my heart in my throat, I moved back against the wall as his ghost appeared next to the bed and he looked in wide-eyed wonder at his wife.

"Kim?" he asked tremulously, and she nodded. Joyously, they fell into each other's arms, their bodies shaking with years of pent-up emotion, and within moments, they vanished.

I crumpled to the ground, moved beyond words to have witnessed their reunion and passing to wherever it is that we end up. To tell you the truth, I bawled my bloody eyes out.

When I had recovered my composure, I took myself to what I had come to call 'Patrick's Park'. Because of the time difference between New York and the UK, it was nearly dawn.

Patrick scowled at me when he saw me walking towards him from where I had appeared some distance away so as not to make him jump.

"Where have you been?" he snapped. "I spent the whole of Christmas day alone."

"I'm sorry," I sighed as I sat down beside him. "I was going to come in the evening but I got held up." In a tired, shaky voice, I told him about Kim and Ray, and an expression of contrition immediately replaced the glower on his face.

"Sorry for snapping."

"It's ok."

"No, it's not."

I didn't answer, and we sat without talking for a while.

"What would your family have been up to yesterday?" I eventually asked.

He sighed. "My mum would've cooked a huge dinner. My brothers would have been around with their wives and kids. The house would have been noisy and messy and joyful and everything Christmas should be."

"And you'd normally be there with your girlfriend?"

He nodded. "Except the last two Christmases."

I told him about my own family's Christmas. "It wasn't the same as usual."

"No. I guess the first Christmas is especially hard for them. It will get easier."

"Aren't you curious to see them – your family I mean?"

"Of *course* I bloody am!" he burst out.

"Then what's stopping you?"

He stared at me as if astounded. "You think I want to see them living their lives without me? You think I'm some kind of a masochist like you?"

"I'm not -"

"Yes, you are," he insisted. "You fecking *haunt* them. Not to mention that poor lorry driver."

I went to open my mouth to deny this, but snapped it shut. He was right. But what was the alternative?

"You think I should haunt my death-place like you

instead?" I scoffed, but without much conviction.

"They need to move on," he stated more calmly. "I just don't want to witness it."

I brooded over this. Maybe I *should* just leave them all alone? Maybe it *would* be too hard to watch them all living their lives without me? But the thought of half a century without seeing Ben's beloved face and hearing his familiar voice left me cold. It would be a hell of a bleak fifty years.

To my relief, since I had returned from my travels, Ben hadn't had any one-night stands. Hopefully, it had just been a passing phase. A distraction from the pain.

"What're you going to do when he meets someone else?" Patrick asked then, as if he'd heard the train of my thoughts.

I shook my head, a sudden ache where my heart should have been beating.

"He'll get married one day. Have kids. Have you thought about that?" he persisted.

"Are you deliberately trying to hurt me?"

"No, of course not," he responded, surprised.

We stared at each other for a few moments.

"It will be an honour to watch him live out his life," I finally told him stiffly, remembering Dean's words about Susie. I don't know if I was trying to persuade Patrick or myself.

"You couldn't even handle a few one-night stands," he reminded me more gently.

"It was the initial shock. It will get easier," I insisted. He looked at me doubtfully, but didn't reply.

We sat watching the sun rise and listening to the dawn chorus. The ducks, swans and geese were already feeding and squabbling on the pond. The first dog walker turned up and started throwing a ball which the spaniel scrambled after enthusiastically, before returning with it eagerly and dropping it at its owner's feet, only to repeat the process again and again. *If only humans were so easy to please,* I thought.

Finally, I sighed and stood up. Without saying a word, I rested my hand on Patrick's shoulder. He nodded, and as I vanished I heard him murmur, "Merry Christmas, Beautiful Nosy Girl."

## Chapter Nineteen

I returned to Ben, who was waiting on his mum to finish cooking him a full English breakfast, and then I decided to visit Al.

I had already checked in on him once since my return. To my delight, I'd appeared beside him in his lorry (a different one from the one he'd been driving when we'd crashed) as he went about his routine deliveries. I hadn't spoken to him, preferring to sit beside him in companionship and more than a little worried about distracting him. I still had the sneaking suspicion that he could somehow hear me or sense me when I was talking to him.

This time, I discovered him sitting at the kitchen table tucking into his own breakfast of bacon sandwiches with Pam. Olly, their son, was nowhere to be seen. I presumed he was where most teenagers would be at ten o'clock on Boxing Day morning – tucked up comfortably in bed.

"Did you have a good Christmas, Al?"

A piece of bacon seemed to get lodged in his throat and he started coughing. Pam jumped up and patted his back almost violently.

"Sorry about that," I said when the commotion was over. Al didn't react, he just stared ahead with a slightly clenched jaw.

"I'm glad you're working again," I told him.

Pam said something about getting Olly out of bed. "Leave the boy," Al snapped, before flushing at her hurt look.

"There's no need to take it out on Pam," I chastised him. He took another bite of his sandwich and started chewing determinedly.

"I know I should leave you alone," I sighed. "I *know* I should. I'm sorry if my presence disturbs you. It's just…I need to…what the hell *happened*, Al?" I finally blurted.

He threw down what remained of his bacon butty and stormed out the back door. Pam looked after him in bewilderment. I made my way over to the kitchen window and looked out. He was sat at the table, already smoking. *Well, that went well,* I thought, tiredly.

*

I spent the rest of the Christmas holiday with Ben and his parents, with occasional visits to my family and friends. When New Year's Eve rolled around, I followed Ben and his friends out for the evening, full of trepidation, and I was relieved when he returned home alone after welcoming in the New Year fairly sensibly (he only threw up once).

When Ben returned to work, I got back into a routine of school and Uni visits, as well as a few outings with Kate and Dean to see films and shows. One day, I popped back to see Huipi and was touched when he greeted me excitedly and started indicating how much the children had grown in my absence. I spent the whole day with him, and learned a few new words - those for 'rain' and 'monkey' particularly stuck in my mind.

Kate and I also spent a day in Paris, and another in Barcelona. In the former, we strolled alongside the picturesque Seine, absorbing the beauty of the language of the sophisticated Parisiennes, letting it flow over us like the cool water of the river; thought ourselves to the top of the Eiffel tower to admire the uninterrupted views of the city of romance – we could see the Arc de Triomphe, Notre Damme, the Louvre and the Sacré Coeur, to name just a few of the capital's famous landmarks; and later we took in a spectacular cabaret show at the infamous Moulin Rouge, full of colour, sequins and feathers against a backdrop of pulsing music and glittering lights.

In Barcelona, we were wowed by the stunning architecture of Gaudi's Basilica of the Sagrada Familia; explored with wonder the magnificent works of art on a tour of the Joan Miró Foundation; and enjoyed the views of the idyllic Montjuic hill before we watched, enthralled, as dancers performed an authentic flamenco show in the Tablao de Carmen, their hands and feet flashing to the beat, their black and red dresses whipping around their lithe bodies.

Kate was wary of travelling further afield in those early days, but Dean came with me to explore the jaw-dropping slash in the face of the Earth that was the Grand Canyon, and the thunderous wonder of Niagara Falls – places he hadn't visited before. I marvelled at the natural processes that must have been involved over huge periods of time to form such majestic features in the Earth, and again felt tiny and insignificant. But I knew I wasn't. My photo was still on Ben's bedside table and that was all the evidence I needed of my continued importance in the world.

Bal finally mustered the courage to ask Amy out on a date, and she said yes. I followed them to a restaurant one Saturday evening and watched as they got on like a house on fire. Bal was charming and teasing, and Amy responded by coming out of her shell more and more as the evening wore on. I sat in the back seat of the car as he drove her home, and as they kissed goodnight I smiled and decided to give them some privacy. I returned home and snuggled against Ben where he relaxed on the sofa in a rare Saturday night in, feeling deliriously happy for my friends.

\*

The anniversary of my death arrived. It was a Sunday, and my mum had arranged for a get-together of my family and friends to visit the rose garden where my ashes were buried. Ben's parents flew over to be with him. He hadn't slept well the night before, tossing and turning or lying awake staring at the ceiling between fits of uneasy sleep, and he looked pale as he performed his morning routine and pecked at the breakfast his mum had made for him. When it was time to go, his dad clapped him on the back and he stood up jerkily and let them lead him to the car. The drive to the crematorium was undertaken in silence.

My mum and dad, Charles and Beth, Vicky, Jules and Asia, and a couple of Ben's friends were already waiting by the entrance. Several of them were holding bunches of flowers, their fresh, bright colours contrasting sharply against the bleak backdrop of the dormant bushes of the rose garden. Deirdre, Phil and Ben climbed out of the car and made their way over to the group, and sombre greetings were exchanged before they all headed around the building.

I forced myself to watch as they approached my headstone and laid the bouquets around it. Then they stood back and stared at it for several minutes, many of them with their hands clasped. A few sniffles could be heard, and tissues were passed around. My dad put his arm around my mum, and Ben's best mate, Stu, put his hand on Ben's shoulder as he scrubbed at his eyes.

"I'm still here, guys," I murmured to them, with a dull ache in my chest.

My dad said a few words then, about how I would want them all to remember me with love, but how I'd also want them to move on. "Some of those she's left behind have got their whole lives ahead of them still. She wouldn't want you to waste it in mourning for her. She'd want you to live your life to the full. Seize every opportunity that presents itself and create a few which don't. Let's not let her death stop the rest of us from living. That's not what she would want. Not the girl that I remember." He looked pointedly at Ben as he said this, and when Ben nodded in acknowledgement, my dad embraced him.

Inevitably, they all went to the pub then.


The next day, Deirdre and my mum helped Ben to clear out my closets and take my clothes and other possessions to a charity shop. It felt weird seeing the empty wardrobes and shelves where my books had been, but I'd known this had to happen eventually. *At least my photo's still in prime position,* I thought, gazing at my smiling face from where it stared back at me from Ben's bedside table.

It was a good photo, a happy photo, taken the year we'd met. My brown eyes were alive with laughter at something Ben had said to me just before the camera clicked, freezing the moment in time forever.

*Oh, Daisy,* I thought. *If only you'd known then what I know now. How different things might have been.*

My mum started crying as the last of my life was bagged up, and Deirdre embraced her in an unusual display of affection, murmuring comforting words to her. Ben turned away, busying himself with the bags. I watched, helpless, until Mum had recovered her composure, and they carted the bags downstairs and began loading the car.

As they all headed off to the High Street charity shop, I headed to Patrick's Park.

The day was fairly fine, for February, and there were several people strolling around the winding paths, making the most of the weather, as well as the usual shenanigans of the birds in and around the pond.

"You've just missed Dean," Patrick greeted me as I sat down beside him.

"Oh, how is he?" I hadn't seen any of my friends for a couple of days. I'd wanted to stick close to Ben for the anniversary.

"Fine, fine. We mostly talked about the football."

"Why don't you join him in the pub one day – watch a match with him?" I suggested. But I was unsurprised when he just rolled his eyes.

I had just started telling him about the visit to the rose garden when he suddenly jumped up like he'd been electrocuted. Startled, I popped up beside him and followed the direction of his gaze. He was staring, bug-eyed, at a couple who were walking on the other side of the pond, hand-in-hand. The woman was striking. She was tall and had flowing dark hair around a model's face, the bone structure sharply pleasing to the eye. She was wearing knee-high boots and a camel-coloured overcoat. The man was also tall and distinguished-looking, but he was blonde. They were a handsome couple.

"What is it?" I asked, but as I said the words, realisation dawned and my heart started sinking.

"It's her," he whispered. "It's my fecking girlfriend. Here. Walking in the park where I died, holding hands with another man."

## Chapter Twenty

"Oh, Patrick…"

We stood, staring, as they circled the pond, chatting in a relaxed and comfortable manner as if they knew each other well, and headed off down another path before disappearing from sight.

Patrick sat down heavily, a stunned look on his face. I sat beside him and rubbed his back. He leaned forward and rested his head in his hands, and we stayed like that for some time. I don't know what Patrick was thinking, but I was ruminating about what a tragedy it was to die young, and the injustice of life moving on. *But it's inevitable,* I thought. *We can't expect people to stay frozen in their grief forever. It wouldn't be fair. No, they deserve a life, with or without us.*

Eventually, the sound of someone whistling for their dog jolted him and he sat upright and scrubbed at his face. "Well, I guess the mountain came to Muhammed," he said resignedly.

"I'm so sorry."

"Me too. Christ, no wonder you took off to the fecking Moon." We looked at each other, then burst out laughing. My laughter turned to sobs, and we clutched at each other desperately, both of us crying. Crying at dying too young, crying at life moving on without us. Crying because that's what you do when there's nothing else you *can* do.

Kate's arrival was what it took to finally pull us apart. I wiped at my face with my sleeve as Patrick exclaimed, "Jesus! It's like a fecking train station here today!" and Kate looked at us in bewilderment. I explained what had happened, and she hugged Patrick, murmuring to him sympathetically, before settling herself onto the bench beside us.

"I expect John will meet someone new eventually," she said matter-of-factly after we'd sat in silence watching the serenity of the birds at play for several minutes.

I clasped her hand in mine.

"The kids need a mother. It's not fair to expect John to do it all alone. He wasn't made for that."

I tried to imagine what it would have been like if Ben and I'd had children, and what it would be like to witness another woman raising them. Could I be as generous as Kate was being in such circumstances?

"I always thought I'd have kids," Patrick uttered with a sigh.

"Me too," I murmured.

"I'm so sorry you never got the chance," Kate said, her eyes full of sympathy.

"What's done is done," Patrick replied stoically.

Momentarily, Kate sighed. "I'd best be getting back home. Poppy's unwell. Nothing serious, but I don't want to be away from her for too long."

We nodded, and after one last hug for each of us, she vanished.

"She's a kind woman. Drops by now and again to check that I'm okay," Patrick said.

"Kate's great," I agreed.

He nudged his shoulder against mine. "So are you."

"Thanks," I smiled.

"Oh, feck it," he said suddenly, standing up. "Will you come with me to see my parents?"

My eyes widened as he held out his hand to me.

"Might as well, now that I've seen…" he added, gesturing in the direction his girlfriend had gone.

I nodded and took his hand, and we disappeared together.

\*

We reappeared in a large Victorian house. There was a bright, modern conservatory attached, the winter sunlight streaming in through the glass ceiling, and in it an older man was sitting reading a newspaper while a similarly-aged woman completed a crossword. They were a handsome couple. I started to walk closer when a strangled sound stopped me. I turned to look at Patrick and saw that his face was contorted in grief. He was shaking his head and backing away, holding his hands up in front of him as if to ward off the pain of seeing his parents after the passage of so much time. I stopped him, put my arm around him and gently urged him towards them.

When he reached them, he fell onto his knees. Then his head bowed and his shoulders started shaking. I crouched beside him, my hand moving rhythmically over his back. His parents continued as they were, oblivious to the scene that was unfolding before them.

*What would it do to them,* I wondered, *to know that their youngest son was here, before them, right now, weeping at the sight of them?*

After some minutes, Patrick straightened up and looked up into their faces. "I'm sorry I've stayed away for so long," he told them earnestly. "I just…" his voice cracked, and he stopped to clear his throat. "I just had such a *great* life, you know? And it's because of *you*. I couldn't have asked for better parents. I hope you were proud of me."

"I'm sure they were," I said softly. He sighed and stood up, then scrubbed at his face. "Might as well do my brothers next since I'm in the mood."

I smiled encouragingly, and we visited both of his older siblings at work. They'd obviously been close; I could tell by the way that he teased them and from the anecdotes he told me about the things they'd got up to together growing up. We watched them for a while. They were both good looking and charming, professional in their interactions with their colleagues, and I could see the resemblance between them and Patrick.

"There are good genes in your family," I told him when I first saw his second brother, Ryan, but Patrick just looked at me in surprise.

He wanted to return to his parents then, so we said goodbye and I transported home to Ben. I spent the evening on the sofa with him and his parents. He'd taken the day off, but he was due back at work the next day and Deirdre and

Phil were flying home first thing in the morning. They retired to bed early, and I spent the night listening to Ben snore, perfectly content to be so close to the one I loved.

*

Spring was here before I knew it. Once again, I observed the signs of new life bursting out of the ground. Green leaves unfurled on the trees, seemingly overnight, and daffodils and tulips reared their colourful heads in their search for the fortifying sunlight. Cool blue skies stretched to the horizon, and my usual sense of new beginnings was confirmed when Charles and Beth announced that she was pregnant.

I actually clapped in excitement when they broke the news over dinner one Sunday in March. My mum cried, and even my dad shed a tear when they announced that if it was a girl they'd decided to call her Daisy. Touched, I had a lump in my throat as they toasted to the pregnancy. Beth was thirteen weeks along, and had brought the image of the twelve-week scan to share. Mum oohed over the bean-shaped baby, and Charles proudly pointed out an arm and a leg.

When the meal was over, I rushed to tell my friends the news, one-by-one. Kate turned weepy-eyed as she reminisced about her own pregnancies and Dean smiled and shook my hand. Patrick hugged me and told me how much he'd enjoyed being an uncle. I felt sad that I'd never get to interact with them in the way he described playing with his nieces and nephews, but just the fact that I would get to see them grow up, and watch over them, was exciting to me. I was going to be an auntie!

When I returned to Ben, I remembered Charles's face as he'd looked at the image of his baby, and for the first time I truly wanted that for Ben, even if it meant someone else would be the mother.

"You'll be a great dad," I told him, as we sat on the sofa watching the football.

## Chapter Twenty-One

Time moved on. Days became weeks. Weeks became months. I followed my routine, the only changes being that I now checked in on Beth and Charles more frequently, and I managed to persuade Patrick to take a few trips with me, now that he'd been forced out of his self-imposed isolation.

He was still spending most of his time on his bench in the park, because, in his own words, "I don't want to fecking *haunt* my family. I didn't spend that much time with them when I was *alive*, for Christ's sake," but he was willing to venture further afield for his friends. He'd watch televised sporting events in the pub with Dean, like the boxing and the rugby, shouting passionately in response to every twist and turn on the screen; pop to Kate's regularly for a chat; and occasionally we'd all go to a show together.

The first trip abroad I managed to persuade Patrick to take was to his childhood home in Ireland. He'd grown up in Kilkenny, and after taking me to the home that he'd been raised in and the school that he'd attended, he spent a day showing me around the tourist attractions in the medieval town.

We toured the grand Norman castle, well-preserved churches and monasteries, the imposing cathedral and impressive Dominican priory. Later, we mooched around the craft shops, studying the paintings, pottery and jewellery that were for sale, then ended up in a sixteenth century pub listening to traditional Irish music played by a live band. The only drawback was that we couldn't sample the beer, a fact about which Patrick grumbled repeatedly.

We returned several times to Ireland after that, and each visit just made me fall more and more in love with the country. I found it rugged and romantic, beautiful and magical. From the Ring of Kerry, with its stunning views of the Atlantic, breath-taking mountains and scenic villages, to the Giant's Causeway, with its thousands of hexagonal basalt columns tumbling down into the Ocean, I couldn't get enough of the 'Emerald Isle'. Patrick loved it too – he was at his most relaxed and light-hearted in his native island – and the excursions across the Irish Sea cemented our growing friendship.

\*

In August, Ben started dating someone from work, a willowy redhead named Nicola. She hadn't been at the office for long, but I had taken an immediate dislike to her. I found her loud and attention-seeking – she was the sort of woman who pouted and kept flicking her hair back when she talked to men – and I wondered what he saw in her. However, I decided to respect his choice, after all, I wasn't a complete cow and I told myself that she had to have *some* redeeming features.

I gave them privacy when they were together, and tried to understand when he put my photo away in a drawer and she started spending the occasional night at the house. On these nights, I'd return to the Moon and try not to think about what they were doing in my bed.

At different times, I persuaded Dean and Patrick to journey there with me, and I took great delight in being their tour guide around the landing sites. We'd sit staring at the Earth in its various phases, and shake our heads in awe at the wondrous sight. It was a chance to get away from it all, to take a break from the intensity of an existence of effectively haunting our loved ones, and it also allowed us to give them some privacy when we felt that it was appropriate.

\*

Beth had the baby in September. I was there throughout the long, arduous labour, pacing around between increasingly close-together contractions and saying encouraging words that she couldn't hear during each painful squeeze of her womb. I cried with Charles when the baby eventually came, bloody and bawling, and the midwife informed them that it was a girl. Daisy Rose Roberts was seven pounds and two ounces, had light-brown skin and her mum's big blue eyes, and I fell in love with her instantly.

When Charles and Beth took her home, I would spend the nights sitting up with a tiredly contented Beth during the almost continual feeds, and I'd hang over Daisy's cot stroking her cheek when she'd cry for seemingly no reason. As the weeks passed and she became more interactive, I would coo and smile over her and later swear to my friends that she could see and hear me. Once, I even felt her hand clutch my finger for a few seconds. It was magical.

Between Daisy, my friends and routine, I barely had time to spend with Ben, who was more and more occupied with the lovely Nicola.

Christmas arrived again, and Ben flew out to Benalmádena to spend it with his parents. I flitted between Spain and the UK, eager to see as much of Daisy's first Christmas as I could, remembering to fit my friends in during the evening. As last year, Dean was happily in the pub with Susie and the regulars, and Kate was content at home with John and the children; but for the first time in four years, Patrick spent the day with his family. I found him at his parents' house and it was exactly as he'd described it – 'noisy and messy and joyful and everything Christmas should be'. I hung out for a while, until his nieces and nephews began to get tired and crotchety and his brothers and their wives decided to make a move.

"Moon?" Patrick suggested, his eyebrow cocked questioningly, and I nodded. We sat gazing at the Earth, our knees drawn up to our chests, and silently watched it rotate against the glittering backdrop. It was a sight I would never grow weary of.

*

I visited the site of the crash on the second anniversary of my death, but I didn't stay for long. It was only a road junction after all. There was nothing particularly interesting about it. Oh, a few people remembered that there had once been a young woman killed there, but life went on.

I hadn't visited Al for a while, so I thought I'd see how he was doing. It was a Monday, and I was expecting to reappear in his lorry as he went about his work day. However, I materialised in his garden, where he was back to chain-smoking by the look of the overflowing ashtray.

"Well, it *is* the anniversary, so I guess I'll forgive you," I told him. He jumped. "I bloody *knew* it! You *can* hear me, can't you?"

He stubbed out his cigarette and his chair scraped loudly as he pushed it back and ran into the house like he was being chased by a hell-cat. I stared after him, gobsmacked, and dropped down onto the step. The thread was still there and I picked it up. "What happened, Al?" I asked no one, and the thread snapped.

\*

A smaller group than last year visited the rose garden – my parents, Ben, Charles and Beth with Daisy, and Vicky. They all shed a tear; even Daisy seemed to sense that something wasn't right and had a good cry at one point. She stopped and smiled when I spoke soothingly to her though.

I noticed that Nicola didn't stay over at the house for a week or two around the anniversary of my death, and Ben seemed moodier.

"I know," I told him softly as he sat staring at the television on Saturday night. "It's a difficult time of year for you."

## Chapter Twenty-Two

As a few more weeks passed and Ben returned to his normal self, I decided to go and visit Huipi again. I would go every few months, and he was always pleased to see me, his eyes lighting up whenever I appeared before him. This time, Patrick came with me.

When we first arrived, he stared around the settlement, wide-eyed with awe. I watched him absorb the sight of the simple huts surrounded by lush trees, the happy children playing near the river, the gossiping women busy preparing meals while squatting on the packed-mud floor. I smiled as I led him around the clearing, and when I spotted Huipi I proudly led Patrick over to him.

After initial caution, Huipi relaxed and took over the tour with enthusiasm. He showed him the men, working together as they hunted and fished, the sound of their camaraderie pleasant against the noises of the rainforest. It was an entirely different world from that to which Patrick was accustomed, the big, crowded city, the grey concrete and bright lights, and I could see that he was fascinated by it.

Much later, when the sun was starting to set beyond the trees and the tribe was settling down for the night, the three of us were preparing to say goodbye when I felt Patrick suddenly go very still beside me. I turned to look at him and saw that his gaze was fixed unblinkingly on one of the huts. Or more precisely, on a young woman who had emerged from within and stood on the threshold, gazing up at the darkening sky. I had seen her many times before. She was very beautiful, with long, straight dark hair and bronze skin. Her eyes glinted in the dim light which highlighted her strong cheekbones.

She was one of those women who draw attention without even meaning to, or even being aware of it, and I had often observed how she moved gracefully about the camp, quietly supervising the children and ignoring the advances and antics of the young men who tried to gain her attention. Patrick was unable to take his eyes off her. I reached over and squeezed his hand, breaking the spell that he seemed to be under. He blinked and looked at me, and I swear that, for a second, I could see all the stars of the night sky in his eyes. He shook himself and gave a low, embarrassed chuckle.

Huipi had watched the exchange in confusion, and I reached over and squeezed his fingers gently too. He seemed to understand that I was saying goodbye, for now, and he smiled and touched his chest before turning and walking away.

"Shall we?" I asked, when I turned back to Patrick. The place where the woman had been standing was empty, a dim, barren hole. He bit his lip and nodded reluctantly, casting a yearning look back through the darkness towards the hut, before we vanished.

*

"You were entranced!" I teased him when we were settled on our bench in the park.

Patrick opened his mouth in denial then changed his mind. "Feck," he sighed, and I think he'd have blushed if he was able to.

"She's very beautiful," I said, matter-of-factly.

We stared at each other for a moment, then burst out laughing. I giggled so much that a few tears leaked from my eyes.

"Jesus!" he announced when we'd calmed down. "I felt like I'd seen the sun for the first time."

"I didn't know you were so poetic," I smirked.

"Shut it, you." His eyes twinkled.

Then we both sighed.

"I'd best be going, Grumpy Irishman," I told him.

He nodded. "Ok, see you soon, Beautiful Nosy Girl."

Smiling, I vanished.

\*

Life, or rather death, moved on. A few years passed. I watched Daisy develop into an adorable, babbling toddler, quick to learn and full of curiosity for the world around her. I whooped when Charles and Beth announced a second pregnancy, a boy this time. Between my family and friends, my hobbies and my travels, I was content, if not joyously happy.

Ben was in his early thirties by now, still in his prime. I'd remained stoic as I'd observed him flit from one short-lived relationship to another, the unimpressive Nicola a distant memory. Wistfully, I imagined what we'd have been doing if I'd survived the accident, or if it had never occurred. We'd have been married by now. Perhaps Daisy and little Teddy would even have a sweet little cousin or two.

"It wasn't meant to be," I murmured to myself, as I sat on the Moon on the fifth anniversary of my death. I was alone. Patrick was visiting the Amazon, the pull of Puna, the tribal beauty, too much for him to resist for any significant length of time. I hadn't mentioned it to him, but I wondered if Puna was the one that he was waiting for. I hoped so. What else could explain the way that he gravitated to her? Perhaps, sometimes, we only meet our soulmate in the afterlife? I contemplated this for a while, before my head started spinning and I gave up. Some things are just too big for us to comprehend. "I'm sure You know what You're doing," I muttered, and as if God heard me, a star winked in the distance.

\*

Ben started dating a woman named Olivia a few months later. She was petite, wore her dark hair in a messy bun and had a gentle, loving nature. She was a librarian at the university, and I liked her immediately. I watched as Ben came fully back to life, his heart opening like the petals of a sunflower under her patient and tender ministration, and was unsurprised when they moved in together six months later, and when he proposed to her within the year.

Although I had got used to seeing him with other women, and although I could see that she was good for him, I still wept when it happened. I trailed behind them as they shopped for an engagement ring and watched as they excitedly shared the good news with friends and family. It was a bitter-sweet time for me. I couldn't help but be wistful for what we would have had, if the accident hadn't taken place, but seeing Ben so content almost made up for it.

Almost.

*That's love,* I thought, trying to be pleased for him. *You'd rather see the other person happy than melancholy, even if it meant they woke up next to someone else each morning.*

The wedding preparations began immediately; Olivia and Ben were both in their thirties, and wanted to start a family as soon as they were married. I watched the other woman live what would have been my life, trying to quash the jealousy that regularly threatened to overwhelm me. Masochistically, I stalked Olivia as she prepared for the big day, trying on wedding dresses and sitting for her hair and makeup trial, all the time thinking that it should have been me. My heart was a stone in my chest, hard and heavy. I began to neglect my friends, and more than once, Patrick, Kate and Dean expressed their concern that I was becoming obsessed.

"It's not fecking healthy," Patrick told me one day after he appeared beside me while I watched Olivia and Ben at a cake-tasting session. Displays of pretty, tiered creations surrounded us, displayed on pastel table coverings, and I stared miserably at a delicate rose made out of icing sugar on the nearest work of confectionary art.

"'Healthy?' I'm already dead," I responded flatly.

"You know what I mean," he snapped.

I stayed silent, and he huffed and pursed his lips. Ben and Olivia laughed as Ben tried to eat a slice of cake that was slightly too big for his mouth. I winced.

Patrick sighed and put his arm around me. "I know it's hard," he said gently, and a small sob escaped before I could stop it. He pulled me in for a bear hug and I shook in his tight embrace.

We stayed like that for some minutes before I pulled away. "Let's go," I said quietly. He nodded, and without discussing it, we vanished, and reappeared on the Moon.

## Chapter Twenty-Three

As the wedding drew closer, I worked hard at accepting Ben's new life. On Patrick's advice, I kept myself busy with my ghost friends, returning to the theatre, sitting in on university lectures and taking short trips abroad. I spent lots of time with my parents and little Daisy, who was the best distraction. Sometimes when I was with her, I managed to forget the upcoming nuptials for short spaces of time. Very short.

But before I knew it, the day was upon us.

"Just don't go," Patrick advised me. "It'll be bloody torture."

"I have to," I told him. And I did. The occasion was like a magnet, pulling me in. Ben was my North, and I was his South. I couldn't stay away from him, even though I knew it would be incredibly painful.

I was right. As I sat in the back pew of the crowded church and watched Ben turn to see Olivia walking down the aisle, his face lighting up like it had only ever done for *me* before, I felt my heart rip in two. He looked so handsome, so very happy, so very much *my* Ben, my darling Ben, who I had loved since I was sixteen. But he wasn't looking at me, not Daisy, who had been dead these seven years, but at this new woman, this replacement, this woman who was so very lovely, but was not me. I bit my knuckles as they exchanged vows, and would have drawn blood if I'd had any flowing within me.

Then suddenly, I was sobbing. Huge, gut-wrenching sobs that only I could hear. Animalistic, like a wounded creature, which I was. I didn't try to stop myself; I couldn't. I indulged my agony utterly. Minutes passed and I was oblivious to anything other than my own anguish. The ceremony finished, but I remained seated, head bowed and shaking, until my despair gradually subsided.

I lifted my head to find the church empty and silent. I sat staring at the beautiful flower arrangements – pink roses and baby's breath – which stood in stark relief to the stern and forbidding darkness of the church's interior. And I waited.

They came hours after the ceremony, as I had planned. They appeared in the aisle beside me, and wore identical expressions of confusion at finding it empty. Patrick cottoned-on first.

"It's over, isn't it? You told us the wrong time," he admonished, running his hand through his mop of dark locks in frustration.

"I needed to be alone, and I knew you wouldn't let me," I whispered, staring at the Bible tucked into the pew in front of me.

"Oh, sweetheart," Kate murmured, a sympathetic look on her face. John had recently started dating again. I patted the pew and she sat beside me, her head resting against mine, her hand rubbing my back. The human contact felt nice, comforting.

Dean sighed and moved to sit on my other side, where he took my hand in his. He didn't attempt to say anything, knowing that nothing could make this day any better for me, but I drew comfort from the solidity of his presence, his calm strength and wisdom.

Patrick remained in the aisle, his hands on his hips, cursing quietly to himself before lapsing into silence, his head down.

Then he started laughing, barking out the most cynical, bitter sound I'd ever heard, in life or death. Dean and Kate stared at him in surprise, but I understood completely.

Death sucks.

I watched as Patrick darted towards the flowers positioned at the front of the church, his fists clenched as he struck out at the display on the left again and again. The arrangement remained undisturbed, but this didn't stop him. He continued swiping at it.

"Come on!" he snarled, and although he didn't look back at me, I knew what he wanted.

I appeared next to him and began boxing at the floral display to the right. It felt amazing – coldly invigorating. Patrick was cackling by now, like a mad man, and I started giggling uncontrollably, almost, but not quite, hysterically. And then, as suddenly as we'd started, we stopped. Patrick launched himself towards me and gathered me in his arms, a sob escaping him. I clutched at him tightly and felt Dean and Kate join us in a group hug.

"Moon," I whispered, and we all vanished.

\*

Olivia fell pregnant almost immediately. Ben was delighted when she announced the news one evening after he returned home from work. It was the week before the eighth anniversary of my death.

My heart bubbled, churning with mixed emotions as I saw the light and love in Ben's eyes, and watched as he grinned and scooped Olivia up and swung her around. She shrieked and giggled and I swallowed back the bitter thought that it should have been *me* in his arms, *me* carrying his baby.

Soon, they were breathlessly discussing names and colour schemes for the spare bedroom, which would become the nursery, and I couldn't take any more. I escaped to the comforting arms of my friends.

\*

On the anniversary, as was my custom, I paid a visit to Al. As usual, he had taken the day off work, and I found him chain-smoking in his garden.

"Hello, Al," I said quietly, as I took my place on the step. Other than a slight quickening of his breath, he showed no response. He was used to my annual appearance.

We sat in silence for a while, before I sighed and updated him on the events of the past year.

"And now she's pregnant," I finished, my expressionless voice belying the emotion which bubbled under the surface.

Al's eyelids drooped slightly and he took a deep drag on his cigarette.

I studied the garden to distract myself from breaking down. It was neater than it had been when I'd first seen it, though it was quite bleak still, spring not yet having made her hopeful presence felt. Rectangular beds sat in uniform rows to one side, but they were empty. *Like my womb,* I thought. *The only difference is that new life will soon be bursting out of those beds, but I will remain forever dormant.* I swallowed, and imagined that I could taste bile.

The back door creaked opened and Pam followed her usual routine of placing a cup of tea on the table before him, before resting her hand on his shoulder and heading silently back into the house. She knew by now not to ask anything of him on this most difficult of days.

I watched the steam curl from the mug, before it disappeared into the frigid air.

"You'd better drink that before it gets cold," I told him flatly after a few minutes. He grunted and reached for it. I watched him slurp some down, before he returned the cup to the table with a gentle clang, unaware that he had inadvertently revealed that he could hear me, a fact that he always tried to hide.

"I need to know, Al."

He shook his head, almost imperceptibly.

"Yes," I insisted quietly, and his lips tightened slightly.

"*Please*, Al."

He started gathering up his cigarette box, lighter and cup. The chair scraped as he pushed it back and stood, ready to head back into the house.

"I had a fucking *life*, Al!" I told his retreating back, and he stopped. His shoulders slumped and his head fell forwards. I opened my mouth to say more, but closed it with a snap when he spoke.

"You did it on purpose," he said hoarsely, without turning around. Only his head was turned slightly to the side.

"*What* did you say?" I asked, startled.

"You fucking crossed into my lane and ploughed into me, head on," he continued, husky-voiced.

"No," I breathed.

"Yes," he uttered, quietly, and I couldn't mistake the sadness and sincerity in his voice. The pain. "Your airbag was deactivated and you weren't wearing a seatbelt. They said you'd suffered from depression for years."

I reeled at his words and shook my head in denial. *No!*

"You killed yourself," he continued softly, as if he knew I needed to hear the words. "I'm so sorry." And then he walked into the house, shutting the door quietly behind him.

I stayed on the step for some minutes, frozen in shock. It couldn't be true… it just couldn't. I would remember… wouldn't I? I'd had an amazing life – a wonderful fiancé, a professional career, a lovely family and friends – what would someone like me have to be depressed about? I'd had my whole future ahead of me, damnit!

Suddenly, I grew angry. A ball of fire began to burn in my chest and I leapt up, determined to confront Al and his outrageous declaration. "You're wrong, Al!" I shouted, fists clenched at my sides as I glared at the uncaring face of the stone-grey house. But it wasn't enough to unleash what was inside of me.

I appeared beside him in the kitchen. He was sat at the worn table, his head in his hands.

"Did you hear me?" I demanded, leaning down to speak right into his face. He jumped. I didn't care that I'd startled him. "You're mistaken, or a you're a damn *liar*, Al!"

A loud scraping noise echoed around the room as he hurriedly pushed back his chair and ran from the kitchen. He headed for the stairs and I met him at the top. "Say it isn't true," I insisted, and he reeled back at the sound of my voice immediately before him. Gathering himself, he rushed through me into the bedroom and slammed the door. I stumbled at the icy nausea that enveloped me.

I found him sat on the edge of the bed, which was neatly made up with a floral quilt and matching pillows. He was grinding his hands against his eyes, and I realised that he was trying to stop himself from crying. The vitriolic words that I had been about to utter died in my throat. Unknown to him, I sat down beside him and let him gather himself together while I tried to calm myself down. It wasn't so much anger that I was feeling, I realised, but panic. Panic that it was true; panic that I had brought this on myself; panic that I had ruined my chance of a life – a family – with Ben. Panic that this was all my own fault.

I rested my face in my hands, my elbows on my knees, and tried to clear my mind, trying to let the memories of my life flow. At first, there were just the memories Vicky and Ben had discussed soon after my death – the fun times, the good times. The holiday in Corfu, re-enacting the Abbey Road cover, swimming with dolphins in the Caribbean. A perfect picture of a perfect life. I frowned as more happy memories flowed and I became aware that I couldn't remember anything really *bad*.

No one's life is *all* good. I began to grow uneasy. Why couldn't I remember a single unhappy time, a feeling, an event, a day?

Al sighed next to me, still unaware of my lingering presence. Then he stretched out on the bed and closed his eyes, which were now dry, but slightly red. I decided to let him rest and thought myself to Patrick's Park.

## Chapter Twenty-Four

"*Oh Christ, Oh Jesus*," Patrick whispered repeatedly into my hair as I shakily revealed what Al had disclosed. He held me tightly, as if I would float away if he let go, and to be honest I wasn't sure that I wouldn't.

"How can it be true?" I asked him desperately. "Surely I would remember something like that."

"I don't know, sweetheart. I just don't know," he sounded confused and frustrated, with an underlying current of sadness.

"Well, they do say God works in mysterious ways," I stated bitterly.

"What do you mean?" he asked, frowning.

But I didn't answer.

"Daisy?"

"I guess He took it away," I finally choked out.

"Took what away?" Patrick responded in bewilderment.

"My memory."

"Why would He do that?"

"Who the fuck knows?" I leaned back and scrubbed my hands over my face.

Patrick seemed to ponder this. "Maybe you're right."

"What do you mean?"

"Well, depression is an illness, like any other – cancer, say – and when you die you no longer suffer with it, do you?"

"But Kate *remembers* having cancer," I frowned.

"Yes, but depression is a *mental* illness," he replied. "Maybe He wipes the slate clean in such cases. You know, so that it doesn't carry over into the afterlife. This is the 'well' you, and the 'well' you is who you remember…maybe because it's for your own good."

I tried to fit this theory into my perception of my wonderful life, but it was difficult.

"I feel like I can't trust my own memory," I told him.

"Your memories are real; you *can* trust them. They're just minus the bad times."

"Oh God," I groaned into my hands. "What have I done? Poor Ben…Poor Al…my poor parents. What a waste; what an absolute *fucking* waste." Tears coursed over my cheeks. I jumped up and kicked at the bench, hoping to feel it, to transfer the pain from my heart to my foot, but of course, it just passed straight through it, ice-cold, and I screeched at the grey sky, "What the fuck, God? What the *actual* fuck?"

Patrick watched me as I paced back and forth, trying to unleash the pent-up energy that threatened to consume me. I had a flashback to the scene of the 'accident' – how had I not noticed before that my crumpled car was slanted across the wrong lane? That I wasn't wearing a seatbelt? That the air bag hadn't activated? Had I repressed the knowledge?

I desperately tried to remember the events leading up to the crash and any hints in the way my friends and family had reacted in the aftermath, but other than that one time Ben had spoken aloud of his anger towards me, there was nothing.

"People don't speak of such things," Patrick finally broke the silence to utter quietly, as if he had heard my thoughts. "They would rather bury their heads in the sand. Pretend it never happened. It's understandable."

"'Understandable'? 'Understandable'? None of this is bloody 'understandable', Patrick!" I told him harshly. I mimicked a news reporter's voice: "Young woman with everything going for her drives head-long into a lorry, devastating her friends and family and demolishing her promising future in one fell swoop!"

"You were ill. It wasn't a choice. You mustn't blame yourself," he insisted. The pity in his eyes was unbearable.

"But I do," I told him expressionlessly, and I vanished.

I reappeared on the Moon and sat staring at the Earth, my knees drawn up to my chest as I rocked back and forth. I felt like I had died all over again; only this time, it wasn't because of a tragic accident, something that had happened *to* me that had been completely out of my control, just one of those unlucky things that happened to some people. No, this time, it was in what I was quickly accepting was a deliberate act, fuelled by a deep depression that I couldn't remember.

*I must have felt so hopeless,* I thought. *And nothing that anyone could say or do had been able to help me. Had I had therapy? Taken medication? And how had my illness affected Ben? Had he been able to cope with me at my worst? What had I put him through? And my parents, what of them? They had outlived their youngest child because she took her own life at the tender age of twenty-six. What did that do to a parent? Oh God, oh God...*

Patrick had said that it wasn't my fault. That I was ill. And I knew that if he'd been talking about someone else, I'd have completely agreed with him. Depression *was* an illness. It wasn't something that a person chose. And it wasn't 'mind over matter', or a question of 'thinking positive', or 'pulling your socks up'. It was clinical; it was chemical; maybe genetic. I knew all this. And yet I couldn't apply these thoughts to myself.

The guilt was overwhelming, a feeling so indescribably painful that I felt ill with it, nauseated and off-balance. I remembered Ben's zombie-like state in the weeks following my death; my parents' tear-stained faces; Charles and Beth's sadness; Vicky's grief; Al's silence. And I was filled with so much self-blame and regret that I could almost taste it.

\*

The gathering at the rose garden took place later that afternoon. Present were my parents, Charles and Beth with Daisy and Teddy, Ben and a heavily-pregnant Vicky, all wrapped up warm against the February chill, bundled up in woolly hats, scarves and gloves. They took turns to place flowers by the stone that marked where my ashes were buried, pretty bouquets of carnations and roses, lilies and freesias, and spoke little; even the children were sombre and quiet. Just another year in what was becoming a long line, where life had moved on without me.

But to me, it was anything but 'just another year'. I stood with my head bowed, unable to look at their faces, ashamed of the grief and suffering that I'd caused. I wanted more than anything to crawl into Ben's reassuring arms and beg them all to forgive me. I wanted to look into my father's eyes and see the warmth and love that used to shine out at me as a little girl. To sit and have one more conversation with my mother. She would tell me that it was alright, that she didn't blame me, and I would be comforted.

But I couldn't.

Suddenly, I was yearning for the peace and simplicity of my childhood, the days, surely, long before I could have been touched by the illness that led to my death. Days of innocent play, when I was oblivious to the cares of the world and surrounded by love.

I wished for it so hard, I felt my head spinning. The world rushed around me. My vision turned blurry and I soon became nauseous. I staggered, and was about to hit the ground when I felt that strange *pop* which signified that I'd vanished. My world turned black.

## Chapter Twenty-Five

I woke up in a strangely familiar room, shaking and still feeling sick. Gingerly, I sat up and examined my surroundings. Awareness dawned on me almost immediately. I was in my childhood home, and it looked just as it used to look when I was a little girl: cheerful patterned wallpaper and a black leather sofa; the gas fire with its brass fittings; navy carpet imprinted with a faint, swirling pattern; big old boxy TV; clock ticking away on the mantle.

*Time!* I thought. *I've travelled through time!*

I reeled from this new state of affairs. Dean hadn't mentioned *time*-travel – but then, perhaps he didn't know? I took a moment to steady myself, then stood up on slightly less-shaky legs. Just as I did, the living room door opened, and a little girl of about four years of age ran in to the room, giggling. She was wearing a flower-print dress and being chased by a dungaree-wearing boy who was a few years older and also laughing exuberantly. Their cheeks were flushed and their eyes were bright. *It's me and Charles!* I realised, staring at the younger version of myself in amazement.

The younger me launched herself onto the sofa and buried her face amongst the cushions. Within seconds, little Charles was on her, tickling her mercilessly. The giggles grew louder, almost hysterical, and I found myself laughing along in delight.

My mum and dad entered the room carrying shopping bags, and they smiled at the antics of the children. I stared at them hungrily. They looked so much younger and more vigorous, their skin smooth, their eyes bright, and the resemblance between my dad and my brother at the same age was uncanny.

I watched the children throw themselves into playing with their toys, a doll's house for little me, the figures and furniture arranged neatly to be just-so, and superhero action figures for young Charles, while my mum and dad went through to the kitchen to put the groceries away. I was fascinated by these youthful versions of my brother and I, and the sense of nostalgia was overwhelming. Tears came to my eyes and I wished that he was here to share this magical experience with me. This gift.

*Thank You, Lord,* I thought fervently, briefly closing my eyes.

I observed my family for the rest of the morning, while they spent time playing together in the sunny garden, making mud pies and bouncing on the small trampoline, the children's voices raised in glee, feeling content and like I had escaped from the excruciating pain of the future. Here I was, long before any tragedy would touch me, happy and safe and secure in my small world. The little girl delicately eating her lunch in front of me now could never know hopelessness, nor despair. She was untouched by the trials and tribulations of life, and mental illness had no place in her innocent mind.

For the first time, looking upon myself, as if at another person, I was able to think more objectively about the circumstances of my death. This little girl wasn't to blame for what she'd grow up to do because of an *illness*. No more than Kate was to blame for her death by cancer, or Patrick for his aneurysm.

"You were sick," I told her quietly. "And the doctors couldn't fix you."

A sense of peace stole over me, but it was fragile, like taped-over cracks.

I stayed with my family for the rest of the day, up until my dad read the bedtime story and the children were fast asleep, their little mouths slightly open, their eyelids fluttering as they dreamed. An idea had occurred to me, and I wanted to see if it would work. I wanted to see what Ben was like as a little boy.

\*

As I pictured a younger version of him, the room started spinning again and a less-intense feeling of nausea overcame me. I closed my eyes, and when I reopened them, I was standing in a park in the sunshine. Not Patrick's Park, but another, unfamiliar recreation ground. There was no pond, but instead there was a tired-looking basketball court and a skate ramp covered in graffiti. A game of football was taking place on a large, open area of grass, with what looked like hoodies being used to create the goals. Pre-teen boys were calling instructions and encouragement to each other and the irregular *thumps* of the ball when it was kicked sounded loudly in the summer silence.

I was drawn over to watch the match and my breath caught in my throat as I spotted a familiar lad. He had shaggy, light-brown hair and I knew that if I looked closer his eyes would be pale green. It was unmistakably my Ben. I examined his slim build, seeing where his shoulders had yet to broaden; I looked at his hands, which would one day touch me so lovingly; his lips, yet to be kissed by mine.

*Oh Ben, what did I put you through?*

Proudly, I witnessed his even-tempered response when he was fouled, his uplifting encouragement to his teammates, his ingrained sense of fairness and sportsmanship shining out of him as he congratulated the other team on their win, patting backs and shaking hands.

I followed him as he walked home at a leisurely pace with a friend, his hoodie slung over his shoulders, and watched as they parted ways before Ben turned into the little cul-de-sac where he would still be living when he met me, roughly five years later. The windows of the surrounding houses observed us, blankly, their thoughts hidden.

I saw his dad, who was washing his car on the driveway, greet him by flicking his sodden sponge at him so that droplets fell on his hair and clothes, making them both laugh. Ben's dimples flashed, and I swallowed past the lump that had suddenly formed in my throat.

I stayed outside as Ben entered the house and the front door closed behind him. His father continued his routine chore, whistling as he worked. The only other sounds were the chirping of the birds in the nearby trees and the distant sound of traffic.

I debated entering the house, but I felt a strong pull to visit another Ben, in another time. Before I knew it, I found myself standing in the common room of my sixth form college. Motivational posters adorned the white walls, and the latest pop music was playing on the old stereo in the corner. I spotted my sixteen-year-old-self, dressed in jeans, ballet pumps and a leather jacket, satchel over my shoulder and curly hair scraped up into a ponytail at the crown of my head, stroll into the large area with a group of friends which included young versions of Jules, Asia and Vicky. The group headed over to one of the seating areas. I spotted seventeen-year-old Ben sitting close by, talking with a friend, but we hadn't noticed each other yet.

In fascination, I waited for the moment. It came a few minutes later. Ben glanced around casually, before doing a double-take when he saw me. I laughed out loud at the comical sight. I must have felt his eyes on me then, because something made me look in his direction. I saw myself blush as our eyes briefly connected, and remembered the burning sensation in my cheeks and my confusion at seeing such a handsome boy staring at me. I sighed, enveloped in the soft blanket of reminiscence.

Momentarily, I saw myself stand and head towards the coffee machine. I watched Ben say something to his friend before he also stood and walked in the same direction. *That's right* I thought, smiling. *Later, you told me that you only pretended you wanted a drink so you could have an excuse to talk to me.* My eyes blurred as I watched him nervously strike up a conversation.

*Oh Ben, we had our whole lives ahead of us, didn't we?*

Wistfully, I observed for a while longer. As I did so, an urge began to grow to find out when and how it had all started to unravel. From a tiny seed, the feeling bloomed until I could no longer ignore it.

## Chapter Twenty-Six

I skipped ahead in time to my university days, watching myself in lectures closely, and as I worked diligently on my assignments. I had always been a perfectionist, I remembered, as I watched myself growl as I crumpled up an essay and started it all over again.

Concerned, I witnessed how irritable I became during exam season, snapping at an ever-patient Ben and barely sleeping. Had this been the start of my depression? I wondered. But then, didn't most people struggle during stressful times?

With growing anxiety, I haunted myself as I settled into my first year of teaching. Passionate and hard-working, though more than a little naïve and idealistic, I watched as I threw myself whole-heartedly into my vocation. I saw myself on good days and bad, days when I was full of energy and everything seemed to go right, and days when I was clearly exhausted and getting through the day was an achievement.

*But that's teaching* I thought *and most teachers would agree that it's not always an easy job. The pupils could be difficult, the marking was never-ending, and you could never quite switch off.*

However, I felt uneasy as I saw myself striving for perfection – every lesson having to be the very best it could be, every student given individual time and attention – and heard the words spoken to Ben about how I never felt good enough.

"There's always more I could do," I snapped at him one Sunday afternoon after he had encouraged me to take a break from lesson planning. We had been living together for a year by this time. "You don't understand!"

Calmly, he placed a cup of coffee on my desk and kissed the top of my head, before leaving me to it. Always so understanding, always so supportive. A tsunami of guilt washed over me, a wave of self-blame.

One day, after I'd had a sleepless night due to lying awake worrying about a pupil whose grades were slipping due to personal problems, I was watching myself teaching when I noticed the inspirational poster that I had proudly tacked up on my first day on the job.

*A teacher is like a candle*

*It consumes itself to light the way for others*

If only I'd known how literal that would come to be, that it was possible to care *too* much. I looked away from the poster.

I flitted about in time, seeing good times, as well as bad: the school holidays, when I de-stressed somewhat and spent more time with Ben, relaxing in cafes, nights out with friends, vacations abroad; occasional breaks from working during term-time, when we would binge on boxsets and share a bag of toffee popcorn; visits to my family; Christmases and spring walks.

But gradually creeping over me was a black cloud, heavy and foreboding. It was easy to see when you could observe someone at different points in time: the chronic insomnia that I began to suffer with; the irritability; the constant exhaustion; the self-doubt, never quite feeling good enough, despite good feedback at school and the loving support of Ben; the bouts of almost crippling anxiety.

I was present for a panic attack one Sunday evening. It sickened me to see myself lose control, and when the memory of the cold dread that had settled in my chest and the sense of impending doom that had quickened my breaths hit me, I reeled. I couldn't stand to see myself almost pass out, and I thought myself out of there as quickly as possible.

Ben had taken me to see my GP the next morning, I recalled now. I had called in sick at school, saying I had the flu, ashamed of what I saw as my failure to cope. The doctor had prescribed anti-depressants and sleeping pills, and signed me off work for the week. Ben had taken a week's holiday from work, and stayed with me constantly. My constant Polaris.

I had remained on the anti-depressants for six months, then decided I didn't need them anymore. I was twenty-five.

\*

The months leading up to my death were bitter-sweet. I regressed even further, lying anxiously awake at night, imagining everything that could go wrong – from small scenarios to big, every worry was given the same importance. I stopped watching the news, unable to bear the daily reporting of one tragedy after another. I withdrew into myself, avoiding social gatherings, making whatever excuses I could as to why I had to stay at home. I felt worthless, like I didn't deserve to exist, and like everyone would be better off without me.

I hid as much of this as I could from my loved ones, but I couldn't hide everything – some of the signs of my internal struggle seeped out of me, like sap oozing from a diseased tree. I would sit staring into space for long periods, and cry at the smallest of things – the discovery of a dead baby bird on our patio, the breaking of a favourite vase, a rainy weekend – and I would be unable to switch off from the sorrow; it would affect me for the rest of the day.

At various times, Ben, my parents and Vicky tried to persuade me that I needed help, but I refused, not wanting to rely on medication to get through life, and believing that therapy was something that other people did, not me. Never me. I saw it as a failure in myself, a weakness. I just needed to try harder, to be better, that was all, but the more I tried, the more exhausting everything became and I watched, helplessly, as I started to unravel further.

As the day of the crash approached, I looked for a trigger, for something that had tipped me over the edge, from low mood to deciding to end it all, but nothing seemed obvious. I was just on a downward spiral into depression, into the far reaches of the basement of my mind, with no escape route. And I had decided I couldn't live with it any more.

*Maybe it was a genetic predisposition, triggered by stress,* I thought. *Inevitable with my perfectionist personality. Everyone is touched by some ailment in their lives…maybe I was just one of the unlucky ones, destined to self-destruct.*

The morning of the crash was grey and miserable, the sound of the rain drumming on the roof loud in the silence of our bedroom. I watched myself rise tiredly from our bed and pull the curtain back so I could stare out of the window for several minutes, my face blank in the glare of the streetlamp, while Ben lay sleeping behind me in the darkened room. The rain sluicing down the glass looked like tears – it was as if the sky was already grieving. When Ben finally stirred, it seemed to jolt me out of a trance, and I watched uneasily as I headed, robot-like and expressionless, for the shower.

When I'd finished, hair washed, legs shaved, I observed myself carefully applying my makeup and painting my nails. I was preparing my body, I realised with a start. I already knew what I was going to do.

My heart clenched.

I watched as I made my way down the stairs to the kitchen, where Ben had made toast for both of us. Perched on the stool at the breakfast bar, I nibbled at one corner. The radio played in the background, but otherwise we didn't talk more than a few words. Ben seemed relaxed and was already setting up his laptop ready to start work.

Soon, I was climbing off the stool and calmly gathering my purse and car keys. I trembled as I watched Ben absent-mindedly kiss me goodbye, before I headed out to the supermarket in my usual Saturday morning routine. But this was a journey which would never be completed.

*Oh Ben, if only you'd realised how low I had become! If only I had shared how I was feeling with you, instead of allowing myself to sink into self-destructive oblivion!*

Could I face what would happen next? I debated with myself, before steeling myself and vanishing before I could change my mind, only to appear almost immediately at the road junction. I *had* to see it for myself. Maybe then I could truly believe it.

I stood waiting on the grass verge, staring in the direction from which I would soon be arriving, my hands and legs shaking. Sunlight was attempting to break through the grey clouds, witnesses to the coming tragedy, but the rain still fell persistently onto the black tarmac.

It was still quite early in the morning. The traffic had yet to build up at the lights. Cars were streaking through the junction every time they settled on green, and a single pedestrian was waiting to cross, the bright umbrella obscuring her face. I braced myself for what was to come.

Within another minute, I spotted my blue VW in the distance. As it got closer, I looked at the traffic lights, willing them to change to red, but they remained stubbornly green. Green like Ben's eyes; green like the palm trees in the Caribbean; green like the spring I had always loved.

I looked in the opposite direction to the VW and spotted Al's heavy goods vehicle heading for the crossroads. He was driving at a good pace, but not faster than the speed limit.

As the vehicles drew ever closer to each other, I gritted my teeth and found myself holding my breath.

Suddenly, just as I thought I had made a mistake, that the vehicles would pass by each other without incident, the VW's driver – I – floored it, and swerved into the lorry's lane. It happened at the last minute, and Al stood no chance of avoiding it.

The resounding metallic *crash* echoed around my head, and I slid to the ground.

Darkness enveloped me.

## Chapter Twenty-Seven

I came to in the rose garden, back in the present day, as my loved ones were just about to depart. I stared, dazed, at the group who were sombrely saying their goodbyes before heading back to their cars. They were all pale, their faces drawn. Vicky's heavy coat blew open as she walked, revealing her seven-month bump, and I would have sworn I tasted bile when I remembered Olivia's pregnancy.

*Eight years,* I thought. *Eight damn years.*

I now fully accepted Al's revelation. How could I not? And Patrick's explanation seemed the most plausible. I had been ill, but illness didn't carry over into the afterlife. To forget had been a blessing, I realised now. To remember was agonising.

*Ignorance really is bliss* I thought sorrowfully, as I watched Ben drive away, away from my cold ashes and back into the warm arms of his wife.

*

I returned to Al then. He was still lying on the bed, but his eyes were open; he was staring at the ceiling. The distant clatter of pans could be heard and I guessed absently that Pam was cooking their evening meal.

"I'm back, Al," I said softly. His eyes closed and he inhaled deeply. I watched his chest rise sharply.

"I-I just wanted to say…" I swallowed past the lump in my throat. I cleared it; it sounded loud in the quiet room. "I just wanted to say 'sorry'." God, it sounded so lame. His eyes didn't open. "I mean, *really* sorry. So very, very sorry. Not just for today, or for…haunting…you, I guess, generally, but…" Why was this so damn hard?

Finally, my voice broke. "I'm sorry I took my life, Al. And I'm sorry I involved you. I-I know now that what you told me earlier is the truth. I was sick, Al. So very, very sick."

He must have been holding his breath, because he exhaled heavily then. His eyes opened and darted around the room.

"I'm standing at the foot of the bed," I told him quietly. His gaze settled in my general direction, but I could tell that he couldn't see me.

"I forgive you," he said hoarsely, and a sob escaped me. I clapped my hand over my mouth and tried to hold back the threatening flood, but it was hard. The sounds of snuffled-back tears filled the room, and they weren't solely mine.

"Thank you," I croaked when I was able to speak. "I promise I won't bother you again."

A look of relief and peace stole over his worn face, the lines of tension relaxing, and I realised fully for the first time the terrible toll that my haunting had taken on him. "Goodbye," I whispered, and I saw him nod and close his eyes, before I vanished.

\*

It was cathartic to tell my friends what had happened: Al's devastating revelation, my eye-opening journey back through time, my apology, his forgiveness. It was like by explaining it, I was fully accepting it, and a weight seemed to lift off my heart and a sense of less-fragile peace stole over me; it was as if the cracks were self-repairing, gluing themselves back together.

"I'm so proud of you," Patrick told me quietly, resting his arm across my shoulders and squeezing. The four of us were stood on the grass verge at the road junction. The sun was setting in the distance, streaks of gold and amber brightening the horizon, glorious against the creeping darkness above. Rows of lampposts stretched into the distance, silhouetted against the dramatic sky, soldiers stood at attention. Cars passed by intermittently, but the sound of their engines seemed subdued, as if in respect. I closed my eyes and rested my head against my friend.

"You're so brave, darling," Kate uttered gently. She was holding my hand.

I saw Dean nod in agreement. He had been looking thoughtfully at the road throughout my monologue, his hands in his pockets, but now he turned to face me. "You were in a dark place, love, there's no denying that, but what's done is done. You weren't to blame."

I smiled a small, sad smile at this, my eyes watering. He reached out and tweaked me on the nose. I giggled quietly, then sighed.

At Kate's suggestion, we headed to the Moon then. It was the perfect place to go whenever one of us needed to talk, or get away from it all, or gain perspective. Life, death and everything in between had been discussed on the dusty, lifeless satellite, as the Earth rotated slowly in front of us, our loved ones sleeping or going about their day, oblivious to the ones who waited patiently for them.

"John's new girlfriend is a nice lady," Kate told us stoically. "She's a widow, with a young daughter. Her husband's struggling to come to terms with it – he's gone travelling for a while – but they seem to be a comfort to each other." I patted her hand, but didn't speak. "It'll be good for the children to have a mother-figure in their lives again," she continued, but this time her voice caught. I put my arm around her waist, and she flashed a shaky but grateful smile at me.

Kate had always been so good at accepting that life would move on without her, but she was only human, and it was not easy to watch the love of your life begin again with a new partner, and to envision someone else raising your children.

Dean watched in sympathy. Susie was much older than Ben and John, who was in his mid-forties; she was in her early-sixties by now, and she seemed more than content with her independence. But Dean had a lot of empathy and I could see that he truly felt for those of us whose loved ones had their whole lives ahead of them.

Patrick was frowning, no doubt thinking about how he'd feel if Puna found a partner. So far, she'd displayed no interest in any of the men in her settlement, spending most of her time working with the women and supervising the children, but things could change.

We sat in silence for a while after that; words weren't always necessary. Sometimes companionship is enough.

## Chapter Twenty-Eight

A week later, I had mulled over the events of the past and had finally found peace within myself, a sense of acceptance. I was visiting Dean in the pub, and we were discussing the possibilities of time travel.

"I'd love to go to Ancient Rome," Dean said with a spark in his eyes. He'd always loved the antiquity of Italy.

"Egypt would be fascinating too," I agreed, thinking of the wondrous sights I had seen there so many years ago. How amazing would it be to witness their construction, their transformation from raw materials to majestic, towering structures, built to last for thousands of years?

Dean nodded. "Or America before the Europeans arrived."

"Or Australia."

"Ancient China!"

"The Stone Age!"

"The dinosaurs!"

We burst out laughing at the absurdity…and in amazement at the possibility.

"What about the future?" Dean asked, once we'd sobered up.

The thought made me giddy. "We'd see flying cars," I gushed after a moment, my imagination running wild. "And robot servants."

Dean laughed, his belly wobbling. "Colonies of humans living on other planets?"

"Yes! And medical advances which mean that sickness is a thing of the past. And we'd have cleaned up the Earth, andand no more wars!" I declared, excited at the possibilities, my eyes wide.

He chuckled and looked over at Susie, who was serving a young couple. "We could visit our loved ones."

This sobered me instantly. Did I want to see Ben, happily surrounded by his new family, before it was forced on me naturally by the passing of time? I wasn't so sure.

Dean seemed to read my thoughts. "You could visit young Daisy; see how she turns out," he suggested gently.

I thought about this. "But what if I witness something bad, and then I come back and I have to watch her growing towards it, unable to change it? I'm not sure I could exist happily with knowledge like that."

He frowned. "That's a good point."

We were quiet for a moment.

"Why don't I do a test-run of just a few days, say?" Dean finally suggested. "I could pop there and back in a jiffy, see if any of this is even possible."

I nodded slowly. It was a good idea. We couldn't not at least *explore* the possibility of travelling into the future.

"OK, then. No time like the present." He seemed to brace himself, then closed his eyes. I watched him closely, remembering that when I'd travelled into the past, I'd reappeared back at the exact same time as I'd left. Perhaps all I would see was him flash out of existence, only to return a microsecond later.

Nothing happened. Had I blinked and missed it?

Dean's eyes re-opened. He looked confused. His shoulders slumped.

"Try again," I suggested. He did so, a look of renewed concentration on his face.

Nothing.

"Hmph! Why don't you try? You've managed to time travel before; perhaps you've got the knack?"

I nodded. I thought of the next day, when I knew that Ben and Olivia would be visiting the hospital for the twelve-week scan. Although it wasn't something I relished the idea of witnessing, it was something concrete to aim for. But, again, nothing happened.

"You don't think something bad happens within the next few days, do you?" I asked, my voice full of apprehension.

"What do you mean?"

"Like, they die or something."

"What, all of them?" he questioned in astonishment. "Susie *and* Ben and Olivia?"

"You're right, it's stupid." I shook my head as if to remove the thoughts of freak accidents and natural disasters. "I guess it's just not possible to travel forwards," I shrugged, secretly relieved.

Dean looked disappointed, however. I patted him on the knee. He sighed. "I suppose it makes sense – the future hasn't happened yet."

I nodded. It did make sense. How could we visit somewhere that was yet to be determined by people's decisions, their free will?

"The past it is then."

We reverted to discussing the time periods we'd love to see, continuing our chat long into the night. Kate and Patrick joined us after a while, and we all laughed to picture ourselves at Henry VIII's court, or in Genghis Khan's harem.

"We could find out who Jack the Ripper really was, and if Lee Harvey Oswald really did shoot JFK!" Patrick declared excitedly.

"Attend Woodstock, or Princess Diana's wedding," Kate suggested more gently.

"When do we go?" Dean finally asked.

"No time like the present," Patrick responded, his eyes shining.

"The past," I corrected dryly, and was rewarded with a wry smile.

"Shall we go together?" Kate enquired nervously, looking at me.

"If you'd like," I answered, reassuringly.

"I'd love to see my children as babies again." She looked

at me pleadingly.

I nodded. "Nappies and night-feeds it is then."

She clapped her hands together and beamed.

I saw Patrick and Dean look askance at each other. "1966 World Cup Final?" Dean suggested, hopefully. They looked at us guiltily.

Kate laughed. "It's fine – I wouldn't expect you to get the same pleasure out of my babies as I would."

"As *we* would," I corrected with a smile. She looked back at me warmly.

"Right then! That's settled." Dean looked at Patrick, the anticipation in his eyes clear to see. "Kick-off?"

"Absolutely."

"Expect to feel a tad sick and dizzy," I warned them before they vanished. They nodded, and within seconds they were gone.

"Shall we?" I asked, looking at Kate in expectation.

"Poppy, in the hospital, a day old," she responded firmly, and we too vanished from the present.

*

Time travel, as I'd discovered, grew easier with practice. I reappeared on a busy maternity ward with Kate lying at my feet; she was groaning loudly. Leaning down, I helped her up. She put her hand to her head and uttered a rare curse.

"It gets better," I promised.

While Kate took a few moments to acclimatise, I examined our surroundings. The white-washed section of the ward we'd arrived in contained four beds, each enclosed by a light blue curtain that hung down from a rail which was attached to the ceiling. Frazzled nurses were bustling about in the corridor, and more than one infant's wail could be heard further away down the corridor.

"Can you remember which bed was yours?" I asked Kate, when she appeared to be more herself.

"That one." She pointed to our right, to one of the beds near the large window, and we thought ourselves to the other side of the curtain.

"Oh!" Kate gasped, as we stood before a sleeping mother and infant. The baby – Poppy – was lying on her back in a transparent bassinet next to her mother's bed, covered from neck to toes by a yellow blanket. Kate, looking only a little younger than she did now, appeared pale but otherwise peaceful, her blonde hair tousled on the pillow, her closed eyes slightly shadowed from exhaustion.

"Was it a difficult labour?" I asked, as she stood staring misty-eyed down at her daughter.

"It was long, but John – and an epidural – got me through it," she replied, without looking up. "And, of course, the anticipation of meeting this little one."

Just then, the baby stirred, her little hands coming up to clutch at the air as her eyes opened. A tiny wail escaped from her rosebud mouth and her mother jolted instantly awake.

We watched as she smiled tiredly. "You're awake are you, my beauty?" she muttered, smiling before pushing back her sheet and carefully swinging her legs off the bed, clearly still in some discomfort from the delivery. "Come to mummy then."

She lifted the doll-like child and put her to her breast. Poppy suckled contentedly. We sighed at the utterly beautiful, utterly peaceful scene.

"Of course, this was before the nipple soreness kicked in, and the colic, and the baby blues," Kate informed me, but without any resentment.

I grunted, unable to talk without giving myself away. Because, suddenly, I was in agony. Because, in a few short months, I knew, this would be Olivia, and the baby would be Ben's. *My* Ben's. Before me was everything I had wanted, picture perfect.

I couldn't help it – a sob escaped me. Kate turned to me in surprise and her eyes were full of compassion when she saw the unshed tears in mine. We reached for each other, and I clung to her as if she was my life raft. I was terrified of losing my grip for I would surely drown.

Kate's breath hitched, and I knew that she too was overwhelmed by the tragedy of it all: my infinite childlessness, her having been cruelly ripped away from her babies. "In five years, she – I – will be dead. What a waste, what an absolute fucking waste!" she wept.

I nodded in agreement, afraid to speak the words which I knew would choke me.

"We shouldn't have come," she said then, her voice full of tears. "This was too much."

We let each other go, and scrubbed at our faces with our hands.

"I guess we should have gone to watch the football," I

said, my voice dry, when I was once again in control of myself.

Kate let out a relieved, but shaky, laugh. "Oh God, no. Anything but that!"

"Woodstock?" I queried tremulously, and she nodded with a smile.

## Chapter Twenty-Nine

Time travel, I discovered, was a lot like ordinary travel. We became tourists, observers of everyday people in extraordinary times, or conversely, voyeurs of extraordinary people in everyday life. And like my early geographical travels, it was an escape, a distraction, from having to witness Ben moving on with his life.

Woodstock, in August of 1969, was a happy muddle of half a million people, including hippies, bikers and Vietnam veterans; epic music; fields of churned up mud and rubbish; and rain. Lots of rain. Open drug-taking abounded, and the atmosphere of 'peace and love' was almost tangible. For three unforgettable days, we remained on the crowded New York dairy farm watching performances by Janis Joplin, Joan Baez, The Who and so many other legends that I lost count. We danced and sang almost non-stop, unable to feel sorry for the music-lovers getting soaked in their filthy sleeping bags, even when a thunderstorm struck – after all, they were making history, for goodness sake!

Princess Diana's wedding took place on July 29th 1981 at St Paul's Cathedral in London. We gasped in awe as she arrived in a gilded horse-drawn carriage guided through crowded streets of cheering well-wishers, and as she walked down the aisle in front of thousands of elegantly-dressed guests, her infamous train stretched out behind her. The exchange of vows in front of the Archbishop, imposing in his silver and white vestments and mitre, made Kate weep. Knowing the tragedy that awaited in Diana's future, however, it was a bitter-sweet occasion to witness.

After that, inevitably, we ventured back to 1969, this time to July 20th. We watched Armstrong and Aldrin's historic Moon landing, witnessing the unspoilt dust of the lunar surface marred for the first time ever by footprints and laughing as they bounced around in the reduced gravity which left us unaffected. We observed for hours, fascinated as they collected moon rocks, set up experiments and planted the American flag. I had only ever seen fuzzy, black-and-white clips on television before; to see it in glorious, real-life colour was exhilarating to say the least.

We whizzed back and forth through time, staying in different periods for different durations – a single event could be witnessed in a few hours, whereas a whole era warranted days or weeks of exploring. We observed with pity young chimney sweeps performing their dangerous and dirty chore in the Victorian days; the historic signing of the Magna Carta in 1215; the epic siege of Troy; and of course, the building of the majestic pyramids by hundreds of over-worked slaves. We travelled for months and never grew tired of seeing the cruelties and achievements of our human ancestors.

Other ghosts avoided us, looking askance at our modern clothing and, at times, in particular at my darker skin.

We were on a beach in South America, observing Francis

Drake's famous exploits against the Spanish, when we made the decision to travel back further than we had ever dared to before.

I was intrigued by the thought of observing early humans and life before we'd evolved. We visited east Africa first, and witnessed our ancestors surviving in the unspoilt wilderness of a world as yet untouched by technology. Families hunted and gathered; individuals survived by sheer tenacity and their reliance on their social group; people lived their simple lives and died with no written record that they had existed.

Life before humans was a savage yet peaceful time on Earth. Predator and prey danced in a never-ending performance of life and death. Plant life flourished, and our pre-human ancestors were no more than scurrying mammals, intent on survival. At one point, the dinosaurs were present on every continent and we were awed to witness their dominance over the land. The herbivores were gentle yet fierce in their battle to protect their young from hungry carnivores. Predators continually fought, and often lost, their fight for food.

Fascinated and overwhelmed by curiosity, we ventured further back, to a time before animal – and then even plant – life had existed. The world was a bubbling cauldron of volcanoes and rock, ocean and sulphur. From the Moon it was unrecognisable as the Earth – even the continents were vastly different in size, shape and location. It was the most disturbing yet most awe-inspiring era we visited. I remember thinking that it was like arriving on an alien planet.

I contemplated life and death, having now a sense of the vastness of time and space. What was the meaning of it all? So many billions of people, so many billions of years since the Big Bang, so many lives, small and insignificant in the grand scheme of things, even those of Kings and Queens and Emperors. What is all this *for* God? I wondered, as I looked out upon a vista of seething magma. I waited, but He didn't answer.

*

We returned to the present, mentally if not physically exhausted from our travels through time. We reappeared in the pub, literally a split second after we'd left. We'd been gone for many months however.

Patrick and Dean likewise reappeared and we gushed about our experiences. The guys had only been gone, subjectively to themselves, for a matter of a few weeks. They had watched the final as planned, cheering at the country's famous 4-2 victory against Germany, and had then gone on to witness key events from both World Wars. Enraptured, Kate and I listened to their vivid descriptions of trench warfare and the bloody Battle of the Somme in the first war, then the evacuation at Dunkirk, the systematic bombing campaign during the Blitz and the launch of the successful Normandy invasion from the second.

We heard tales of unimaginable courage set against a backdrop of horror and bloodshed; tragic stories of young men whose lives were cruelly cut short, far away from their loved ones. The scale of the devastation was difficult to imagine.

Hours later, they listened, gobsmacked, as we recounted our own tales.

"My God!" Patrick exclaimed, when I nonchalantly told him about witnessing a ferocious tyrannosaurus rex take down a triceratops.

Dean just sat with his mouth hanging open.

Kate and I looked at each other and burst out laughing.

"Oh, you were only joking!" Patrick exhaled in relief.

"Nope," I confirmed, the hint of a smug smile still lurking on my lips.

"Fecking hell!"

"I guess we're just more daring than you," I provoked.

"You bloody are not!" he spluttered. He looked at Dean in disbelief and a new determination. "Come on mate, let's head back."

Dean appeared to consider this. He seemed torn between wanting to experience more of the past, and remaining with Susie, at whom he kept casting longing looks; after all, to him it had been weeks since he'd been able to spend any time with her.

"Maybe in a few days," he finally replied.

Patrick glanced over at Susie and clapped him on the shoulder. "Understood, my friend."

Suddenly, we were all eager to be alone with our loved ones. We said our farewells, promising to meet up again soon, and Dean watched as we vanished.

I reappeared at Ben's workplace and stayed with him for the remainder of the day, mentally preparing myself for the visit to the hospital, which was to take place in less than twenty-four hours. "You'll be a wonderful father," I told him quietly, as I watched him gather his things at the end of the day in preparation for returning home to a woman who wasn't me.

## *Chapter Thirty*

Ben had arranged to have the day off work so that he could attend the twelve-week scan. I watched as he and Olivia hurriedly completed their morning routine and headed out to the car. Trying to be happy for them, I sat in the back and listened to their excited chatter as I stared out of the window.

I was thinking about beginnings and endings, and how they were turning points in the story of our lives. They changed us, irrevocably, so that we would never be the same again. Everything that came afterwards was a ripple that spanned out from that moment, unstoppable and irreversible. A sigh escaped from my lips, unheard by the others.

Once we had arrived at the Women's Hospital and they had checked in at the ultrasound department's reception desk, I watched as Ben and Olivia nervously found two empty seats in the waiting area and settled themselves in for a wait of unknown length.

Rows of green plastic chairs filled the space, and in most of them were women each in various stages of pregnancy, from those possessing still-flat bellies to those whose tummies were gently bulging to women who looked ready to burst. Some were sat with a partner, some alone or accompanied by a female friend or relative. Brightly-coloured posters adorned the walls, promoting varied messages from following a healthy diet and giving up smoking to encouraging breast feeding and participation in research trials. A quiet hum of conversation filled the area.

Ben and Olivia waited patiently to be called through, talking in hushed voices, while I paced around restlessly.

When Olivia's name was finally called, after nearly an hour had passed, I debated with myself as to whether I should join them in the imaging room. *Why am I torturing myself like this?* I wondered. *Why am I haunting an innocent woman?*

*Because it should have been you,* a sly voice answered, and, unable to resist, I trailed after them into the dim chamber.

The sonographer, a young woman with a professional, efficient air about her, welcomed them and instructed Olivia to lie down on her back and reveal her tummy, before tucking a paper towel into her waistband. Olivia gasped when some cold gel was smeared onto her stomach and they all laughed. Next, a probe was being pressed into her abdomen and we all waited expectantly as the young woman fulfilled her routine tasks, calm and efficient.

Minutes passed, and I started to grow uneasy as I noticed a frown line appear between the woman's eyes but she didn't speak. Eventually, she turned to Olivia, and said in a quiet, sad voice, "I'm so sorry, but there is no heartbeat."

I reeled in shock, and Olivia's face crumpled. Ben paled and reached for her hand. No words were spoken for a few minutes as Olivia began to cry and Ben rested his head against hers.

I barely heard the sonographer as she started to gently explain about 'missed miscarriages' and the options that they now faced. My heart and mind were too filled with pity and sadness. Unable to bear the sounds of their grief, which tore at my innermost being, I thought myself to Kate, knowing that only another woman could offer me the comfort that I needed.

\*

Travelling through time had taught me the insignificance of each individual life – including my own – in the grand scheme of things. Billions of people had lived and died, leaving barely a ripple in the fabric of time. But the loss of this life, this one life, extinguished before it had barely even begun, hit me like an express train. The loss of any baby was devastating, but this was not just any baby. This was Ben's baby. This was the baby that would have been half him, half the love of my life, half of my soulmate. My heart wept for him, and for Olivia.

Kate listened compassionately and her eyes shone wetly as she expressed her sympathy for them. I told her of my shock and sorrow for my Ben and his new wife, unable to hold back the tears that slipped down my face, each one an echo of the heartbeat that was no more. While I had wished from the beginning that *I* was the one to carry his baby, I never would have desired this outcome.

"I can't even begin to imagine how Olivia must be feeling," I said softly, my voice breaking, and Kate murmured her agreement. We were sat on the edge of John's – their – bed. Teeny-bopper music could be heard emanating from Poppy's room, and the repeated *thud* of a ball as John and

Sam played footie in the garden. I stared down at a fold in the deep purple bedspread.

We sat in silence, Kate's arm across my shoulders, listening to the sounds of her family. I don't know what she was thinking as we sat there, but I was contemplating the randomness of life. Randomness which took away a mother from her children, as in Kate's case, and a child away from its mother, as in Olivia's. I prayed silently to God, asking him to comfort both her and Ben, and bless them in the future, once time had begun to heal their hearts.

\*

Back at home, I found Olivia lying under a blanket on the couch, silent, but with swollen red eyes which spoke volumes of her heartbreak. The rattle of a teaspoon could be heard in the direction of the kitchen and soon Ben was entering the room carrying two steaming mugs. His hair was rumpled, his face haggard, and when he got closer I noticed that his eyes were bloodshot. *My poor darling,* I thought, wishing I could comfort him and cursing my helplessness. He placed the tea on the small side table next to Olivia, stroked her hair and then lifted her feet so that he could sit at the other end of the couch with them in his lap. Absent-mindedly, he rubbed them.

The blanket slipped down, revealing Olivia's hand resting lightly on her tummy.

They didn't speak for several minutes as the tea grew cold; each seemed lost in their own thoughts. *Perhaps they've already said everything that needed to be said,* I thought, but I was wrong.

"We can try again," Ben broke the silence to state.

Olivia closed her eyes in response.

"When the time's right, I mean," he continued, but still, Olivia remained mute.

*Let her grieve,* I thought. *Time will heal her heart and then she'll be ready to hope again.*

Time mended many things, or at least made them more manageable, I had learned. Knowing this didn't make it any easier when the pain was fresh though, as it was in Olivia's case.

Over the next few days, Ben tended to Olivia as they let nature take its course and fresh tears were shed by all of us. They were cathartic tears, healthy tears, and they seemed to wash away the sharp edges of their grief.

In the following weeks, Olivia grew stronger, a sense of acceptance replacing the initial shock and anguish, and she began to talk about trying again in the summer.

Once I could tell that they had passed the worst of their grief, I began to spend more time away from them. I got back into my old routine, seeing my friends regularly and travelling with Patrick to visit Huipi and Puna on several occasions, the change of scene and pace of life refreshing. I was with Vicky when she gave birth to her first child, a whopping ten pound boy that she named Noah; I checked in on Bal and Amy, who were now married with two children and more in love than ever; I popped to see Jules and Asia, who were still together after all these years; and, of course, I spent many hours with my family, especially Daisy, who was now seven, and Teddy, who was four.

I even went time-travelling again, with both Dean and Patrick, but for shorter durations. We saw the Beatles performing in the Cavern Club in Liverpool; observed Henry VIII's skill at jousting; heard the cries of dying men at the Battle of Hastings; and of course, I accompanied them even further back, and witnessed their awe on sighting their first dinosaur.

## Chapter Thirty-One

Olivia fell pregnant again in July. She and Ben were more restrained in their joy this time, but cautiously hopeful, and I willed with all my might that this pregnancy would have a better outcome. *Please, Lord,* I thought. *Please bless them with a happy ending this time.*

It wasn't to be. She miscarried in the tenth week, and my heart broke for them all over again.

It was almost unbearable to see them suffer so for the second time in less than a year.

Helplessly, I watched as Ben attempted to comfort his wife, and as Olivia lapsed into a prolonged depressive state. She took to spending long hours in bed, curled up in the foetal position, and only showering at irregular intervals, when she was forced to. Her parents, who lived in Scotland, came down for an extended stay, and this seemed to help somewhat, but Olivia was changed. She was quieter, slower to smile, more likely to have a faraway look in her eyes, so that she frequently didn't hear when people spoke to her.

Ben often looked at her, as she sat there in her own world, with a helpless and anguished expression on his face. He seemed tortured by her grief, and no wonder…her depression must have reminded him so much of what he'd gone through before, with me. He started staying later at work, and could only relax at home if he had a glass of something strong in his hand. He was older now, and, sadly, more aware of the consequences of life's battles.

I watched, helpless, as their relationship slowly began to unravel.

"It's just temporary," I told Ben one evening as he sat brooding in front of the television. He wasn't really watching it; he was just staring at it as he sat sipping from a tumbler. "Something like this is bound to affect things between you…it will get better," I promised.

And it did.

A year passed, and although the relationship never got back to the light-heartedness and ease of the early months, they settled into a new, somehow deeper yet more fragile love. It was a love which was as delicate as gossamer, and indeed it was if their hearts were knitted together by fine strands of the silky thread, and each thread represented a tear that they had shed in their grief for their lost babies.

When Olivia fell pregnant for the third time, it was clear that she was too filled with anxiety to enjoy any aspect of it. Ben treated her like she was made of glass and Olivia did everything that she could to stay healthy and safe in order to prevent another tragic outcome, but to no avail.

She was alone in the house when she started bleeding in the ninth week. I watched the light leave her eyes as she calmly took herself to the bathroom and then phoned the hospital. Ben met her there, and the miscarriage was confirmed.

Three children lost. Three little mirror-images of my Ben, my soulmate. I wondered what they would have been like, those children, their personalities and dispositions, their hopes and dreams. How would they have changed the lives of those around them? What ripples would their existence have left on the world?

Now we would never know.

There were no tears this time. It was like the sorrow was too deep for outward displays of emotion. But I knew it must be bubbling under the surface, and I feared the eruption.

It didn't come until a few months later.

They had spent the winter living like roommates – almost strangers – sharing the same house but with no real apparent bond to speak of. It was eerie to watch their polite, but distant, interactions, and I wanted to scream at them to cry, to throw things, to do something – anything – to break down the wall that had developed between them. It was a wall made of grief and guilt and dashed hopes, but instead of their shared experience bringing them together, it was tearing them apart.

I hated that wall. I wanted to take a bulldozer to it. I wanted to smash it until there were only fragments left scattered across the ground. I wanted to force the two of them to stumble through the debris into each other's arms, to comfort each other, to cry together, to show the love that had first knitted their hearts together.

But all I could do was watch, and witness.

The arguments started around the time of the tenth anniversary of my death. It was always a difficult time of year for Ben and I noticed that he started drinking more heavily in the week leading up to it.

Olivia was usually very attentive at this time of year, sensitive to his needs as he became quieter and more withdrawn, but this year she seemed to have forgotten, or was too caught up in her own sorrow to have the patience, strength or capacity to deal with someone else's. She had been through several tests, but the doctors had yet to identify the cause of the miscarriages.

They started bickering about little things – the way Ben did the laundry, the way Olivia parked the car, the way the dishwasher should be loaded – things that had perhaps mildly irritated before suddenly became contentious issues in the relationship.

And then there was Ben's drinking. It didn't return to normal levels after the anniversary. If anything, it increased. Olivia pointed this out one day in March, during a particularly nasty argument which had started over something so mundane I can't even remember it now.

"She's been dead for over a decade!" she suddenly screamed, spittle flying out of her mouth. "You need to get over it. I'm sick and tired of living in her shadow!"

It was the first time she had alluded to me in such a negative way, and I reeled in shock at the intensity of it. Ben paled, then threw his glass, hard, into the fireplace, where it shattered loudly, before storming out of the room. The slam of the front door signalled that he had left the house. Olivia, pale-faced, collapsed onto the sofa and buried her face in her hands.

I stared at the amber droplets on the hearth. *Whiskey tears,* I thought, my heart aching for them, *to replace the salty ones that they should be shedding together.*

I stayed with Olivia for a while, as she gradually composed herself before collecting a dustpan and brush from a cupboard in the kitchen, her eyes tired, her shoulders slumped. Slowly, she swept the scattered shards of glass into a pile, and I had the melancholy thought that the pieces were like their hearts, broken irreparably, never to be the same again.

I found Ben in the rose garden, staring broodingly at my headstone. It was raining heavily, and he wasn't wearing a jacket. His shirt was stuck to his skin, making it translucent, revealing patches of pink beneath, and water dripped from his hair and mixed with his hot tears.

"Go home," I told him, my heart aching for him. "Go home to your wife. She needs you now."

"I'll never get over losing you," he whispered, and my breath caught. Had he heard me?

But he said no more, and we stood beneath the thundering downpour, staring at my grave side-by-side, each lost in our own thoughts of what might have been.

## Chapter Thirty-Two

Ben's drinking only got worse. He would consume whiskey heavily throughout each evening after work, then wake up in the morning with tired, puffy eyes. He started taking mouthwash into the office with him to disguise any lingering smell of alcohol.

He and Olivia were barely speaking by this point. While he sat drinking in front of the television night after night, she would retire early to bed, where she would read or watch her own programmes. The weekends were not much different, with the exception of the completion of – separate – chores and Olivia's visits to friends or family. Anything, it seemed, to get away from the house, which had developed an atmosphere of gloom and tension, if not outright hostility. I viewed it as a tangible presence. I envisaged a malevolent monster wrapped around the house, its tentacles reaching in through the doors and windows, suffocating and extinguishing the love with which it had once been filled.

Sorrowfully, I watched them travelling towards an outcome which seemed inevitable. It was like a train hurtling along a track, the course unchangeable, the station signifying the end of the line.

Sure enough, Olivia moved out at the end of the summer.

She announced her intention quietly as they sat eating their evening meal one Friday evening. I say eating – Ben barely picked at his, preferring as he now did to drink the final meal of the day.

A brief flicker of surprise came and went in his eyes, before he schooled his features into one of indifference. "If that's what you want," he responded calmly.

"It is."

"Where will you go?"

"To Jen's. She said I can stay in her spare room until I can sort a new place out."

He mulled this over, perhaps absorbing the realisation that she meant this to be a permanent move. He confirmed this with his next question.

"You're not coming back then?"

"No."

He nodded, and that was the end of the conversation.

The next morning, Ben sat in his armchair, already drinking, his face carefully composed to appear indifferent, while Olivia packed her clothes and toiletries into a suitcase. When she'd placed her luggage by the front door, she informed him matter-of-factly that she'd be back for the rest of her things when she'd sorted out somewhere to rent.

"Bye then," he said in an abrupt voice, without looking at her.

She opened the door, then paused and turned back to him.

"Try to cut back on the alcohol, Ben. I'm saying this because I still love you. It's not doing you any good."

He didn't answer, and she lifted her suitcase and walked out the door. It clicked shut softly behind her and Ben reached for the bottle.

\*

Over the next few years, I watched, frustrated and saddened, as Ben lapsed into the routine life of a functional alcoholic. He remained single, a divorcee, and seemed uninterested in the company of others, preferring to spend his spare time alone with a bottle, a brooding expression on his face.

"He's been through a lot," Patrick quietly reminded me one day as we sat on his bench and I tearfully lamented what had become of my childhood love. He was a shadow of the man I'd known – my strong, vibrant Ben, who'd had so much life in him, so much hope and excitement for the future. I remembered him banging the pots and pans to loud rock music just before he'd been informed of my death, his energy, the light in his green eyes, eyes that were now dulled by alcohol and loss. He was in his early forties now, but he looked ten years older.

"I feel so helpless," I sniffed into Patrick's chest. "All I can do is watch, and it's *shit*!"

He sighed. "I know sweetheart, I know."

"Why is he doing this to himself?"

"People cope with things in their own way. This is his. Is it healthy? No. Does it dull the pain? Yes. Let's just hope that it's only a phase."

"A phase? It's been going on for *years* though," I protested.

"Sometimes that's how it goes. Try to see the big picture – we know from our travels through time that things never stay the same. Bad times pass; good times pass. Life is a cycle. You don't know where he'll be this time next year, or in five years, or ten. Be patient."

"If only he'd ask for help."

"Maybe he's not ready for that. Give him time. And don't forget, alcoholism is a *sickness* that people can and do recover from, when they're ready to admit they have a problem."

"He must *know* he's got a problem! It's not normal to drink that much day after day!"

"Perhaps, deep down, but not on the level where he's ready to do something about it."

I sighed in frustration. "If only he could hear me." I thought of Al then, and the temptation to revisit him and beg him to talk to Ben for me was overwhelming. But I had promised that I would leave him alone, and I had vowed to myself that I would never break my word; he had suffered enough. Besides, I wasn't sure that Ben would believe a stranger turning up out of the blue and announcing that he could communicate with the dead. Who would?

I watched the ducks and geese squabble noisily over the scraps that people threw them. It was early spring again, but I couldn't enjoy the sights of new life springing up around me. I couldn't feel the sense of renewed hope that the season usually inspired in me. The flowers which sprouted freshly from the ground held no joy; the pale sunshine brought no sense of relief; even the sound of children's laughter was bitter-sweet.

It was as if a storm cloud had gathered over my existence, and no matter where I ventured, it remained always above me.

## Chapter Thirty-Three

Because it was so difficult to witness his self-destruction, I had taken to spending more time away from Ben, unable to watch him slouched before the television with a glass in his hand evening after evening, and more time with Daisy. She was thirteen by now, and her youthful energy and optimistic outlook were a welcome relief from the burden of watching the man I loved self-implode. She had her whole life ahead of her, and she already knew what she wanted.

From the age of four, Charles and Beth had enrolled her in a ballet class, which she had taken to like a duck to water. I had thrilled in watching her master the graceful posture, positions and movements of the dance, her little body strong and lean. I shared in Charles and Beth's pride, as if she were my own daughter; her natural talent at making a difficult skill seem almost effortless was a joy to behold.

It wasn't just her innate ability that made my heart feel full when I watched her, it was her determined concentration. From a young age, she had been tenacious in everything she tried to master, whether it be walking for the first time, learning to form letters upon starting nursery, or standing on pointe for the first time. Her motivation and self-discipline were striking in such a young child.

The pleasure I received in watching her, the delight in seeing her lost in the swelling music as her graceful body seemed to float across the stage during performances, was a counter to the pain of witnessing Ben's deterioration.

I had come to terms with the circumstances surrounding my death. I had accepted my illness, and knew that the past couldn't be altered. What was done, was done. But Ben was *alive*; he could still effect a change, before it was too late. His life was passing him by, and it was torture to see him exist in a state of self-obliteration and ever-increasing isolation.

The contrast between my visits to Daisy and my time with Ben couldn't be starker – one was all energy, hope and optimism, the other all listlessness and capitulation. One brought smiles to my face, the other frowns.

I lay with Ben one night as he slept in his usual alcohol-fuelled semi-coma. I stroked his face, knowing that if I could smell him, he'd reek of stale whiskey beneath minty mouthwash. I was glad that I couldn't.

"It's just a phase," I whispered repeatedly to him. "Everything's going to be alright. You'll get through this. I'm here, my darling. I'm always here."

He whimpered in his sleep, and the sound was so full of pain and sorrow that I closed my eyes against it. I stayed with him until dawn, gazing at him and seeing the boy I'd once known in the damaged man slumbering before me, and then headed to the Moon to brood on life and lost opportunities.

Patrick had once told me that life was inevitably a tragedy. That we were all just travellers on the journey to loss. We would all lose loved ones; we would all die. It was inescapable that all our hopes and dreams would come to nothing in the end. But I had to believe that there was more to it than that, otherwise what was the point of this afterlife in which we were existing? Why else didn't we just disappear into nothingness when we passed? Into dark oblivion? No, there was something *more*. Something *other*. Something *better*. I thought of Leticia and Kim then, and smiled.

*Hold on, Ben,* I willed. *Hold on to hope.*

\*

My parents, Charles and Vicky had kept in contact with Ben throughout the years, and I would see the concern in their eyes whenever they managed to get him to meet up for a coffee, and when they saw him at the annual rose garden gathering. Each had tried in their own subtle way to address the issue of his drinking, to no avail.

He was in a busy café with Vicky one Saturday when she decided to be blunter than she'd ever been before.

"You can't go on like this, Ben," she suddenly announced, putting her cup down in its saucer with a clang. He looked at her in surprise. "Have you seen yourself in the mirror lately?" Vicky continued, her lips pursed. "You look like shit."

"I'm fine," he responded tightly. But she was right. There were dark bags under his eyes, a permanent tinge of pinkness to his nose and cheeks, he'd gained weight, and there was a general air of dishevelment about him, unlike the Ben of the past.

"You're *not* fine. You smell, for one thing," she told him, wrinkling her nose. "And no amount of mouthwash or aftershave can disguise it, whatever you may tell yourself."

Ben blinked, and his cheeks flushed redder with a mixture of embarrassment and growing anger.

"I don't need to listen to this," he muttered through gritted teeth. His chair scraped across the floor as he stood up suddenly and made to leave.

"Oh yes you do," Vicky snapped. "Sit yourself back down!"

Ben paused, then slowly eased himself back down into the chair. He stared at her sullenly. There was a minute of silence as Vicky seemed to gather herself.

"You've got to stop feeling sorry for yourself," she said more gently then. "Have you had some shitty things to deal with? Yes. Is drinking yourself into an early grave the answer? No."

"It's better than feeling the pain," he told her quietly.

"Pain is a part of life. We choose how we deal with it. This isn't the way. You're forty-three, Ben, you have so much time ahead of you. There's still a chance to find love again, to have a family, to *live*."

"I don't want to. I'm happy on my own."

"Happy? Is that what you call this nothing existence of yours?"

He opened his mouth as if to answer, then closed it. He looked away.

"You can't even lie to *yourself*, can you?"

Vicky picked up her leather shoulder bag and rummaged through it, before pulling out a folded piece of paper. "Here.

This is a leaflet I picked up at the doctor's surgery. There's a helpline number, and a website."

Ben stared at the leaflet for a few seconds as she held it out to him, before reluctantly taking it and shoving it into the inside pocket of his jacket. She nodded, satisfied, then she stood and began gathering her things together. As she passed him, she bent to kiss him on the cheek, and, resting her hand on his shoulder, I heard her murmur, "I'm rooting for you, and so is Daisy." My breath caught and I watched her weave her way between the tables and exit the café, then she was on the pavement, pulling her coat more tightly around herself, before she moved out of sight down the street.

I turned back to Ben. He was sat with his eyes closed. "She's right. I am," I told him quietly. His eyes opened, and he reached for his coffee cup, then sat turning it in his hands, staring into it expressionlessly. I joined him in watching the small amount of remaining cold liquid slosh in slow circles within the cup, becoming hypnotised by the repeated undulations of the coffee.

I thought of Patrick's words regarding life being a cycle of ups and downs then. Ben was in a trough at the moment – was there another peak awaiting him? I crossed my fingers and prayed that there was happiness in store for him – the sooner the better.

However, when we arrived home, before even taking off his jacket, he headed straight for the recycling bin and unceremoniously dumped the leaflet inside, before reaching for a bottle. Unable to watch, I thought myself to Daisy and spent the rest of the day distracting myself by observing her go about her usual day.

I found her in the ballet studio, practising at the barre. Her corkscrew hair was worn in its usual sharp bun, her feet encased in flat ballet shoes, her pink tights and black leotard showcasing the smooth contours of her youthful body. Sideways on, she was exercising first one leg, then the other, before repeating the process. I watched her perform such movements as *plies, ronde de jambe* and *grande battement*, her poise mature and her strength and stamina impressive.

When she moved to the middle of the studio and began to practise *Adage* steps, including a graceful *promenade* and beautiful *arabesque,* I was enthralled by her balance, control and musicality. Her extensions, which she had worked hard on for years, now appeared effortless.

The lesson moved on to combinations, performed at a faster tempo, incorporating movements such as *pirouettes* and *waltz steps*. Jumps and turns were added in during the *Allegro* part of the lesson – featuring *saute, changement, jete* – the movements becoming bigger and faster as time progressed. Daisy whirled across the sprung floor of the studio, her light brown skin shining with a healthy layer of sweat, her blue eyes flashing.

My heart swelled as she finally performed *Reverence,* curtseying to the instructor and the other dancers, before heading to collect her towel.

*How beautiful she is,* I thought, smiling. *She's a fresh flower, just opening from a bud. No sign yet of aging. No wilting under duress. Just innocent and hopeful as she turns her face to the sunlight of the future.*

## Chapter Thirty-Four

I followed Daisy to the car park, where Charles was waiting for her. He beeped the horn of his Honda and she skipped over and climbed into the passenger side. I thought myself onto the backseat and listened contentedly as they chatted and laughed on the drive home, their bond unmistakable.

Twenty minutes later, I followed them inside their three-bedroom semi. Beth, who was wiping her hands on a tea towel, greeted them in the hallway and Daisy teased her about the smidge of flour on her cheek. Rolling her eyes, Beth wiped at it then reached for an envelope that was sitting on a shelf.

"This came for you," she informed Daisy, and I could see the curiosity in her eyes. Daisy had only just turned fourteen and it was unusual for her to receive a letter.

Nonchalantly – too nonchalantly – Daisy reached for the envelope. Beth seemed to hesitate, then finally handed it over. As Daisy casually headed up the stairs, Charles raised his eyebrows at his wife, who shrugged.

One of the advantages of being a ghost is that you can spy on people without them knowing. I thought myself to Daisy's pretty, pale-yellow bedroom, the walls of which were adorned with sepia pictures of ballet dancers striking various poses, and watched her tear open the letter. Peering over her shoulder, I read along with her. The contents were brief, but very clear in meaning. Following on from her scholarship application, Miss Roberts was invited to an audition to attend a prestigious school of ballet in London.

"When did you apply for this, madam?" I asked, reluctantly impressed by her independent spirit. A wide smile spread over her face, but I noticed that the letter shook slightly in her hands. She was both excited and nervous.

A knock sounded at the door then, and Beth entered, clearly unable to resist the temptation to discover the contents of the envelope. Without saying a word, Daisy handed it over and stood waiting as her mother read, her hands clasped behind her straight dancer's back.

Beth's hand flew to her mouth and she looked up at her daughter. "Why didn't you tell us?" she asked, bewildered. "We'd have helped with your application."

"I thought you'd be upset." Daisy bit her lip.

"Oh, my darling, never. If it's what you really want, we'll support you all the way."

"It is," Daisy responded firmly.

"Then I guess we'd better share the news with your dad."

"Do you think he'll be mad at me?" Daisy asked, a little frown line appearing between her brows as she continued to nibble at her lower lip.

"Mad? No. Disappointed that you didn't tell us? Maybe. But he'll get over it."

I followed them downstairs. Charles reacted with surprise and consternation to the news of his daughter's secrecy, and peppered Daisy with questions to make sure that she understood that gaining a place at the school meant living away from home, as well as a gruelling training regime. But Daisy was adamant.

"Then go for it," he smiled when he was satisfied, and, with a squeal, Daisy launched herself into her father's arms.

*

Time flew by and the day of the audition finally arrived. I joined my brother's family as they climbed into the car and sat in the back with the children as Charles dropped Teddy off at a friend's house and then drove the two hours to London. Daisy's leg jittered up and down and she sat chewing at her nails. Her nerves were contagious and I found myself struggling to sit still.

"You're going to be fine," I told her, patting her free hand. "Your routine is perfect. You've got this."

With the help of her dance teacher, Daisy had been practising relentlessly for the audition. "And don't forget, they've already seen you perform in the video you sent in with your application and they liked what they saw." It turns out Daisy had sent in a recording of herself in the lead role of *Cinderella*, which was the school's summer production, and in which she had shone like no other. She had also filled in the section of the form which requested details of her parents' income to prove that she was eligible for the scholarship. Although she'd been incredibly deceptive, I couldn't help but be proud of her determination and ingenuity.

I chattered on for the remainder of the drive, not caring that no one could hear me. It eased my nerves.

Before we knew it, Charles was pulling into the car park of an impressively grand building, which was set in beautiful wooded parkland. As Daisy climbed out of the vehicle, I saw her look up at the imposing entrance with wide eyes. Her apprehension seemed to freeze her to the spot. But then Beth was calling her name, her arm outstretched encouragingly, and she was soon joining them in climbing up the stone steps and into the ballet school, her mum's hand resting lightly, supportively on her back.

I stayed close to Daisy as she was signed in and they were led to a dark, wood-panelled waiting area. Four other young teenagers, perfectly postured, were already sat with their parents and 'hellos' and 'good mornings' were exchanged in a tense murmur.

Soon, they were called one-by-one to change into their ballet outfits and warm up. Daisy was last.

When she was finally summoned for the audition and Charles and Beth had kissed her and wished her good luck, I watched her take a deep breath then I tagged along as she was led by the tiny, elegant lady through to a large, mirrored studio.

Once inside, she was greeted warmly by a panel of three and asked a few questions about her reasons for applying and her previous training, which Daisy answered easily, their kind and open manner making her visibly relax.

As soon as she was directed to the barre and asked to demonstrate a series of movements, starting with *plie*, she seemed to enter a world of her own. Her serene expression and confident, graceful positioning were a complete contrast from the jittery girl of the car. I watched, enraptured, as she performed *battement tendu, battement glisse, ronde de jambe, battement fondu, battement frappe* and *petit battement*, *developpes* and *adage* work before ending with *grande battement,* her body lean and agile.

When she'd finished, she was offered water and then she prepared herself for her choreographed piece, which was to take place in the centre of the studio.

Again, she took a deep, steadying breath, then entered and held her starting position, arms extended, toes pointed, and waited for the music to commence. If I'd had a body, my heart would have been pounding out of my chest as I stood against the wall behind the judging panel and Daisy started to dance.

She began with light, flowing steps, a *promenade,* gradually building up to turns and jumps. I recognised *jete* and *pirouette* as well as others that she had worked relentlessly to master over the past ten years. The music swelled and she began to move faster, all the while maintaining her balance and demonstrating her strength and flexibility. I couldn't look away.

When the music drew to an end, I burst into a round of applause and discovered that tears were streaming down my face. I watched, blurry-eyed, as Daisy bowed and the panel smiled and thanked her and told her they'd be in touch very soon, then she was exiting the room.

In the waiting area, Charles and Beth rushed to embrace her, anxiously asking how it had gone. Daisy shrugged. "I didn't make any mistakes," she told them simply, and that had to be good enough for them.

## Chapter Thirty-Five

The wait for the outcome of Daisy's audition seemed interminable, but in reality it was five days. The letter arrived on a Thursday, when Daisy was at school and Charles and Beth were at work, and wasn't opened until the whole family was home. They arrived together, Charles and Beth having collected Teddy from football practice and Daisy from her after-school dance class, and when they found the official-looking letter addressed to 'Miss Daisy Roberts' on the mat, they took a collective breath.

"You open it for me," Daisy begged her father, and she began gnawing at her thumbnail as he carefully tore open the envelope and scanned the contents. A large smile blossomed on his face, and Daisy and Beth squealed and began jumping up and down.

"Let me read it!" Daisy insisted, once they'd hugged and kissed. I looked over her shoulder as she scanned the letter.

*Dear Miss Roberts,*

*We are delighted to offer you a full scholarship to attend our ballet school. We were extremely impressed with your application and audition, and would like to commend you on your obvious dedication to mastering the finer points of the dance.*

*Attached are the particulars regarding enrolment. If you have any questions, please do not hesitate to contact us. We look forward to welcoming you at the beginning of the new term, and once again, congratulations.*

It was signed by the Head of the school.

"I'm so very proud of you," I told her quietly, my eyes shining, and Charles and Beth unknowingly echoed me.

"Let's celebrate with a take-away," Charles suggested then, and I stayed with them for the evening, listening to their happy chatter, before heading to the Moon to tell my friends the news.

"You should have seen her; it was like watching a fairytale princess," I finished, after giving Kate, Patrick and Dean another blow-by-blow account of the audition while we sat watching the Earth slowly rotate below us.

Kate sighed. "How lovely to have one's whole life ahead of one, *and* to know what you want out of it."

"And to have the talent and determination to succeed," I agreed.

"I always knew what I wanted," Patrick stated.

"Oh? And what was that?"

"Money and a fast car and lots of sex," he winked. I rolled my eyes.

"I just wanted to be a mum," Kate said quietly.

I patted her hand. "And you're a great one." She smiled at me gratefully. "What about you, Dean?"

"Me? Oh, I always wanted to be a train driver growing up, but I was happy driving my taxi in the end. You meet a lot of interesting people when you're a cabbie, including the odd famous person." He gave us a knowing look.

We listened eagerly as he shared names and anecdotes, commented on how polite or rude the celebrities were and, importantly, how much they tipped. We laughed at some of his more colourful descriptions, and frowned and shook our heads at the miserliness of a *very* rich singer.

"Speaking of which," Patrick began, "Don't forget we said we'd all take a trip to the eighties to watch Live Aid soon. I want to see Queen perform *Bohemian Rhapsody*." And that started a whole new conversation.

Eventually though, I sighed, and told them it was time for me to be heading back to Ben. They all looked at me sympathetically, and I uttered a soft 'good night' before vanishing.

However, when I returned home, I discovered that Ben was not asleep, as he usually was at 3 a.m. Instead, he was sitting in the darkened lounge with the 24-hour news channel on low. In his hand, instead of the usual tumbler of amber liquid, was the leaflet that Vicky had given him. He must have fished it out of the recycling bin one day when I wasn't around.

I sat beside him and gazed at his face as he stared down expressionlessly at the folded sheet of paper.

"What's going on in that head of yours?" I asked gently.

I reached out and stroked his cheek, and he closed his eyes as if he felt it. I rested my head against his shoulder, and we stayed like that for over an hour, before he finally retired to bed, leaving the smoothed-out leaflet on the coffee table.

*

The next morning, my heart full, I watched as Ben poured all the alcohol that was in the house down the sink, each bottle glugging loudly as it was emptied, as if to signal an emphatic ending. Then he called in sick at work before ringing the GP's receptionist and booking an appointment for later that morning. As he pulled on his exercise clothes, which hadn't been worn for some time, and headed out for a jog, I smiled widely. It was a first step, but it was a big one, and I was proud of my man.

*

Ben returned home half an hour later, red-faced and with dark sweat patches under his arms. He showered, and then it was time to drive to the doctor's surgery.

Rock music blasted out of the car's speakers as he drove. Sitting in the passenger seat, I felt like I'd travelled back in time to when I was alive, some sixteen years earlier, and we were just heading out on a routine errand – perhaps to the supermarket or the local Do-It-Yourself centre, I imagined, closing my eyes. We'd hold hands as we meandered at a leisurely pace along the aisles, consulting each other on our prospective purchases – nothing grand or exciting, just blissful normality. With the exception of my time with Daisy, I felt happier and more hopeful than I had felt for longer than I could remember.

Inside the surgery, I watched Ben check in at Reception, then we headed in to the pale green waiting room. There were several other people already in there, sitting quietly on the blue plastic chairs, some flipping through magazines, some staring at their phones. A baby woke up and shattered the silence just before Ben was called through, and I cooed over him and he soon settled down, to the relief of his tired-looking mother.

I followed Ben into the doctor's office. Anxious now, I sat in the chair next to his and listened as he revealed his reason for coming. His voice shook a little, but he held firm in his intention, and he was honest when the GP questioned him about the amount of alcohol that he'd been consuming and the physical effects that it was having on him.

I'd known about some, the more obvious signs, but I was surprised to discover that there were other, less overt symptoms of his dependence on alcohol: stomach upsets, nausea when he hadn't had a drink for a while, short-term memory problems, and increased tolerance so that he needed more and more alcohol to gain the same effect. I rubbed his arm as he outlined the illness's effect on his life: his increasing social isolation, his loss of control, his constant craving and his irritability if he didn't get to have a drink for an ever-shortening period of time.

The doctor listened closely and asked a few questions, before quietly praising him for taking this first step in seeking help. They discussed withdrawal symptoms, medication, and the dangers of suddenly stopping drinking, and devised a plan for Ben's recovery – including referral to Alcoholics Anonymous. He was also told that he should have a blood test to check that his liver function hadn't been impaired. I left the appointment feeling extremely encouraged, but I knew that this was just the beginning of Ben's fight to win back control over his life.

## Chapter Thirty-Six

Ben took the week off work, and I stayed with him throughout the early stages of withdrawal. He became pale, his hands shook, and he vomited on more than one occasion. He didn't eat, had an almost constant headache, and often lay on the bed with the lights low, a cold flannel on his forehead.

Both mentally and physically, he was in a battle – with himself psychologically *and* with the drug's effects on his body. The craving he was resisting was like a form of torture. I imagined it as a sly antagonist, like the bad guy in a story, provoking him and luring him in for his own evil purpose. I talked to Ben constantly, willing him to be strong, to not give in, to win the battle. I knew it was to be the first battle in a war which would last a lifetime.

One night, as he lay awake, he quietly started weeping. It was hard to see him reduced so. I held him and spoke softly to him. I told him how brave he was, how he would get through this initial phase, how I was here for him, how proud I was. I kept talking until the tears finally stopped falling, and he drifted into an uneasy sleep.

I lay next to him for the rest of the night, contemplating

the human mind and its coping strategies. *We protect ourselves from pain,* I thought, *but sometimes the way that we cope with life's difficulties is even more destructive than facing them head-on would be. It's like avoiding a storm, only to run head-first into a hurricane.* Ben had run headlong from grief, only to land in the grasping arms of addiction.

I mused on this until Ben woke up. He had tired shadows under his eyes and he'd already lost weight, but he looked better than he had for years. Pleased, I watched as he got himself up and took a shower, then as he managed to eat some breakfast. He sat trying to read for a bit, a thriller, with some success, and then it was time to gather his keys and wallet and head to his first meeting of Alcoholics Anonymous.

I debated as to whether I should stay away and give him privacy, but decided to tag along and then leave if I felt at any stage that I was intruding on something that was too personal.

We walked the short distance to the church hall through the tree-lined streets. It was autumn, and I admired the warm, multi-hued colours of the leaves, wishing I could kick through them with abandon like I had as a child and stop to collect the biggest, shiniest conkers and admire their smooth, rich-brown coating. It was a sunny day, and mild for the time of year, just the merest hint of coolness in the breeze; I judged this by the ruddiness which developed in Ben's cheeks, and the fact that he'd zipped up his jacket.

"I miss feeling the sun and the wind," I told him with a sigh as we walked. "I miss the simple pleasures the most. It's amazing what you take for granted when you're alive." And then, "Do you remember the snowball fight we had that first winter at college? We had so much fun. I remember feeling the ice trickling down the back of my neck when you got me on the back of my head. I'd give anything to feel that sensation again." Or his hands that had rubbed my cold ones when we'd headed back inside the common room. He'd bought me a hot chocolate then, and stood behind me with his arms wrapped around me while I sipped and the liquid warmed me from the inside. They were good times, happy times.

We soon reached the church hall, which was a modern building tacked onto the side of the much older church, and found our way inside, where Ben was greeted warmly by a man who introduced himself as Frank and asked if it was his first time attending a meeting. Frank was a large, fit-looking man with rich ebony skin and a deep voice; I warmed to him immediately and Ben visibly relaxed the more they talked. Frank fetched a Starter Pack for him and led him over to a table where he could help himself to tea or coffee, before he was encouraged to take a seat and the meeting began.

I listened closely to Frank's introduction as he welcomed the newcomers, of which there were three, and as a couple of speakers shared their personal stories. All had struggled, all had lapsed, all had persevered and were still persevering. I was inspired by their strength, impressed by their self-awareness, humbled by their candid descriptions of how they had inflicted pain on others, of their years of secrecy and guilt, of the intensity of their regret.

Ben chose not to share his personal journey with alcohol on that first day, but he did acknowledge that he had a problem, and that was a huge first step, for which he was congratulated. He blushed as he was applauded, and ducked his head, and I beamed with pride.

The meeting ended, and more tea and coffee was drunk as people lingered to chat. Frank spent time with Ben, giving him his phone number and earnestly telling him to call anytime – day or night – whether he was struggling with the need to have a drink or not.

For the first time in years, Ben walked with a bounce in his step as we returned to the house. He seemed re-energised and had a new look of determination about him. He began a much-needed cleaning of the kitchen, scrubbing at the counters with a vengeance and whistling as he worked, before putting on his favourite rock music and moving on to repeat the process with the other rooms.

I knew that this wasn't the end of his fight, merely the beginning of a long journey, but hope bloomed in my chest: hope that he was now on the road to recovery; relief that he was no longer having to battle alone; and love for the strength of the man who had stolen my heart at the tender age of sixteen.

*

I stayed close to Ben in the following weeks. I was there when he phoned Vicky and thanked her for her intervention, telling her about the progress he'd already made. I was there when he first opened up in an AA meeting about his relationship with alcohol, about the pain of losing the love of his life when he was still a young man, about the second chance that he'd had with Olivia, who was now happily remarried. I listened, proud and sad and hopeful all at the same time.

To my surprise, he also opened up to his boss about his struggle, and I was relieved and encouraged by the supportive response that he received; he was promised whatever time and assistance he needed. I thought back to how I had been too ashamed to admit the truth of my depression to my own boss, and admired Ben's courage. *If only I had asked for help,* I thought. *Perhaps I too would have received the support I needed to climb out of the trough.*

But I couldn't. I didn't.

## Chapter Thirty-Seven

My new routine was interrupted by Patrick's sudden appearance one evening. I was sat watching a nature documentary with Ben, when he appeared in front of the TV. I could tell by the look on his face that he had bad news.

"What's wrong?" I asked, jumping up.

"It's Huipi," he said, and swallowed as if around a huge lump in his throat.

"He's gone." It was a statement, not a question, but Patrick nodded.

"I couldn't find him anywhere and then I discovered that his wife had passed away. And now Puna has the same fever that she had."

Shocked at the sudden influx of troubling information, I took a moment to process what he'd said. I hadn't seen Huipi for a while, and while I was glad that he was now reunited with his loved one, I was sorry that I hadn't got to say goodbye. I knew I would miss him.

The news of Puna's illness was more disturbing. She was only in her thirties, I estimated, and though I knew that death was not the end, it was still tragic for someone so young to lose their life. There was also the matter that, if she passed, I was pretty certain that Patrick would disappear with her. What would I do without my best friend, my Grumpy Irishman?

Shaking myself, I reached out and clasped his hand in mine. "Let's go," I said, smiling in what I hoped was a reassuring way, and we vanished.

We reappeared in Puna's hut, where she lay on her woven pallet, tended to by her sister and niece. Her face was flushed and shiny with sweat, and she shivered and muttered unintelligibly. Patrick moved forward and lowered himself until he was sat in a space beside her, reaching out his hand to place on top of hers.

Suddenly, her eyes opened and she seemed to stare right at him. They gazed into each other's eyes, and a wide smile broke out on Puna's face. Her hand came up, as if to touch his face, and then it dropped as her eyes drifted closed once again. Patrick and I looked at each other in awed amazement. His eyes were shining.

We stayed with Puna for three days and nights, as she tossed and turned and murmured incoherently. Patrick would alternate between sitting by her side and pacing around in the small space, too anxious to converse much.

His love for the woman he had never encountered in life shone at its brightest during that time. I saw the side of Patrick that he rarely revealed – his intense passion, his tenderness, his vulnerability. I felt that I was privy to something special, something rarely witnessed, the depth of a man's love for his soulmate. I was touched to be permitted to be an observer of, and trusted companion during, his constant vigil over her.

"She's strong," I told him on the second night. "She'll get through it."

And she did.

When, to our immense relief, her fever finally broke, and she lay talking quietly with her family members and taking sips from a carved wooden bowl, we decided to take a break on the Moon.

"Thanks for staying with me through that," Patrick uttered in a low voice as we sat gazing down at South America. He looked so tired, his face strained and relieved at the same time.

"That's what friends are for," I replied, feeling my own emotional exhaustion.

"You're a great friend, the best."

I nudged my shoulder against his. "Ditto."

"I…I thought it might be our time, you know? I thought she wouldn't make it."

"It was touch-and-go there for a while," I agreed.

"It made me realise how much I'd miss you and Dean and Kate."

"We'd miss you too."

"I wonder if we get to see each other again – wherever we end up."

"I hope so."

"Remember when you first met me? I was so stubborn, so foolish – and rude. God, I was so rude to you."

I laughed. "You told me to 'buzz off!'"

He grimaced. "I never thanked you for persevering with me. You wouldn't give up on me. If it wasn't for you, I'd probably still have my arse glued to that bloody bench. And I'd never have encountered Puna."

"Oh, I don't know about that. I think that part was meant to be. You're soulmates," I said simply.

He smiled at this. "You made me believe. You made me hope. And I'll be forever grateful to you, Beautiful Nosy Girl."

Embarrassed, I stayed silent at this, and he placed his arm over my shoulder and I leaned against him. The Earth kept turning majestically below, and I thought of all the billions of lives being lived out before us. Somewhere, someone was falling in love. Somewhere, someone was birthing their first child. Somewhere, someone was saying goodbye to a loved one. The world was full of joy, and pain, and loss, and hope. It was a cauldron of emotion, and we were all just ingredients thrown into the pot. But would I change anything, if I could? No, I decided. I wouldn't.

You may be surprised to hear this, but, over time, I had come to believe that everything happened for a reason, and that all we could do was have faith, and trust that He would look after us all. It was impossible not to.

We soon returned to Puna, who was sitting up and drinking some broth out of a container that her sister held for her. I kissed Patrick goodbye, then watched him settle at her side, before heading back to be with my own soulmate.

I found him at work, and after sitting with him for the

afternoon, I checked in with my friends and family. Daisy was at ballet class and Teddy was at football practice, while Charles and Beth finished up their work days. My mum and dad were Christmas shopping. Vicky was talking on the phone with her mum. Kate was sitting in on one of Poppy's lectures at university, and Dean was in the pub.

I updated the latter two on the events of the previous days, and stayed to chat with Dean for a while. However, although he made all the expected responses to my news, I could tell that something was bothering him. He kept glancing over at Susie with a wrinkle between his brows. Eventually, I asked him if anything was wrong.

He hesitated before answering. "I don't know. I hope not," he finally uttered, with doubt in his voice.

"What do you mean?"

"Susie's been to see the doctor and he's sending her for tests."

My heart sank. First Puna, now this. "Why?" I asked, placing my hand on his arm.

"She's lost weight and she's tired all the time. And she keeps getting bruises and she can't remember how she got them."

I frowned at this and looked closely at Susie for the first time. She was pouring a pint, but without her usual cheery banter; she had shadows under her eyes and her clothes seemed looser on her than usual. I couldn't see any bruises, but she was wearing trousers and a top with long sleeves. I held Dean's hand. "Do you want me to come with you when the results are back?"

He thought about this for a few seconds, then shook his head. "No thanks, love. You've been through enough lately. Hopefully it's nothing serious."

I reassured him that I was there for him if he changed his mind, and he nodded gratefully. We chatted quietly for a while longer, then I headed back to Ben.

\*

That night, as Ben lay sleeping, I thought about the fragility of the human mind and body. About how everyone seemed to be touched by one ailment or another in their lifetime, and how some people made it through to the other side, like Puna, and how some people didn't. But of course, we were all destined to be fatally affected by something in the end.

I thought of my depression, Ben's alcoholism, Puna's fever and now Susie's concerning symptoms, not to mention the conditions that had caused my friends' deaths. I suppose it's inevitable that a biological machine, made up of trillions of cells, would have flaws, would malfunction at some point. Afterall, we couldn't live forever, not in our earthly bodies anyway. I thought of Leticia's words then, *'He will wipe away every tear from their eyes, and death shall be no more, neither shall there be mourning, nor crying, nor pain anymore, for the former things have passed away'* and felt comforted.

That weekend, Ben drove the few hours to visit Charles, Beth, Daisy and Teddy, a journey he hadn't undertaken for a while. He was greeted warmly, like one of the family, and spent time talking candidly with the adults about his recovery and playing football with eleven-year-old Teddy in the frosty garden, before sitting down to a roast dinner. I could see that

Charles and Beth were pleased and relieved that Ben had finally sought help, and as he was leaving, Charles patted him on the back and told him how proud he was of him. "Daisy would be too," he added softly, and he wasn't talking about my niece.

Ben nodded, his eyes suddenly wet. They hugged, and then Ben was promising to come back soon, before heading out to the car.

# Chapter Thirty-Eight

Christmas passed, the usual affair of festive trips to see friends and family, and the New Year brought both good and bad with it.

The good news was that Daisy started at her new school with the commencement of the new term. I watched as Charles, Beth and Teddy helped her settle into her dormitory room, which she was to share with two other third-year students, before tearful goodbyes were exchanged.

I stayed with her as she unpacked and chatted with the two friendly girls, named Himari and Chloé. Himari was Japanese and Chloé was French, and the three hit it off immediately, united by their love of ballet and pop music. The girls looked over Daisy's timetable and squealed at the number of classes that they shared, then promised to show her around London when they all had some free time.

Smiling, I left them to get to know each other.

The bad news was that Susie was diagnosed with an acute form of leukaemia. I listened to Dean as he outlined the doctor's explanation of the diagnosis, the treatment options and prognosis. Other than a slight tremble in his hands, he remained stoic.

"The doctors'll do their best, other than that it's in His hands," he said heavily. "I just hate to see her suffer."

\*

Susie started her first round of chemotherapy almost immediately, and on more than one occasion I sat with Dean as he stayed by her side throughout. She received the drugs through a vein in her arm at the hospital, during the administration of which she would sit trying to read, always a cosy mystery, or chat with the staff and other patients.

I admired her incredible bravery as she suffered the after-effects of the cell-destroying treatment: the vomiting, her head hanging over the toilet bowl as she retched and shook; the exhaustion, so that she would lay in bed for hours, weak and pale; the eventual hair loss, enough that she took to wearing a colourful scarf around her head. I never heard her complain, though she cried once.

Dean was beside himself when he saw her breakdown. "I just want to comfort her," he said, helplessly, as she lay in bed after a session of chemo and wept. He wrung his hands and paced around the room without taking his eyes off her. "I don't know what to do!"

"Shall we pray for her?" I asked suddenly, and I don't know where the words came from.

He nodded, and we settled down next to each other at the side of her bed. We bowed our heads and said our own private words. Mine involved asking God to relieve Susie of her pain, and to give Dean the strength to see her through the illness. I didn't pray for her to be healed; I was sure that there was a plan, and when it was someone's time, it was their time. By now, I trusted Him implicitly to look after us all.

After a break, during which we all took a collective breath, Susie went through a second round of therapy, and again Dean never left her side. The strength of his love for her shone through in every look he gave her, every gentle word that he spoke to her when she was suffering, every small movement made towards her when she wept. The force of it was like a physical presence in the room, almost as if I could reach out, and touch it.

Then more tests were administered, and I was with them when Susie received the results.

"I'm sorry," the doctor said. "The condition hasn't responded to the chemotherapy as well as we'd have liked." She went on to outline the options that were left to Susie, including further chemo, and the possibility of a stem cell transplant if a donor could be matched. But Susie waved the doctor's words away.

"No," she stated flatly.

"No?" repeated the doctor. Dean looked on in shock, but I had suspected that something like this might happen.

Susie, strong, stubborn woman that she was, shook her head but said no more. The doctor attempted to persevere in her explanation, and Susie held up her hand.

"I've had enough. No more. I'll go out on my own terms, thank you very much."

And Dean, who had been so stoic throughout her rounds of chemotherapy, who had never shed a tear in all the years that I'd known him, buried his face in his hands and wept.

*

How can we bear to watch a loved one slowly dying before our eyes? How do we find the strength and resilience to face their pain, their suffering? I never discovered the answers to these questions.

Dean refused to leave Susie's side over the next few months and I was reminded of Letitia's patient vigil over Derek. The power of love shone between them, so potent it was almost tangible; it crackled in the air like static electricity.

When the pain became too much, and Susie shed tears, Dean would stroke her hair and murmur comforting words until her medication kicked in and she would drift off to sleep, the lines on her face relaxing. Throughout this time, we observed the unfailing dedication of her home care team, the way they tended to her gently and attempted to keep her spirits up. Patrick, Kate and I took turns to stay with them throughout her final weeks, offering Dean comfort as he in turn offered it to Susie.

When it was time for her to enter a hospice, my respect for the compassion of palliative carers shot up even more. I wondered how they could bear the repeated pain of forming relationships with people who were at the end of their lives, people who were suffering, people who inevitably, tragically, passed away. How did they face having to tell loved ones over and over again that it was time?

Susie had been married once, years before, but she had never had children. It was her brother's family that regularly visited, offering the practical support and physical comfort that we could not. But on the night when she passed, only Dean and I were present.

I was sat on an armchair in a shadowy corner of the room, and Dean was on a straight-backed chair next to Susie's bed. A lamp shone on the bedside cabinet, illuminating the space around it with a soft glow. We were silent, each thinking our own thoughts as she slept, her even breaths the only sound in the room.

Suddenly, I realised that I could no longer hear anything. I looked over at Dean just as Susie's ghost appeared before him. She looked so beautiful, so much the Susie of a year ago that my breath caught. *This is what happens,* I thought, thinking of my own illness. *We revert to our true selves in death.*

I watched, trembling, as Dean's face broke into a smile of unmitigated joy, and he reached out and clasped her hands in his.

"Dean?" Susie whispered tremulously.

"Yes, love," he answered softly, and he leaned forward and kissed her hand. His eyes were shining.

"I've missed you," she breathed.

"We're together now, forever and always."

And just before they disappeared, I saw a smile of the purest delight spread across her face.

I cried then. Cried with happiness, cried with sadness, cried with relief that Susie's suffering was over. I cried for all the years that my friends and I had spent waiting for our loved ones, for the pain of watching them go on without us. I cried for those of us who were left behind, for the years ahead of us.

I cried for Patrick and Puna, who had never known earthly love; for Kate and John, especially Kate, who had to watch another woman take her place as a mother; and finally, I cried for me and Ben. I cried for the children we'd never had, for the suffering he'd endured, and I prayed fervently that only good things were ahead for him. I cried until I'd exhausted myself, and then I visited my two remaining ghost friends, and broke the news.

It was expected; we had prepared ourselves for it, but we still wept together. We sat on our refuge, the Moon, and comforted each other. We speculated about where Dean and Susie were now, what Heaven was like, what God's purpose was. We talked until the early hours of the morning, and then returned to our own loved ones.

## Chapter Thirty-Nine

Dean had spent twenty-five years waiting for Susie. He had once told me that it was an honour to watch her living out her life, and over the next few years I finally began to feel the same about my loved ones.

Two more years passed. Two years in which my friends and I adjusted to life without Dean, our foursome now down to three. Two years in which I witnessed Ben regain his health and lend his support to others who were struggling with addiction, mentoring them as Frank had done so well for him. Two years in which Daisy settled into the gruelling regime of ballet school, juggling academic lessons and mastering more advanced dance skills, which she showcased in increasingly prominent roles in the school's performances. Two years of contentment.

It was a contentment that arose from being at peace, with myself, my situation, my history, my companions, and from seeing my loved ones living their lives in such a positive and healthy manner.

*Those years were like the eye of the storm,* I thought later, when I looked back on my decades of existence.

Because then one day, I was sitting on Patrick's bench in the early hours of a summer morning, discussing Daisy's recent selection to be part of an exciting three-month exchange with a group of New York dance students, when my mum suddenly appeared in front of us.

I blinked and stared at her, at first unable to believe my own eyes.

"Daisy?" she uttered, her voice shaking, and that pulled me out of my trance.

"Mum?" I choked, and I launched myself up and into her arms.

We held each other tightly, and I revelled in the feeling of unmitigated joy at having my mum's arms around me again, as I took the time to process what must have happened.

"I'm dead, aren't I?" she finally asked, but it was more of a statement.

I pulled back and looked at her; her eyes were wet, like mine. I nodded.

"The last thing I remember was going to bed at my usual time. The next thing I knew I was standing at the side of it, looking down at myself. I tried to wake your father, but I couldn't. Then I thought of you, and here I am."

"Oh, Mum," I said, reaching out for her again. She was seventy-five and had always seemed healthy. I wondered what had happened, perhaps an aneurysm, like Patrick, or a heart attack, like Dean? "I'm glad you didn't suffer," I told her then, thinking of Susie.

But was it really better to go suddenly? Yes, it was over

quickly, but you never got to say goodbye to loved ones, to touch them one last time, to tell them how much it had meant to you to have them in your life – all the things I wished I'd had a chance to do. At least Susie had the time to tell her brother and his family that she loved them, and to set her affairs in order.

I introduced her to Patrick then, and he quietly expressed his sympathy, his face saddened. She thanked him, her smile wobbly, then turned back to me.

"Your poor dad," Mum sighed. I nodded. I wasn't sure how he'd cope without her; they'd always done everything together. I remembered my first journey back in time, when they'd unloaded the groceries together, and how they used to garden together; even small tasks were always shared between them. "I should be with him when he wakes up."

"Let's go," I answered. We held hands, murmured our goodbyes, and I coached Mum into channelling her emotions – her concern for my dad, her desire to be with him, her love for the father of her children. Soon, we vanished.

We reappeared in their darkened bedroom, where the light was just beginning to creep in through the curtains as the sun rose, tentacles of sunrays edging towards my father and fated to awaken him, only for him to discover that the love of his life was gone. Dad was breathing loudly, peacefully, and I braced myself for what was to come.

Within half an hour, the first tentacle reached him and he began stirring. We watched as he took time to fully awaken, and then he slowly sat himself up and scrubbed at his face as if to rid himself of the final remnants of sleep, after which he pushed back the bed cover, swung his legs to the side and eased himself into a standing position, before making his way out of the room.

"He always brings me a cup of tea first thing in the morning," Mum said quietly.

"I remember."

A few minutes later, he returned with two cups and placed one on my mum's bedside table.

"Tea's ready, Jackie."

When she didn't answer, he put his hand on her arm. "Jackie."

I think he must have thought that she was in a deep sleep, because he left her then and returned to his own side of the bed. He turned the lamp on and sat reading a novel while he drank his tea. At one point, he looked over at her, but didn't seem to realise that anything was amiss.

It was only when he'd finished his own cup, and was perhaps worried that my mum's tea was getting cold, that he put the book down and tried waking her again. This time, with more determination.

"Jackie, wake up love. Tea's here." He put his hand on her arm again and shook her. When she didn't respond, he frowned.

My mum and I started sniffling as the realisation that something was wrong hit my father. We watched as he tried again to wake her up, much more vigorously, and then as he pulled the cover off her and checked for a pulse. Finding none, he reached for his phone, his hand trembling as he called for an ambulance. Once he knew it was on its way, he followed the operator's calm instructions and commenced CPR.

We watched. We waited. Nothing happened. Dad persevered until the paramedics arrived, then stood back breathlessly, expectantly, as they performed their checks.

"I'm sorry. She's gone," the lady told my dad quietly, and he finally broke down. He sat, heavily, on the end of the bed, and held my mum's foot with one hand as he wept into the other. Mum bent down and placed her forehead to his, her arms around his shoulders, and I rested my hand on her back, rubbing gently, as our own tears dripped from our chins and our breaths came in loud gasps that only we could hear.

We stayed close to dad during the following days. We were there when Mum's body was taken away, when he called Charles and told him the news, when he went through the sombre process of organising the funeral. We never left his side, and neither did Charles, who had dropped everything and travelled up to be with him as soon as he'd received the phone call.

The day of Mum's funeral was one of the hottest days of the year. The kind of day when everything has to be done slowly, or not at all. The sun was bright and high in the Mediterranean-blue sky, and most of the mourners wore sunglasses and removed their jackets, their skin glistening with a fine sheen of sweat.

My dad complained of feeling unwell in the car on the way to the crematorium, and Charles encouraged him to drink from a bottle of water that he'd thought to bring along. Dad leaned on my brother as they entered the calm and hopefully cooler sanctuary, and Mum and I looked on with concern. It wasn't just the heat; the shock of the past few days had aged him.

The simple but beautiful service was over within an hour, and as the mourners filed out solemnly, ready to head to the wake, my dad asked Charles if they could sit for a while longer. Beth, Daisy and Teddy lingered, but Charles sent them off with Ben and Vicky, saying they'd be right behind them.

Dad had been pretty breathless all day, but as he sat struggling more and more, I suddenly realised that it wasn't just the heat that was affecting him. Charles noticed too.

He was just encouraging our dad to loosen his collar further, when Dad suddenly clutched at his left arm and keeled over onto the floor before Charles could grab him. Mum screamed and we rushed forwards as Charles whipped out his phone and dialled 999.

\*

At the hospital, Charles paced and mum and I kept a vigil at Dad's bedside. He never regained consciousness, and, as we sat beside him, I was reminded of Derek's final days.

Within a few tense hours, he passed.

Dad's ghost appeared before us as a bustle of noise and a rushing of staff commenced around the bed. We ignored the scene, and Mum and I launched ourselves towards him as he looked at us first in wide-eyed surprise and then in delight. He opened his arms and we fell into them.

"Daddy," I breathed.

"Daisy, my Daisy."

He kissed us both tenderly, and we looked at each other and smiled. And then they were gone.

## *Chapter Forty*

It's a strange feeling, being without one's mother and father. I was so used to seeing them in my regular visits, and even though I couldn't interact with them it was a comfort just knowing that they were there. I felt like an orphan, and I could sense that Charles did too. Losing that generation put *him* as the head of the family, and that was a big psychological adjustment to make.

*It's the cycle of life,* I thought, as I watched fourteen-year-old Teddy and seventeen-year-old Daisy holding hands at their grandfather's funeral, their second in a matter of weeks. *One generation gets replaced by another, and then they're replaced, and so on and so on. It's up to each generation to make their mark in their own way, and to pave the way for the ones who come after them.*

I'd never known my grandparents, but I thought of them then and all the ones who had gone before them, their life stories, their hopes and dreams, their regrets. An urge overcame me to explore my family history, and I promised myself that I would once the dust had settled.

And I did.

Initially driven by curiosity about getting to know my

mum and dad when they were young, I first travelled back to see them each in childhood. My dad, I discovered, was a rather mischievous child, always up to tricks and getting into trouble both at home and school, and my mum had been quiet and painfully shy. I flitted through the years, watching them grow up, as my dad matured into a more self-disciplined young man and my mum gained confidence, blossoming in her teenage years, then I zipped in and out of time until they met. They first encountered each other in a pub, when they were both on nights out with friends, and I saw how much my dad made my mum laugh as he struck up a conversation. It was to be the same for the next fifty years.

I was curious about my grandparents then, having watched them raise their children, each with completely different parenting styles. I was fascinated by my paternal grandmother in particular. She was Jamaican, like Leticia, and had been a single parent for most of my dad's life. She was a large, formidable woman, quick with her hand and opinions, but also quick to smile. She worked three cleaning jobs to support her two children and ruled the home completely. I absolutely adored her and was sorry I'd never had a chance to know her in life.

I tracked her back to when she'd first arrived in England on a ship from the Caribbean, and then before that, to her parents' home in the Jamaican countryside. My great-grandparents lived a simple life on a small farm. They were hard-workers, and I admired their quiet, peaceful life amidst the dense green rainforest and misty mountains.

My great-grandfather always wore an old straw hat as he worked the land, and, rain or shine, my great-gran sold produce, such as mangoes, bananas, ackee and breadfruit from a roadside stall. I would sit with her for hours listening to her relaxed chats with the laid-back customers. No one ever seemed to be in a rush.

For a few generations, life was pretty much the same. It was when I got back to the days of slavery that things changed dramatically for my family.

A couple of hundred years is nothing in the vastness of time, as I had learned, but the passage of just one generation was devastating to my family.

Suddenly, my ancestors were toiling for hours beneath the hot sun under the careful eyes of often brutal masters. I watched in horror as beatings were administered and the slaves were ordered to work harder, faster. I saw children born into slavery die enslaved to the same masters, or sold on, having been cruelly ripped from their parents. I witnessed them live-out their short lives on plantation after plantation, before dying from over-work and the poor conditions in which they lived. I watched, and I wept.

Perhaps the cruellest lesson was the discovery that one of my ancestors themselves was a slave-owner, an entitled master who impregnated a young slave girl. The knowledge made me feel sick to my stomach.

The girl was called May, and she was fourteen. The child was sold before he reached the age of five. He was the first of several that she birthed, squatting on the floor of her hut and groaning lowly, her face etched in pain, and she didn't get to keep a single one of them. They were property, a commodity. Sub-human.

May was dead by the age of thirty-two.

Horrified, I drifted further back in time, to a many-times-removed great-grandfather who was the first of my family to be taken from Africa. I witnessed the gruelling journey across the Atlantic Ocean to the Caribbean by ship, the crowded, diabolical conditions, the slaves chained below decks for the entire voyage, many of whom did not survive to see their new 'home'. I watched him sold at auction, after being checked over like a horse by one master after another.

Although I wept, I admired his dignity as he stood there, being poked and prodded, his face expressionless, his back straight, and it brought to mind the reeds around the pond in Patrick's Park, blown about by the wind, bending, but never breaking.

It was a relief to go back further, to follow his parents and grandparents in west Africa. To see the tribes living freely. Were their lives easy? No. But were they masters of their own destiny? Absolutely. For the first time, I truly appreciated my twenty-first century life.

I thought of Daisy, of how she was able to follow her dream so completely, little aware of the history of broken bodies that she danced upon. If it wasn't for their tenacity, their ability to survive in the harshest of conditions for generation upon generation, she and I wouldn't have even existed. *If only they could see her,* I thought, *living freely, seizing life and every opportunity she could to realise her ambition. They would be so proud.* Suddenly, I was filled with the certainty that, wherever they were now, they could, they were.

*

On my return to the present, I shared what I had seen with Patrick and Kate.

"The things people do to one another," Patrick said quietly, his lip curled. "My own Catholic ancestors were persecuted too, though I've no wish to go back and see it. I don't know how you bore it."

"It was difficult," I acknowledged. This was an understatement, but I had no words to express the true sense of horror that I'd felt.

"My brother traced our ancestry back to the Huguenots," Kate said. "They were forced to flee France in the seventeenth century."

"It's a wonder He hasn't given up on us," Patrick replied.

We were silent then, each wrapped up in our own thoughts. *People are capable of great cruelty,* I mused, *and yet the opposite is also true.* I remembered the slaves' support for one another, their friendship and comradeship, the way they would pray for each other, the way they would mourn. Every soul was important, every soul was valued. In the darkest of circumstances there was kindness, and hope. Yes, people were capable of great cruelty, but they were capable of something much more powerful. Love.

## Chapter Forty-One

The new school year started, and Daisy turned eighteen. I watched her celebrate with her school friends, and then as she prepared for her New York exchange. She was full of nerves and excitement, and she and the other students who were part of the programme spent hours gushing about what it might be like in 'The Big Apple'. I remembered my time there with Kim fondly, and looked forward to returning. There was no way I was going to miss out on seeing Daisy experiencing such an amazing opportunity.

On the day of her departure, I left Ben with a kiss, comforted by the fact that I would return to him regularly. Content, I watched him head out for his morning run, admiring his fit physique, healthy-looking skin and clear eyes, then zipped across the Atlantic to meet Daisy's group off the plane.

There were fifteen of them in total, all chattering and wide-eyed as they first stepped out of the airport and spotted the row of yellow taxis waiting at the curb. A minibus collected them, and on the journey their faces were glued to the windows, their eyes wide. They marvelled at the vast height of the skyscrapers and squealed when they caught a glimpse of Central Park. Their excitement was contagious, and I found myself laughing out loud at their reactions.

Soon, they arrived at the ballet school and I watched them settle in. They were given a tour and then had the remainder of the day to rest, before their hard work would begin.

Daisy took to New York instantly. She threw herself into the routine of classes, made friends easily and spent her free time exploring the city. I was impressed by her adventurous spirit as she took herself off to such attractions as the Museum of Art, home to Van Gogh's *Starry Night*; Ellis Island, symbol of the American Dream for millions of immigrants; the Empire State Building, with its vast views of 'the city that never sleeps' from its famous observation deck; and Times Square, bustling and bright with its myriad digital screens, shops and theatres. If none of her mates were available, Daisy would venture out alone. I trailed her everywhere, experiencing everything as if it was the first time, vicariously feeling her wonder and curiosity.

It was autumn, or 'fall' as Daisy's new friends called it, and one of her favourite things to do was to stroll through Central Park, admiring the changing colours of the leaves and feeling the increasingly crisp air in her lungs. Often, she would be accompanied by a pretty Belgian girl named Mila. They would discuss everything, from their favourite books to their dreams of dance excellence, and soon they were inseparable.

They would practise together in one of the empty studios, their lithe bodies synchronised in their graceful movements. Teasingly, they would play at mirror-imagining each other, and even choreographed their own impressive routines.

As I watched them grow closer through the weeks, it didn't surprise me when Mila kissed Daisy one Sunday evening. They were in Daisy's bedroom listening to music and laughing, when she suddenly leaned forward and planted her lips softly against Daisy's. Surprised, Daisy hesitated, before tentatively returning the kiss, and, smiling, I decided to leave them alone.

I returned to Ben, and snuggled against him as he lay asleep in bed, thinking about young love and first experiences. I remembered the tender fumbling that had been our own first time, the closeness that it had created between us, and sighed with contentment.

The three months soon flew by, a whirlwind of intense ballet training, exploration of the vibrant city and the shy discovery of first love. It was a sweet love, fresh and tender, innocent and beautiful, like the first opening of the petals on a bud, tentative but hopeful of being greeted by the sunlight.

They spent every spare moment together, dancing, relaxing and exploring, never falling out, never exchanging a cross word, comfortable and confident in their young love.

When December arrived, and it was time for Daisy to return to London, I watched as she said her private goodbye to Mila, both blinking back tears as they hugged. They promised to talk and message regularly, and over the years they did indeed keep in touch, though they were never together in the same way again.

\*

"Have you ever experimented like that?" I asked Patrick one day as we sat on his bench. It was winter by now, and a sparkling blanket of pristine snow covered the grass and the pond was partially frozen, the ice appearing sheet-like, smooth and translucent. I watched, fascinated, as early-morning dog-walkers passed us by, wrapped in heavy coats and woolly scarves, their breaths fogging in the chilly air as they created the first footprints in the virgin white powder, barely remembering what it felt like to experience the cold seeping into my lungs, sharp and invigorating.

Patrick looked at me aghast. "Feck no. And anyway, who said she was experimenting? She could be gay."

"She could," I acknowledged. "I guess time will tell."

"Have you?" Patrick asked after a pause.

"No, but maybe I should have."

"Why?"

I shrugged. "Why not? Life is for living. I think everyone should try to experience as much as possible. When we limit ourselves, we limit the richness of our world."

Patrick thought about this. "I wish I'd learned to juggle."

We looked at each other, and burst out laughing.

\*

The twentieth anniversary of my death arrived. This was the first year that my parents were not among the group of my loved ones gathered in the rose garden. Instead of my dad, Charles led a small prayer, while Beth, Daisy, Teddy, Ben and Vicky bowed their heads.

He spoke of how I had been reunited with my mum and dad, how it was a comfort knowing that God was looking after the three of us. He explained how he'd always felt like I was watching over them, protectively, and how I would understand that life moves on, and that it was okay for the living to have a life; it didn't mean that those who had passed were forgotten. He talked of how he could imagine me willing them all to go for their goals, to be the best people they could possibly be, and to be proud of the people they'd become.

I listened, my eyes wet, touched by the simple words.

They headed for a quiet meal in a local restaurant then, during which they raised a toast to missing loved ones. Ben joined in with his water glass.

As they ate, Ben and Vicky questioned fifteen-year-old Teddy and eighteen-year-old Daisy about their plans for the future. Daisy was hoping to be offered a position at both the Royal Ballet and the New York City Ballet, with the aim of working her way up to being a principal dancer one day. As her school trained its students to the age of nineteen, she still had a year until she would have to make her decision.

Teddy was studying for his GCSEs, and, as he loved Maths and Science, had an interest in going into engineering.

I observed, pleased, as Ben listened attentively to my niece and nephew, smiling at their eager hopes and dreams for the future. I could tell that he liked them a lot. *Our children would have been their cousins,* I thought, and I wondered if the same thought had crossed his mind when he got a distant look in his eyes.

His reverie was interrupted when Charles asked him about his plans to participate in his first half-marathon, and Ben talked enthusiastically about his passion for running, and how he was hoping to raise money for three charities that were close to his heart. A lump formed in my throat when he listed the names of a mental health charity, a miscarriage association and Alcoholics Anonymous.

After everyone said their goodbyes and dispersed, I was drawn to the site of my crash. I hadn't visited the junction for years, but something pulled me there on this occasion. I stood watching the traffic stop and start at the changing signals, orderly and regimented. It was later in the day than when I had taken my life on that fateful morning, therefore much busier, but the weather was uncannily similar. Pale sunshine attempted to peek through the grey clouds, and rain fell persistently onto the black tarmac.

I was staring at an oily slick on the road, which combined with the weak sunlight and water had created a metallic rainbow effect that was oddly beautiful, when someone walked through me. I shuddered, stumbling, then looked up and did a double-take when I recognised Al heading towards one of the traffic lights. He looked older, greyer, more physically fragile, but it was unmistakably him.

I opened my mouth to call to him, then closed it with a snap, remembering my promise to leave him in peace. Instead, I watched as he used a piece of string to tie a bouquet of flowers to the post. My heart felt full in my chest as I saw him step back and bow his head as he thought his own private thoughts. His faded scar was barely noticeable by now.

I hoped that my absence had brought him the peace that he deserved.

When he walked away, his shoulders hunched, his hands

deep in his pockets, I stepped up to the flowers. They were peonies in varying shades of pink and white. I looked at the string and remembered how I'd once thought of another such thread as tying my heart to Ben's.

"It's still there," I murmured, touching my chest.

## Chapter Forty-Two

Time flew by. Ben raised over three thousand pounds for his charities and began planning for his next half-marathon. Teddy aced his GCSEs and commenced Sixth Form College. Daisy immersed herself in her final year of ballet school, and I spent many hours watching her classes; *pas de deux* and *repertoire* sessions were particularly entrancing.

*Pas de deux* involved working with a partner to perform a dance duet, and *repertoire* allowed the students to practise and perform sections of ballet from the classical repertoire, such as *Swan Lake*, *Sleeping Beauty* or *Giselle*. I entered another world once the music began and would become lost in the beauty and grace of the dance, only coming back to myself once the performance had ended.

Proudly, I took Kate and Patrick to watch her Christmas performance. She had the role of Clara in a production of *The Nutcracker* and Charles, Beth and Teddy had front-row seats. I held my breath as Tchaikovsky's overture filled the auditorium and the curtains opened to reveal Daisy on the stage.

We watched in awe as she expertly portrayed Clara, wide-eyed with excitement at her family's preparations for their Christmas party. Soon, I was lost in the festive scene, and then in the magic of the toys' performances, the Sugar Plum Fairy's solo and the Mouse King's final defeat.

When the ballet was over, we joined in with the rest of the audience as the dancers received a standing ovation.

Following on from her lead performance, Daisy received offers of a position at both the Royal Ballet and the New York City Ballet, though the latter was her preference, having enjoyed her time in the Big Apple so much. She took some time to make her decision though since it was a big step to move to another country and leave her family behind. In a deep conversation over dinner one Sunday however, Charles and Beth urged her to follow her heart.

"New York it is then," Daisy declared, beaming, and they all clinked their glasses together.

She was to start as an apprentice, but Daisy had big ambitions. She wanted to be the title role in *Giselle*, Odette in *Swan Lake*, The Sugar Plum Fairy in *The Nutcracker* and Princess Aurora in *Sleeping Beauty*. Her eyes sparkled with determination as she outlined her ambitions, and we all laughed at her exuberance.

On the day of her flight, Charles, Beth and Teddy escorted Daisy to the airport. They took turns to hug her, a tearful Beth in particular finding it hard to let go, and then watched until she'd disappeared into the crowd heading through Security.

"My little girl's all grown up," Beth sighed, her breath hitching as she dabbed at her eyes with a tissue, and Charles put his arm around her and squeezed gently. She leaned into him, and then they turned and made for the exit.

From then on, I spent most of my time flitting back-and-forth between the UK and US, splitting my attention between Ben and my friends on one side of the Atlantic, and Daisy on the other. A room had been prepared for her in a shared apartment, and she was soon established in her new home.

Although Mila had moved back to Belgium, Daisy settled back into New York life quickly, and though she was in the most junior position in the company's pyramid, Daisy worked just as hard as, perhaps even harder than, the more experienced, more senior professionals. She would watch them closely, emulating and then innovating with their choreography in what little spare time she had.

When she got the chance, she would question the director closely about any changes that she made during rehearsals, to the corps structure and formations, or to the choreography itself, always eager to learn, to experience. Her hard work and enthusiasm paid off, and she was often selected to fill a spot in the corps lines.

Ben's life was quieter, more mundane on the surface. He had a regular routine of morning jogs, work and attendance at AA meetings. He obtained a rescue dog that he lavished with affection. He named him Barney, and he would take him out twice per day – once on his run and once for a walk in the evening. He seemed content, if not joyous.

Patrick divided his time between the Amazon and the UK. He was fascinated by the tribe's simple life in the jungle, head-over-heels in love with Puna, and sustained and comforted by the way that she had looked at him and smiled during her fever.

Kate was busy watching over her family – John, who was

single again, Sam, who was specialising in oncology after completing his medical degree, and Poppy, who was now a History teacher.

I met up with my friends regularly. We still felt Dean's absence and talked about him often, remembering his many words of wisdom and reminiscing about the adventures we'd been on together. I must admit, it was a welcome relief to us all to be able to interact with others. Voyeurism can be a comfort, and it can be enlightening, but there's only so long a person can go without having someone to talk to, to engage with. Watching our loved ones go about their lives was indeed a privilege, but I was so grateful for my ghostly friends. It would have been a long, lonely existence without them.

*

One Sunday, Ben was having a spring clean when he came across my photo in a drawer. He sat down on the bed and ran his finger down my smiling face. The touch was so tender that I felt its reflection on my heart.

After a while, he placed the frame on his bedside table, where it used to sit, and then he pulled our old photo albums out of a cupboard and spent the rest of the afternoon perusing them with a soft smile on his face. I looked over his shoulder and chuckled at some of the silly poses that we'd pulled. We seemed so young, so full of energy and life. Now Ben was pushing fifty, and although he was fit from all his running and from eating a healthy diet, he had more than a little grey mixed in with his light brown hair, and the lines on his face had deepened over the years.

His quiet perusal was interrupted by a knock at the front

door. I followed Ben downstairs and stood back as he opened it. It was Frank. The two had become good friends since that first meeting at AA and they often met up for coffee.

"Alright, mate? Just dropping round that book I mentioned since I was on my way to church," Frank explained.

"Oh, brilliant. Thanks," Ben smiled, taking the offered novel, which was a spy thriller by the look of the front cover.

"Do you, er, want to join me?" Frank nodded his head in the direction of the church.

Ben seemed on the verge of refusal, before something changed his mind and he nodded, then reached back to collect his jacket off the hook.

"Great!" Frank beamed, clapping his hands together.

They chatted companionably as I followed them down the tree-lined street. The sun was shining, and cotton-candy clouds drifted lazily across the blue sky. It was quiet on the roads, with only the occasional sound of a car's engine as it passed to disturb the peaceful day.

When they arrived at the church, although he had been to the adjoining hall many times for AA meetings, Ben began to look uncomfortable – he started fidgeting with his collar and glancing around anxiously. Frank seemed to sense his nerves and clapped his hand on his shoulder before guiding him into a pew.

"Just relax, and listen. No expectations," Frank told him, before bowing his head and beginning his own silent prayers.

I sat next to Ben and put my hand over his where it lay on his lap. "I'm here, my darling," I told him, as he looked around curiously at the stained-glass windows. The light was shining through them, casting a rainbow mosaic of colours onto the wooden floor beneath. It was very beautiful. I felt my spirits lift.

When the last of the congregation was seated, the service began. The vicar had chosen the topic of loss for his sermon. He began by explaining how difficult it can be to accept the passing of a loved one; how we find it hard to think beyond this life, to imagine them in another place, reunited with their Heavenly Father.

"'Why did he take them?' we ask ourselves. 'What's the point of it all?'"

I looked at Ben as he asked these questions, and saw that he was concentrating hard on what the clergyman was saying. The vicar continued, describing God's love, and when he added a quote from the Bible that I recognised, the words made me sit up.

"'He will wipe away every tear from their eyes, and death shall be no more, neither shall there be mourning, nor crying, nor pain anymore, for the former things have passed away.'"

Hearing Leticia's words again made my eyes burn. It couldn't be a coincidence. I looked back at Ben, and saw that he had moisture in his own eyes.

The vicar talked on, describing the Bible's teachings on faith, comparing those who doubt to waves tossed and blown about by the wind.

When the sermon was over, Ben bowed his head and joined in with the prayer.

From then on, he regularly joined Frank in attending Sunday services. They seemed to comfort him, and a sense of peace stole over him. I often tagged along, and they brought me solace too.

## Chapter Forty-Three

That year was the year that my Ben turned fifty, and he ran his first full marathon on his birthday. I stood among the excited crowd, cheering him on as he set off amongst the racers, many of whom were dressed in colourful and outlandish costumes. I remember spotting Batman and Super Mario, a giant sausage and a cross-eyed chicken, the light-hearted sights making me smile in amusement. It was good weather for a marathon, mild, with a cool breeze and slightly overcast.

I zipped ahead to different points along the course, shouting encouragement as I watched him approach each time, before he would pass me and I'd zip ahead again. I knew that he couldn't hear me, at least not in a physical sense, but I hoped that he'd at least sense my support on a spiritual level.

*Go, Ben!* I urged, inwardly. *Go, my darling!*

As the race approached the later stages, I could see that Ben was drawing on every ounce of strength that he possessed so that he could finish. He was covered in sweat and his skin glowed pink. The elite runners had long crossed the finish line by the time it came into sight for us, and I increased my encouragement along with the cheering crowd and Ben put on a final burst of energy. He raised his arms as he crossed the line, then checked his time. He'd completed the course in just over four and a half hours, which is around average. *Not bad for a fifty-year-old,* I thought.

Proudly, I watched him receive his medal. This time, he had raised over ten thousand pounds for his charities. Charles, Beth, Teddy and Vicky and her family had been in the crowd near the finish line, and they joined him in celebrating. It was a perfect day.

That night, I sat with my friends on the Moon, telling them about my Ben's achievement.

"In a way, life is like a marathon," Patrick mused, once I had stopped for breath.

"How so?" asked Kate.

"You go through different stages, at your own pace, and only some reach the finish line."

"What's the finish line in this analogy?" I queried.

"Old age, I guess," he shrugged.

I thought about this. I had given up my own race a third of the way through.

"Well I hope Ben reaches it."

"Me too," uttered Kate quietly, "and John and Puna of course."

I hummed my agreement.

Patrick grunted. "Puna's tribe don't have many elderly people – although they have a healthy lifestyle, they have a shorter life expectancy without the aid of modern medicine."

I put my hand over his, and we all lapsed into silence as we stared down at the sparkling Earth.

*

Daisy completed her apprentice year and gained a position in the corps de ballet. She was one step closer to achieving her dream of being a principal.

As usual, she didn't stop at learning her own choreography. She often found a spare studio and practised the principal and solo parts, having watched them closely in rehearsals.

One day, she was alone practising the Lilac Fairy Variation from *Sleeping Beauty*. It was from the section of the story when the royal court panics, and the Lilac Fairy, who had not yet given her gift to the new young princess, promises that if Carabosse's curse ever materialises, then Aurora will not die, but will fall into deep sleep for one hundred years, awakening once she is found by a Prince from a faraway land who shall give her true love's kiss.

Lost in our own world, I watched as the music swelled and she danced the routine, her grace and beauty as she performed a flawless *arabesque* and effortless *pirouette* leaving me breathless.

She had just taken her final position, and the music was ending, when a slow clap sounded from the doorway. Startled, we both turned to see one of the principal male dancers leaning against the jamb. His shoulder-length blonde hair was tied back in a ponytail, and his handsome face held an expression of boredom.

"Very impressive, little flower," he drawled in a slightly

accented voice. "Now do it again – *without* the mistake."

Daisy pursed her lips and stuck her chin out and, without saying anything, moved to restart the music. I watched closely as she repeated the performance, but I couldn't see anything different about it from the first time around…but then, I wasn't the expert, was I?

When she was once again in her final position, before the music had even stopped, the young man simply nodded, "Better." Then he was gone.

Daisy trembled as she stood staring at the now-empty doorway, her face pink.

"Well at least he knows your name," I commented dryly. The principals were the elite, and not above ignoring anyone below soloist. Daisy grabbed her towel and headed to the showers.

I watched Anton Christensen closely during the next rehearsal. He was incredibly focused and talented, confident bordering on arrogant, and, when he was relaxed, quick to smile. I saw that he had high expectations of those around him, but even higher expectations of himself. He was extremely strong, as male dancers needed to be, and when he danced a sense of vitality and virility shone from his performance. It was breath-taking to witness, and more than a little intimidating.

Of course, all the girls had a crush on him. Well, all except one. Daisy barely looked in his direction, except when he was performing on stage. A fact that he didn't fail to notice.

\*

Daisy's twenty-first birthday soon arrived. Charles, Beth

and Teddy flew out to spend the weekend with her. It was September, still warm in the city, and Daisy took delight in acting as tour guide as she showcased her favourite places.

On the Saturday evening, they watched the company's performance of *Sleeping Beauty*.

When Daisy appeared by their seats after the final curtain had dropped, they gushed about how wonderful it had been, and she led them back stage to meet her friends in the corps de ballet.

Daisy's family was welcomed warmly, and the dancers received their praise with gratitude and humble smiles.

Just as she was leading them away, however, Anton appeared in the hallway. "Aren't you going to introduce me, Daisy?" he asked, looking expectantly at the group.

Daisy blinked, her cheeks turning pink, but turned to make the introductions. "This is my dad, Charles, my mum, Beth, and my brother, Teddy. Guys, this is Anton Christensen, one of our principal dancers."

"Yes!" Beth enthused as Charles shook his hand. "I recognise you from the performance – you were superb."

"Thank you. Are you a dancer too?" he asked, looking at Teddy enquiringly.

"Me? Oh no, I want to be a mechanical engineer."

At this, Anton's eyes lit up and he began questioning him closely about his chosen career, displaying a surprising knowledge of mechanics. Daisy watched with raised eyebrows.

"Excuse me," he said to the others after a few minutes had passed by and he realised that he and Teddy were excluding the rest of the family, "but I have a passion for fixing up old cars. It's a pleasure to talk to someone who has similar interests, someone knowledgeable about the workings of machinery. You don't really get many people like that in a ballet company."

"Well, we're about to head off to a restaurant," Charles told him. "If you don't have any plans, why don't you join us? You can continue your conversation over dinner."

Daisy opened her mouth as if to remonstrate, but before she could utter a single word, Anton had accepted the invitation.

Charles, Beth and Teddy waited while Anton and Daisy changed into their regular clothes, then the five of them headed out and along the street to a small Italian bistro. As they walked, Anton once again engaged Teddy in talk of cars, while Daisy strolled ahead chatting with her parents. From the set of her shoulders, however, I could tell that she was far from relaxed.

They entered the elegant restaurant, which was crowded with theatre-goers, and settled into their seats. Anton ended up between Daisy and Teddy. As they perused the menus, he chatted easily with her parents, while Daisy sat quietly.

Then, while the family were distracted by the waiter arriving to take their orders, he suddenly turned to her.

"I didn't know it was your birthday! Why didn't you say anything?"

Daisy merely shrugged. "Why would I?"

"The company like to celebrate special birthdays. You've

been very naughty, *lille blomst*."

"What does that mean?" interrupted Teddy, who had overheard the last part of the conversation after giving his order.

"It's Danish. For 'little flower'," Anton explained, and Daisy blushed.

Charles started asking him questions about his childhood in Denmark then, and Anton eagerly launched into a description of life growing up in beautiful Copenhagen, and his regular visits to his grandparents who lived in the countryside.

Despite herself, I could see that Daisy became engrossed in his vivid and colourful description of what sounded like an idyllic childhood.

When the meal ended, Anton offered to walk Daisy back to her lodging and, after goodbye hugs all around, Charles, Beth and Teddy headed off to their hotel. Daisy stood looking around awkwardly once they had disappeared around a corner.

"Shall we?" Anton gestured in the opposite direction. Without looking at him, Daisy nodded.

## Chapter Forty-Four

"Why won't you look at me, little flower?" Anton asked as they walked and he'd made several failed attempts at conversation.

Daisy hesitated. "You make me uncomfortable," she finally answered.

He looked at her in surprise. "Do I? Why?"

"I-I don't understand you."

"What do you mean?"

"Well, you're always watching me for one thing."

"So? I like looking at pretty flowers. And," he added after a pause, "I see great potential in you, *lille blomst*. I think that one day, you're going to be a big star."

Daisy looked at him in surprise, and a tinge of pink stained her cheeks.

"Ah, now I can see those pretty blue eyes of yours again," he told her in a satisfied voice.

"I'm not interested," she said firmly, looking away again.

"You *were* in the restaurant. You couldn't take your eyes off me."

"I was engrossed in your description of what it was like to grow up in Copenhagen. It sounded wonderful."

"Lies," he answered, with a dismissive wave of his hand.

Daisy looked at him in surprise. "*Lies*?" she repeated.

"Yes. I had a terrible childhood," Anton replied flatly.

"Oh…I-I'm sorry," Daisy said softly. "Do-do you want to talk about it?"

He shrugged. "It's an old story. I never knew my grandparents. My father used to beat my mother and I regularly. I couldn't wait to leave the country."

She placed her hand on his arm. "I'm so sorry," she repeated, and he looked at her warmly.

"My mother's happily remarried now."

They continued walking in silence for a few moments.

"What was *your* childhood like?" Anton finally asked.

"Good," Daisy answered. "Normal." Then she seemed to rethink. "Well except for…"

"Except for what?"

She shifted uncomfortably. "Well, I-I always felt a bit in my aunt's shadow. She died before I was born and I was named after her." I looked at Daisy in surprised sorrow as she said this, and saw a guilty expression on her face.

"Was she a ballerina too?"

"No, she was a teacher, and everyone loved her, but she suffered with anxiety and depression. She killed herself when she was just twenty-six."

*Oh, Daisy!* I thought. *I never considered the impact of my legacy on you.*

"Good God," Anton swore softly.

They reached Daisy's apartment building then, and Anton waited as she fished her key out of her handbag and opened the door. Suddenly, she turned to him. "How did you know where I live?"

"Because I live in the adjacent building," he answered, gesturing over to it casually.

"Have you been spying on me?" she asked with narrowed eyes.

He barked a laugh. "No, *lille blomst*. Just keeping an eye on my future dance partner. You and I are going to do great things together." And with that, he turned and sauntered off down the street.

Daisy was left staring after him, her mouth hanging slightly open.

I left her then, and thought myself straight onto the top of the Statue of Liberty. My heart was aching from her words. *I never knew*, I thought, staring out at the vast darkness of New York Harbour. *All those years of being forced to visit the rose garden, to mourn for a woman you'd never known. All those years of bearing the weight of carrying the name of someone who'd died under such a black cloud. All those years you'd kept your discomfort to yourself.*

Daisy was so important to me, the closest thing to my own child that I'd ever have. And yet to her I was just a photo in a frame, a story of a stranger. I'd always felt that sharing a name connected us on a special level, but to her it was perhaps something regrettable, a weight to bear, a curse. For the first time, I put myself in her shoes, thought about it from her point of view instead of my own, and the realisation of how differently Daisy viewed the connection brought tears to my eyes.

Patrick appeared at my side then, and when he saw my face, he opened his arms to me. In a voice shaking and full of self-pity, I outlined what Daisy had told Anton.

"And the thing is, I'd only ever thought about it from *my* point of view. How selfish of me! I thought I was this precious presence in her life, connected by a beautiful name, the aunt she would have been best friends with, when in reality I'm a-a giant, unwelcome *spectre* casting this huge shadow over her!"

Patrick sighed sympathetically, and offered words of comfort while I poured out my heartbreak. He stroked my hair soothingly.

When the tears finally stopped, and I had reassured him that I would be okay, we sat next to each other with our legs crossed and stared out towards the inky ocean. A few welcoming lights were visible out there in the harbour and even further out, ships that were travelling through the night. I wondered where they were going. *It's like life,* I thought. *We're all passengers on a journey, a voyage through uncharted waters, only the final destination is unknown.* I thought of my parents then, and Dean, Kim, and Leticia, and wondered what it was like where they were. I couldn't even begin to imagine.

It had been nearly fifty years since my birth, over twenty since my death, and I suddenly felt eager for this limbo existence to be over. Daisy's revelation had shocked me to my core, and I realised I'd been living vicariously through her, haunting her. I wondered if I should leave her in peace, and just stay close to Ben for his remaining years on Earth. I shared my thoughts with Patrick.

He looked at me aghast. "You can't stop now; it's just beginning to get interesting!"

"What do you mean?" I asked in confusion.

"I want to see if Anton manages to win her over."

"It's not a soap opera, Patrick."

"It's as good as."

I shook my head but didn't say anything. If I was honest, I was curious to see the outcome of that story myself.

We sat without speaking for a few minutes, before I finally thought to ask Patrick why he'd come. He shrugged. "Boredom."

"Not because you missed my witty repartee then?"

"Nah, I had nothing better to do." He nudged my shoulder with his, and smirked.

"Puna's asleep then?"

He nodded.

"Want to go travelling?"

"Time or distance?"

"Either," I shrugged. "I could do with a break."

He thought for a few seconds. "Do you want to see what Lucky's up to these days?"

My eyes lit up. My favourite elephant would have reached adulthood by now.

It was already daytime when we appeared in the middle of the vast African savannah. Muted yellows and soft oranges still painted the sky, watercolours outlining the silhouettes of a distant mountain and the nearby acacia trees. We stood amongst the tall grasses, and spotted Lucky nearby using his trunk to strip leaves from a shrub.

He was much larger than when I'd last seen him, his tusks much bigger. I walked closer to him and put my hand on the wrinkled grey skin of his side, while I gazed into his wise eye. I leaned against him and closed my own eyes, thinking of the passage of time and wondering what happened to elephants when they died.

My reverie was interrupted by Patrick.

"Where's the rest of the herd?" he asked, looking around the savannah with a puzzled expression.

"Adult males often live alone. They only re-join the all-female herds temporarily, to mate," I explained, dreamily distracted.

"How do you know all this?"

I shrugged. "Nature documentaries."

"Sounds lonely."

"Some human males might think it sounds like Heaven," I answered dryly, and he threw back his head and laughed loudly. Usually this would cause birds to erupt into the skies, and skittish animals to jolt and run for cover, but not in the ghost world.

We stayed with Lucky for the rest of the day, and the peace and tranquillity of his life on the grassland soothed my soul. It allowed me time and space to reflect on Daisy's words and I gradually came to a calm acceptance of her perspective of me. I decided that I would still watch over her; I had too great a love for her not to.

## Chapter Forty-Five

Time moved on. Ben became more and more involved in the church's activities and Daisy persevered in mastering the gruelling routine of life in a professional dance company – and in avoiding Anton Christensen.

I couldn't work out what was going on in her mind. She was usually so confident, so poised, but around Anton she appeared the opposite. Were the blushes a sign of attraction, or merely awkwardness? Did she avoid him because she didn't want to encourage his overtures, or because he came on too strong? Not for the first time, I wished that I could read minds.

Despite her time with Mila, I was pretty certain that Daisy was rather inexperienced, especially when it came to men. I puzzled over whether she had a lack of interest in them generally, or just in Anton…or was it merely shyness around someone who was far more experienced and confident?

Another girl would have taken advantage of his interest in order to climb the company's hierarchy more quickly – he was clearly determined to partner her one day. But it either hadn't occurred to her, or she was too honourable to use him. Either way, I was proud of her for her integrity.

She was alone in a studio, using her free time to practise her choreography for the corps de ballet, when he once again came to lean against the door and watch. She ignored him until the music finished, and then as she collected her towel and wiped her face and neck.

He walked forward, holding out a bottle of water to her without speaking. She took it and murmured her thanks, still not looking at him, and he watched as she drank thirstily.

When she'd drained the bottle, she made to walk past him, but he caught her hand and gently pulled her to a stop.

"Look at us," he said quietly, gesturing towards the mirror which spanned one wall of the studio.

She stopped and looked. They were side-by-side, holding hands. A confused wrinkle appeared between Daisy's brows; she opened her mouth, perhaps to ask what it was that he expected her to see, but then he spoke.

"We're perfect together," he said, simply. And they were. While he was all masculine strength and height, she was petite and softly feminine. Where he was cool fairness and light, she was warm olive. Only the blue of their eyes matched.

They stood looking at their striking reflection for a minute or more, and my breath caught at their youth and beauty.

Suddenly, Anton turned to her. "Dance with me," he said.

And as if in a trance, Daisy allowed him to lead her to the centre of the studio, where he left her alone only to change the music, before he returned to her. I recognised the *pas de deux* as the balcony scene from *Romeo and Juliet* immediately; it was one of my favourite pieces.

I watched, enthralled as he lifted her effortlessly, and as they moved fluidly around each other, the music swelling and flowing around the room as if it were a third dancer. Tears came to my eyes as I witnessed the beautiful magic that they were able to create together.

As usual, Daisy entered another world, her expression dream-like. They gazed into each other's eyes as they seamlessly glided from one flawless position to another, their strength and grace showcased at their best.

Then, when they had taken their final positions, and the music stopped, Anton, his eyes burning, reached for her and began to kiss her hungrily. For a few seconds she responded, then, suddenly, she was pushing him away.

"No!" she said in a panicked voice.

Immediately, Anton dropped his arms and stepped away. He was breathless, his cheeks flushed. He put his hands on his hips and swore softly.

"I want you to go," Daisy told him.

"Very well," Anton answered after a pause, "but if you expect me to walk away permanently from chemistry like that, you're in for a surprise." And he turned and stalked out of the room. Daisy buried her face in her hands.

When she took them away, her face was so full of confusion that I wanted nothing more than to embrace her in that moment. To offer her the comfort and confidence of a loving aunt. But I couldn't. All I could do was observe, and empathise.

\*

On the Moon that night, I contemplated the mystery of love. What made us attracted to one person and not another, regardless of looks? What made us yearn for that one person above every other? How did we *know* when we'd found 'the one'?

I remembered the old lady in the hospital then, back when I was freshly deceased and avoiding my family's grief – the one who'd 'gone' straight away with no one waiting for her, as most people did according to Leticia. Did it mean that not everyone had a soulmate? And, if that was the case, *why* was it so?

Patrick and Kate joined me when their loved ones were asleep and I broached the matter with them.

"It's true," said Patrick. "There would be more ghosts hanging around if everyone had a soulmate."

"Perhaps it's like twins, you know, identical ones," suggested Kate, her voice thoughtful.

"What do you mean?" I queried.

"Well…most people are born alone, but identical twins start out as one egg, which splits into two individuals. Perhaps it's that way with souls too. Perhaps we were once one with our soulmates, and we return to being one when we die."

"We're half of a whole?" Patrick uttered thoughtfully.

"It makes sense," I admitted.

"I've always thought of John as 'my other half'," Kate smiled.

Comforted by the thought, we sat in silence for a while. Then it was time to return to our loved ones.

Months passed. Daisy avoided Anton, and he in turn seemed to be giving her space. Space for what, I wasn't sure. To miss him? To regret her rejection? To reconsider? To apologise?

Or was it that she had hurt him?

His distance and her avoidance didn't stop them from watching each other however. Whenever Daisy wasn't looking, Anton would cast her lingering glances from hooded eyes. And whenever he performed, it was clear that Daisy couldn't take her eyes off him.

The company was rehearsing *Giselle*, the ghostly romantic tragedy of a beautiful young peasant girl who falls for the flirtations of the deceitfully disguised nobleman, Count Albrecht, who is betrothed to another. Giselle dies of heartbreak, and joins the Wilis, spirit maidens who had been betrayed in life by their lovers and aim for vengeance by dancing men to their deaths.

It was the day of the opening performance, the cast were gathered together for final rehearsals, when a call came in that the ballerina who played Myrtha, Queen of the Wilis, had fallen and broken her ankle. The director immediately turned to the gathered dancers in the corps and asked who knew the role. Daisy, who had been practising several of the parts in the preceding weeks, was one of three who raised their hands.

"Daisy can do it," Anton, who was cast as Albrecht, declared immediately, stepping forward, his face serious, his arms folded across his chest. "I've seen her practising. She could do it in her sleep."

The director nodded, his respect for his principal's judgement making the decision for him. Daisy was cast.

I could tell that she was nervous as the director talked to her quietly, giving her quick instructions, but as the other dancers headed into their backstage positions ready for the rehearsal, she listened attentively and nodded at each point that he made. Then she took her place in the wings.

I waited impatiently as the performance started and the dancers moved through their scenes. When Daisy emerged onto the stage, looking regal, icy and full of malice, I held my breath. Confidently, she led the Wilis in a dance around the graveyard, before introducing a new Wili, Giselle, who rose, enshrouded, from her tomb.

I watched to the end, when Myrtha's spell over Giselle, which entrances Albrecht into dancing with her, almost succeeds in exhausting him to death, however he is saved by the rising sun, which causes the Wilis to retreat. Before disappearing into her grave however, Giselle points him towards his betrothed, Bathilde, and he reaches out to her.

I stood and applauded as the rehearsal came to an end, and I could see the relief on the director's face as he gathered the dancers together and talked of his pleasure at their performance. He gave a special mention to Daisy, and she blushed in pleasure.

## Chapter Forty-Six

The opening night was a success, and backstage, as the dancers relaxed and gathered their things together, Anton sought out Daisy for the first time in months.

"You were terrific!" he beamed, swinging her around, and she couldn't help but laugh out loud.

"Thank you," she said breathlessly when he'd put her down. "And thanks for recommending me."

"How could I not? I told you, little flower, you're going to be a big star."

"Well, all the same, I'm grateful to you. You didn't have to," she insisted.

Anton rolled his eyes and slung his arm around her shoulders.

"Want to get something to eat?" he asked casually.

Daisy hesitated, then finally agreed with a nod. I could tell that she was mixed between feeling gratitude for what he'd done for her and not wanting to encourage him, but she was on a high after her first professional role outside of the corps, and it would have taken a strong will to resist the intoxicating buzz of such a night worthy of celebration.

Clearly delighted, Anton grabbed his coat and the two of them walked the short distance to a nearby French restaurant. It was dim inside, the sort of place that had chequered table cloths and accented waiting staff, and, as to be expected, busy with theatre-goers, but they managed to obtain a table for two after a short wait. They settled into seats at the candlelit table, and Anton watched as Daisy perused the menu.

"You look beautiful in candlelight," he told her when she looked up, his eyes gleaming.

"Don't start please."

"What? Can't a man tell a woman how lovely she looks these days?"

"Not when he has an unwelcome agenda, no."

"I don't like the word 'unwelcome'; it makes it sound like I'm harassing you. I've stayed away from you for months. Doesn't that count for anything?"

"Yes, but you haven't given up, have you?"

"I can't. I *must* and *will* have you for my dance partner."

"*Just* a dance partner?" she asked in a suspicious tone.

"If that's all that's on offer."

"It is."

"Then I accept, but, you understand, I'll always want more."

Daisy sighed at this. "I'll never be able to give it to you."

"Why not?"

"Because…because I-I've only ever been with a woman," she blurted, blushing.

Anton raised his eyebrows. "If you've only ever been with a woman, then how do you know you won't like being with a man?"

At this, Daisy's jaw dropped. "Are you saying that a woman has to go with a man to be sure that she prefers women?" she snapped.

"No, of course not. I'm just asking you, very poorly, to have an open mind."

This calmed Daisy somewhat, and she settled back into her seat. The waiter arrived to take their order, and this interlude eased the tension further.

"Don't you find me attractive at all?" Anton asked after the waiter had left.

"You're very handsome, as you know."

"That's not what I asked. I asked if you found me *attractive*. One can find a person handsome without finding them attractive, and vice versa."

She hesitated, then opened her mouth as if to answer but closed it again, and an expression of confusion appeared on her face. She looked so vulnerable, my heart went out to her. Anton seemed satisfied. "You don't know *what* you want, *lille blomst*," he told her softly.

He took pity on her then, and sat back and started talking of the performance. Gradually, with the help of wine and the change of topic, Daisy relaxed and began chatting enthusiastically about the production.

When the meal was over, he again walked her to her apartment building and watched her go inside. Then he headed over to his own block, his hands in his pockets, whistling off-key.

\*

Daisy was soon promoted to soloist. She cried when she phoned Charles and Beth to tell them the good news, and I could hear Beth's excited shrieks through the handset. They promised to visit again soon so that they could watch her perform. She was twenty-two.

Ben joined the choir at his church and ran another marathon, raising even more money for his charities. This time he finished two minutes faster, and I couldn't have been prouder of him.

Kate was spending more time with John, who remained single. He was in his sixties, and not in the best of health after suffering a mild stroke.

Patrick could usually be found in the Amazon. Puna was aging gracefully, but I know that he was concerned about the lack of modern medicine. The tribe relied on the medicinal plants that they could forage in the surrounding rainforest, which were gathered and administered by the women, but they were no substitute for western medicine.

My fiftieth birthday came and went, and I spent some time reflecting on what my life would have been like if I'd lived. I would, perhaps, have grown-up children of around Daisy's and Teddy's ages; I'd have made it to Head of Department at school; we'd have visited New York regularly to watch Daisy perform; Ben may not have needed to turn to alcohol.

Or maybe I was imagining a fairytale. Perhaps life would have been a struggle, with my uncertain mental health and Ben's drinking fated to always cast shadows over our life; perhaps, like Olivia, we would never have been able to have children. The possibilities were endless. It made my head spin to think of all the 'might have beens'.

Kate and Patrick joined me on the Moon, and I received birthday hugs and kisses from each. We sat discussing what we'd be doing if we'd lived.

"I'd be in my mid-fifties. I like to think I'd have encountered Puna, somehow, but it's very unlikely. So I'd probably be on my fourth wife, a twenty-two-year-old model, and rich as Croesus, and driving a Ferrari," Patrick told us, with a twinkle in his eye.

Kate giggled, and I rolled my eyes at him but smiled.

"What about you, Kate?" I asked, nudging her.

"I'd be in my early sixties. I'd be enjoying being a grandparent."

I smiled at this. Poppy was pregnant with her second child, and Sam's first was due any day.

"How's John doing?"

She sighed. "He's lost a lot of confidence since the stroke; I think it made him feel vulnerable. He's still struggling with concentration and his short-term memory isn't great. Poppy and Sam are doing a super job of keeping an eye on him, but their lives are so busy, there's only so much they can do. If I was there…"

She didn't need to finish the sentence; Patrick and I

understood completely.

One of the worst things about being able to see our loved ones without being able to communicate with them, was that we were so helpless when they were in need. Ben's alcoholism, Puna's fever, and now John's stroke, all had made us feel desperate to intervene, to do something, anything, to show our love and support. But all we could do was watch, and pray.

## Chapter Forty-Seven

A week later, John had another stroke. It was much worse this time. He suffered complete paralysis of one side of his body, and his speech was severely impaired. Fortunately, Sam was with him when it happened and so he received medical attention straight away. Kate was beside herself.

I sat with her in the hospital, holding her hand and watching over him as he slept. One side of his face had dropped, and he suddenly looked much older than his sixty-odd years.

John stayed in hospital for several weeks and his programme of rehabilitation commenced while he was still an in-patient. Physiotherapists helped him to begin the process of moving again and strengthening the muscles on his affected side, but it was clear that he abhorred his helplessness. There were times when tears would slip out of his eyes, and the staff would gently talk to him about the hope of recovery.

One day, after a particularly difficult session of physio, he lay in bed staring blankly at the wall. Sam arrived for a visit and showed him a notepad and pen he'd brought him so that he could communicate more easily. John ignored it and Sam, who could obviously tell that his father was in a despondent mood, chatted lightly about his day in an attempt to bring him out of himself.

When it was time for Sam to leave, he leaned forward and tenderly kissed his father on the forehead, before patting his shoulder and telling him that he'd be back the next day. For a few minutes after he'd left, John continued to lie staring at the wall. There was a crack in the paintwork, long and spidery, and I wondered if he was studying that, or if he was looking at something else entirely, something inside his mind. Then he seemed to remember the notepad and pen and picked them up with his good hand. He gazed at them for a while, before awkwardly removing the pen's lid and starting to scrawl slowly on the pad. Kate was leaning over him from the side, her blonde hair hiding her face as she tried to make out the message.

"What's he writing?" I asked her curiously.

After a moment, she turned to me. Her eyes were moist. In a wobbly voice, she said, "It says, 'I want to be with Kate'." And her face crumpled.

\*

Time passed. John was eventually released from hospital and continued to be supported by carers and physiotherapists in his home. Kate rarely left his side, and Patrick and I would visit her regularly. The love with which she watched over her husband, the quiet patience of her vigil, often brought tears to my eyes.

Occasionally, I would manage to persuade her to take a break. For a complete change of scene, we travelled to places we hadn't yet visited. Venice stands out as one of the highlights. We drifted along the canals in a beautiful gondola, observing the sunlit architecture of the Venetian houses; toured St. Mark's Basilica with its opulent, mosaic-covered interior and Byzantine treasures; and explored the Doge's Palace, which was once the political heart of the city. Our breaks did Kate good, and she would return to John re-energised.

\*

Charles, Beth and Teddy flew over to New York to see Daisy in her first solo role. After the show, Anton once again spent time chatting with Teddy about his degree, and this time it was Daisy who invited him along to the restaurant. He seemed to have accepted that their relationship would be that of friends, for now, and Daisy had relaxed significantly in his company, often laughing at his colourful humour.

Patrick, of course, was disappointed at the lack of drama. "That little love story was one of my only forms of entertainment," he whined one day while we sat in the auditorium watching the company's rehearsal of *Swan Lake*.

"He may win her over yet," I said thoughtfully. It was clear to me that she did find him attractive, but felt incredibly confused by it.

He grunted, but said no more. We watched the dancers tell the story of Princess Odette, the Swan Queen, who was cursed to only appear in human form at night. Only the hope of Prince Siegfried's love could break the spell, but the evil sorcerer, Baron von Rothbart, tricks him by transforming his own daughter, Odile, to look like Odette. Siegfried declares his love for Odile, and dooms both himself and his true love to death.

"Why do these ballets always have to be so tragic?" Patrick muttered as the performance reached its finale.

"They don't *all* end in tragedy," I told him.

"Romeo and Juliet, Giselle, this…" he listed, gesturing towards the stage.

"Sleeping Beauty, Coppélia, Cinderella…" I countered.

"Hmph!" he uttered, disgruntled.

"It reflects life. Sometimes there's joy and a 'happy ever after' and sometimes things just don't work out."

"But it's supposed to be *entertainment*," he insisted, with a bewildered look.

"It is, in its way. Audiences want to *feel* something; it doesn't matter if it's pleasure or pain. They want to be transported to one extreme or the other. It takes them away from the mundanity of their own lives."

He considered this, his head to one side. "They should be grateful for the small things in life. Feeling the wind in their hair, the sun on their skin, the scent of a flower, the taste of fine food, the touch of a loved one. All the things that *we* used to take for granted."

I sighed in agreement at this, and thought of all the things that I missed. The smells: hot coffee and bacon first thing in the morning; freshly cut grass, sweet and heady; my mum's lightly floral perfume. The tastes: that first burst of flavour on the tongue – of smooth chocolate, or tangy salt and vinegar on chips, or the tart dryness of a glass of white wine. The touches: the grainy texture of sand between my toes; the softness of a new pillow; the warmth of Ben's arms around me. Small pleasures, small sensations, but the loss of them… my God it was one of the worst parts of dying.

Being a ghost is a half-existence. We can see our loved ones, we can hear them, but we can't interact with them. We can see the world, we can hear it, but we can't smell or taste or feel it. For the first time in a long time, I fully realised what I had lost.

Patrick must have seen the emotion on my face then, because he put his arm around me and I leaned into him. We sat silently in the empty theatre for several minutes, until I decided it was time to check in with Kate and John.

I found them in their local park. Sam was pushing John along the paths in his wheelchair and chatting good-humouredly about his new role as a father, while John listened and grunted at some of Sam's stories.

It was early summer and the grass was lushly green; the flower beds were bursting with colour; the sun was shining warmly in a soft blue sky; and John and Sam wore only their t-shirts.

Kate and I trailed behind them, chatting about our most recent excursion to the south of France. We had transported ourselves onto a yacht, where both of us found the vast openness and the rhythmical *hushing* sound of the sea soothing to our souls. *If only we could have smelled its briny scent, and felt the splashes of the cool waves on our sun-kissed skin,* I thought. *It would have been perfect.*

I sighed, and the walk soon came to an end. I kissed Kate goodbye and headed off to see Ben, who was helping an elderly lady from the church with her gardening. His gloveless hands were covered in dirt, his nails filthy, and I remembered how much he enjoyed the feel of soil on his bare skin. He was planting marigolds, removing them from their pots, shaking out the roots and placing them carefully into small holes that he'd already created. Their bright, warm yellows and oranges reminded me of sunshine. Ben looked relaxed, chatting companionably with his acquaintance as he worked.

I stayed with him until sundown, the stillness of the day and the simplicity of the chore lulling me into a semi-dreamlike state as I lay on the grass with my hands behind my head. *How many days would we have passed like this?* I wondered. *How many days of peace and tranquillity, performing mundane tasks in perfect contentment?* Many, I decided. Many.

## Chapter Forty-Eight

Another year passed, an uneventful one except for the sad passing of Ben's mum. Her ghost form did not remain. I attended the funeral in Spain with Ben, who encouraged his dad to return to the UK. Phil refused; he was settled in Benalmádena, had friends there, a life. We stayed for a few weeks, until Ben was sure that his father would cope on his own, then returned home.

The rest of the year was peaceful. I again enjoyed observing the slow changing of the seasons while I watched over my loved ones. In September, in the last days of the summer heat, and just as the leaves were starting to hint at changing from green to their more mellow autumnal colours, Daisy's hard work finally paid off when she was promoted at last to principal dancer. Her first role was that of Juliet in Prokofiev's version of *Romeo and Juliet*. Anton was to be Romeo. I remembered the first time they had danced together, and the kiss that the performance had ended with, and knew that they would create an amazing chemistry on stage.

I was right. As soon as they began rehearsing together, sparks seemed to fly between them. It was like no performance I'd ever seen before; there was something magical about the fluidity with which they moved around each other, the way they gazed into each other's eyes.

Daisy trusted Anton completely, and he lifted her with ease and grace. In total harmony, they seemed as one being. With Daisy at his side, Anton shone as never before, her darkness contrasting beautifully with his fairness. And with Anton as her partner, Daisy blossomed into everything she was capable of being.

The opening night received rave reviews, and suddenly Anton and Daisy were the talk of the town. Interview after interview was requested and, when Anton revealed his unrequited love for her in one of them, the ballet world went wild.

Daisy was less than pleased. "Why did you do it?" she hissed once the interview was over and they were alone backstage.

"He asked, I answered," he replied with a shrug.

"You could have *lied*," she pointed out in exasperation.

"What for? Only good can come of it. Audiences will be flocking to see poor, lovelorn me mooning after you as Romeo, knowing that in reality you, unlike Juliet, resist me at every turn."

Daisy rolled her eyes, her lips pursed. "That's manipulative."

"That's *marketing*," he corrected. "Besides, I'm not ashamed of how I feel about you. Why would I hide it?"

She didn't have an answer for this and turned her back on him and started gathering her bag and jacket ready to leave.

"What are you going to do with yourself until tonight's

performance?" he queried.

"Why?"

"I thought we could spend the afternoon together."

"Don't you spend enough time with me as it is?"

He cocked an eyebrow. "I can never get enough of you."

Daisy sighed. "I was going to go for a walk in Central Park, maybe grab a coffee on the way."

"Sounds good."

With no further protest, they left the building, side-by-side. The street outside the theatre was busy with people going about their business. A siren could be heard in the distance. New York was never quiet. They walked in the sunshine under a pale sky filled with skyscrapers and pearlescent clouds, and talked companionably about company life.

After grabbing coffees-to-go from an artisan delicatessen, they strolled into Central Park South and began meandering around the paths of the over-eight-hundred-acre lush oasis. The park was a wonder of green serenity nestled in between the bustling Upper West and Upper East sides of Manhattan.

Daisy and Anton spent hours wandering through elm-lined avenues, rolling meadows, flowering gardens, over uniquely-designed bridges and past glassy lakes and ponds. Topic after topic was discussed, and the sound of their laughter could be heard often. Passers-by would look at the attractive young couple who were so engaged with each other, and smile.

At one point, about half way through the afternoon, Anton took Daisy's hand in his. At this, Daisy rolled her eyes at him but smiled, and Anton beamed cheekily. The rest of the afternoon passed companionably in this manner.

After the walk, they returned to Daisy's apartment building. They stopped outside the entrance, and Anton kept hold of Daisy's hand.

"What?" she asked in bemusement as he stood looking at her without releasing her.

"Do you think you'll ever grow to love me?" he asked quietly, an earnest look in his eyes.

Instead of answering immediately, Daisy put her hand on his shoulder and went up onto her tiptoes to place a soft kiss on his cheek. "Perhaps," she murmured, and then, without looking at him, she pulled away from him and hurried through the door, which another resident had just opened. Anton stood gazing after her, a look of surprised, hopeful pleasure on his face.

That night, as the audience gave them a standing ovation, Anton kissed Daisy again. This time, she linked her arms around his neck and returned it, and whistles and cheers erupted from the spectators.

From that point on, they were inseparable.

*

"Yes!" Patrick punched the air when I told him that Daisy and Anton were officially an item. "A happy ending. Thank feck!"

I laughed. "You're a big softie, really. Aren't you?"

"Shh! Don't tell anyone – you'll ruin my street cred," he said in a stage whisper.

We were sitting cross-legged on the Moon. I outlined the

walk in the park, the conversation in front of Daisy's building, the kiss at the end of the performance, and we sighed together wistfully.

"I wonder if I'll ever get to kiss Puna," Patrick uttered after a while.

"Why wouldn't you?"

"Well, from what you say, we only have a few seconds with our soulmate in this form before we go to wherever it is that we end up. What if we then transition to a form where we're not able to touch in that way?"

I thought about this. What *did* we become in Heaven? "Perhaps we become something *other*, something *more*, something we can't even envision, where mere kisses pale into insignificance," I suggested.

He quirked an eyebrow at me. "Kisses become insignificant? Doesn't sound like Heaven to me."

I huffed, mock-annoyed. "Here I am trying to be all-all *profound* and everything and you just joke!"

"Who's joking?" he asked, all wide-eyed innocence.

"Hmph!"

He nudged me, and we linked arms good-naturedly and began to discuss other things: John's slow recovery; Kate's patient vigil; Daisy and Anton's glittering future; Teddy's dreams of working for Formula One; and Puna's routine life in the village.

"You should see her gut a wild pig," he said in an awed voice. "I'd hate to get on the wrong side of her."

I shook my head in amazement. Patrick hated the sight of blood. "I have no idea what you two have in common."

"Our spirits," he shrugged, and I felt a warmth flood my chest. I smiled at him and he smiled back.

Kate popped up in front of us then. She looked panic-stricken. Patrick and I jumped to our feet.

"He's had another stroke," she told us shakily as she wrung her hands, and we rushed to her side to offer what comfort we could. As one, we vanished, and reappeared in an ambulance, its sirens blaring. John lay, motionless, on a stretcher, and a tearful Poppy was by his side juggling the grizzling baby and her confused toddler.

Sam met them in the ambulance bay. He took one look at John and said to Poppy, "Call Eric and ask him to collect the kids. You need to stay."

Patrick and I supported Kate as we followed John into a medical bay and watched the doctors do their work, their expressions grave. When they were finished, Poppy and Sam were allowed inside, and the news was quietly broken that John was unlikely to survive. After tearful reactions, they sat together silently, their hands resting on their unconscious father.

"Do you want us to go?" I asked Kate quietly as the minutes slowly ticked by. We were standing facing the bed.

"No," she answered, without taking her eyes off John. "I'd like you to be here."

"Then we'll be here," Patrick reassured her, and I nodded in agreement.

John took his final breath within the hour, and Sam reached for Poppy as it became apparent that their father was gone. The sound of their weeping was all that could be heard as John's ghost appeared in front of Kate. All signs of his stroke had vanished, and he stood staring at his wife with so much love, so much joy that my whole body trembled to see it. He reached out a hand and touched her cheek, and Kate leaned into it, smiling softly. Patrick and I held hands, spellbound, and within a few more seconds, they vanished.

Moved beyond words, we left Poppy and Sam to grieve. We reappeared on the Moon. Patrick was too full of emotion to sit still, and he paced around restlessly, blinking back tears. I allowed mine to flow.

After a few minutes of this, he scrubbed at his face and came and settled down beside me. He raked his hand through his already-dishevelled hair and spoke.

"You'd described it to me, what it's like to see someone pass, but I'd never imagined it was so…so…"

"Moving?"

"Yes! I feel like I've experienced an earthquake, and the whole world has shifted around me, never to be the same again."

"It's life-changing," I agreed. I remembered how I had felt after my first time of witnessing the reunion of soulmates, Kim with her husband, Ray, and understood Patrick's feelings exactly.

We were quiet then, each lost in our own thoughts. Perhaps he was wondering, as I was, what it would be like when our own soulmate passed. Would we talk of our love, like Dean and Susie, or would we say everything that needed to be said with a touch, a look, like Kate and John? Would there be surprised confusion, or acceptance in their eyes?

"I'll miss Kate," Patrick broke the silence to say.

"Me too," I sighed.

"There's only the two of us left now."

"Mmm."

"We'll be driving each other mad," he smirked, and I chuckled quietly. Then, more seriously, he added, "It'll be lonely for the last one of us that's left."

This sobered me. I thought of having to spend days, months, years without my ghost friend; no one to talk to, no one to interact with, to laugh with, to cry with. Patrick must have been thinking along the same lines, because he took my hand in his and we sat staring sombrely at the Earth together.

## Chapter Forty-Nine

More years passed. They were busy years, happy years. Daisy and Anton became a world-renowned partnership, often travelling to other countries as guest performers with other ballet companies, to huge accolades. Ben was well and truly settled into the life of a confirmed bachelor; he worked, he ran, he attended church services and events. Barney was his closest companion, but he still saw his old friends, and of course, Frank and Vicky. Teddy entered the graduate programme for a Formula One racing team, and Charles and Beth couldn't have been prouder of their two children.

Patrick and I divided our time between our loved ones and travelling. We saw the Taj Mahal, situated next to the Yamuna river, its ivory marble gleaming majestically in the sun; we explored the ruins of Machu Picchu high up in the slopes of the Andes, with its more than two hundred granite structures; we ventured into the Skaftafell ice cave, which was surrounded by the beautiful volcanic landscape of Iceland, its gorgeous blue ice seeming to glow with its own internal light.

We travelled back in time again. Ancient Rome filled us with wonder; we witnessed the violence of gladiator battles in the Colosseum in the second century AD, and the excitement of chariot races in the Circus Maximus. In Ancient Greece we watched theatre performances and the first ever Olympic Games. We were astounded by how advanced the Ancient Chinese were; they invented gunpowder, porcelain, cast iron, paper, the magnetic compass and many other items, and they were expert astronomers.

We observed battle after battle in different times and places. We saw great discoveries and joined intrepid expeditions.

Each era taught us something new about our history, our world and human nature. As a species, we were capable of great innovation, great feats of organisation and courage, great love, but we were also capable of destruction, a thirst for power, cruelty.

Patrick and I lived a thousand lives due to our travelling, and we never grew tired of it, but our favourite time and place was always in the present, at home, with our loved ones.

\*

In the year that Ben turned sixty, his father died. Once again, I accompanied him to Spain and remained with him as he arranged the funeral and said his final goodbye to his last remaining parent. The cycle of life was turning. I thought about how each generation left its own mark on the world, their ripples spanning out to affect the next, who would in turn create their own, which would then influence the lives of the ones who came after. We could only hope that the ripples were kind.

That same year, Daisy and Anton retired from performing.

They were in their thirties, the age when ballet dancers tended to call it a day, and wanted to start a family. They were to become much-sought-after choreographers.

I watched their final performance, *Giselle*, and cried when they received their standing ovation at the end of it, as did Daisy. Even Anton seemed to have moisture in his eyes. The company threw a party for them, and there was much dancing and laughter. *It's not an ending* I thought *but rather the beginning of a wonderful new chapter in the book of their life together.*

As I watched them hug their friends and colleagues goodbye, for now, I wondered how easily they would adapt to being out of the spotlight after so many years of unremitting adulation, and was grateful that they had each other to lean on through the transition.

Needing a much-deserved break after so many intensive years, they were to take a vacation in Florida before commencing their new role. It was a holiday full of relaxation, fun and love. It made me recall the holidays I had taken with Ben, when we would lie on sun loungers next to each other, reading or resting, while the waves lapped at the sand. He'd often reach across the small gap between us to touch me – a stroke of my heated skin, a squeeze of my hand, sometimes a kiss, as if he couldn't go too long without giving in to the need to feel me, to connect with me in some small way. I smiled at the memories.

On their return to New York, Daisy and Anton threw themselves into the business of choreography, working for both their old company and many others around the US and the rest of the world. They were innovative and bold, unafraid of challenging the status quo, and were soon established as the team to approach for companies that wanted to try something new and different.

During this time, they got married. It was a small, simple ceremony at the City Clerk's Office, with only close family and best friends in attendance. I wept as they exchanged their vows, as did Beth, and even Charles had to wipe away moisture from his eyes.

They waited two years before they began trying for a baby, and Daisy fell pregnant within a few months. Her hands shook when she held the positive test out to him one morning, and Anton's smile lit up the room. Of course, I cried. They were tears of pure joy.

It wasn't an easy pregnancy; Daisy suffered from terrible morning sickness in the early weeks and the gruelling routine of their new life of being always on one aeroplane or another exhausted her. But she tried to remain cheerful, and Anton was always by her side, nurturing, supporting, loving her.

Things changed when the baby came. The labour was difficult and resulted in an emergency caesarean section; Daisy's milk didn't come through properly and she resorted to bottle feeding, something she'd been dead set against. The baby, whom they named Rose, was colicky and fretful, and Daisy became anxious and rarely slept. Anton took as much of the burden off her as he could, but he was away a lot, fulfilling their contracts and continuing to earn a living for them.

Charles and Beth flew over to meet their granddaughter and tried to help, but eventually, they had to leave.

"We could employ a nanny," Anton suggested, after waving his in-laws through airport security, but Daisy stubbornly refused. I could tell that she saw it as a failure in herself that her baby wouldn't settle as easily as her friends' infants had.

*She's always excelled at everything she's tried to do,* I thought, *and now that she can't control things by sheer force of will, it's affecting her confidence. Being a mother is a whole new role, and she doesn't have the choreography to follow. It must be so bewildering for her.*

Rose would only sleep if Daisy held her, or pushed her in her pram, and Daisy soon had dark shadows under her eyes. She struggled to have any time for herself, even showering was difficult, and she was continually beating herself up for not doing a better job.

"You're doing amazingly," I told her gently one afternoon as she sat on the couch with a teething Rose and cried. "They don't call it the hardest job in the world for nothing." But of course, she couldn't hear me.

Anton returned from Europe later that day. He took one look at her and tossed his bag to the side and reached for the two of them. Then he took Rose from Daisy's arms and ordered her into bed. Instead of protesting as she normally would, Daisy complied immediately. She was exhausted. She had almost reached breaking point.

For five days, Anton took charge of the baby, and Daisy got more rest than she had in the previous five months put together. He persuaded her to see their doctor, who diagnosed post-natal depression and prescribed anti-depressants, which she accepted with reluctance, her expression clearly doubtful that they would help. However, it was soon time for Anton to leave again.

"Do you want me to cancel?" he asked her, with a line between his brows.

"No, I'll be fine," she insisted, and it did indeed seem that she was somewhat refreshed and had a new determination about her.

"Ok, *lille blomst*, but call me if you need me and I'll drop everything and come back."

She nodded, and he lifted his bag and kissed her and little Rose, and then he was gone.

When he'd left, Daisy unceremoniously threw the medication in the bin.

"Right, my lovely," she said to Rose in a sing-song voice, "we are going to have a fresh start." And she prepared the changing bag and headed out to a mother and baby group.

## Chapter Fifty

Daisy was an incredible actress, she had to be to perform the roles that she had so well, however I could see past the too-wide smiles, the forced jollity, the over-the-phone reassurances to Anton and her parents that everything was okay.

"Rose is great; we're doing great," she would say firmly.

In reality, she was soon struggling again with lack of sleep; she tried transitioning Rose to solids, with little success; she was frustrated, and felt guilty; she cried often but just kept going, and going, without asking for help.

The parallels with my own depression were obvious: the perfectionism, the self-blame, the unwillingness to accept help, the aversion to taking medication, the refusal to admit that anything was wrong. My own anxiety level spiked as I witnessed the runaway train that was Daisy's mental state.

Charles and Beth returned to New York. Initially, they fell for Daisy's performance, however, within a few days, they began casting each other worried looks and whispering quietly to each other about the best course of action to take. They tried talking to her, to no avail.

"There's nothing wrong," Daisy insisted, picking up a grizzling Rose and rocking her absently. But she looked exhausted.

They called Anton and expressed their concerns, but assured him that they would delay their return to the UK, at least until his current contract ended, and that he needn't come home.

In the end, they decided to just take charge. Charles would send Daisy to bed at eleven p.m. and would stay up all night with Rose resting on him as he watched television with the subtitles on, then he would sleep in the day. Beth supported Daisy with weaning, and her patient perseverance and suggestions of new flavours to try eventually paid off.

Daisy seemed torn between relief at getting the help and guilt at needing it. *The psychology of new motherhood is very complex,* I realised. *You have to suddenly get used to a helpless little person being completely dependent on you, night and day, at the same time that it can feel like you lose your identity as an individual. You're trying to learn a whole new skill, which is supposed to come naturally to you, at the same time as suffering from sleep deprivation. You're expected to feel only unconditional love, but instead your emotions can be mixed – your instinct is to nurture, but you may also feel guilt, frustration, resentment.* My heart went out to her, and not for the first time, I wished I could help.

Daisy became very quiet, almost withdrawn. She began to spend a lot of time lying on her bed, sleeping or staring up at the ceiling expressionlessly, leaving Charles and Beth to care for baby Rose.

Charles gradually managed to transition his granddaughter

into her cot at night by placing her into it once she'd fallen asleep and then returning to pat her reassuringly when she woke up – which occurred frequently at first and then less and less often. The first time she slept all the way through was a breakthrough moment, but Daisy barely reacted when he shared the news.

The only event that she bestirred herself for was a daily walk with her mother, which Beth insisted upon. They would stroll through the busy streets of the city and into Central Park, with Beth doing most of the talking. Daisy seemed to prefer to silently take in the beauty which surrounded her. It was early autumn, and the sun was low enough in the sky to highlight prettily the golden browns and russets of the leaves which were in the process of drifting lazily to the ground. It was Daisy's favourite time of year.

One day, Beth was bedridden with flu and Charles was out shopping for groceries, and she suggested weakly that Daisy undertook the walk without her. I watched as she complied, gathering her coat and the changing bag, strapping Rose into the pushchair and heading out of the apartment.

She seemed distant as she did this, as if in a trance-like state. I hoped that the walk in the fresh air would invigorate and enliven her.

They made it to Central Park and strolled around the paths for the best part of an hour. Occasionally, a passer-by would smile at the mother and child, but Daisy walked on, oblivious. At one point, Rose bucked about in her pushchair, as if she wanted to get out. She started crying, but Daisy didn't react, and eventually she cried herself to sleep, her little face pink, her cheeks tear-stained.

Still in a trance, Daisy turned towards one of the gates and proceeded to exit. I frowned when I realised that it wasn't the gate that she usually used; this one was further from the street where they lived, but I conjectured that she was going to skirt around the perimeter of the Park and get home that way.

The streets in New York are laid out in a grid pattern. I watched, confused as Daisy made towards one of the roads which ran perpendicular to the park, and screamed when she stepped out into the traffic.

Cars swerved, horns blared, but Daisy kept on walking, slowly pushing Rose down the middle of the busy road, looking straight ahead as if hypnotised, her face expressionless. People on the street stopped and stared, with horrified looks on their faces; a woman shouted for someone to get help.

A cab screeched to a stop in front of them, and the driver jumped out as if to remonstrate. However, he took one look at Daisy and his demeanour changed. He started to gently cajole her off the road. He ignored the horns and shouts of other drivers, and guided her into the back of the vehicle, then unclipped Rose and lifted her out of the pushchair before handing her in to her mother. Daisy took hold of her as if she was on auto-pilot. The pushchair was quickly folded up and shoved into the boot, and then the driver carefully pulled back out into the traffic.

Shaken, I thought myself into the cab and quietly thanked God for sparing my niece and her daughter. Within minutes, the taxi pulled up in front of a hospital.

Inside, the driver led Daisy to a seat and then spoke quietly to the lady on the front desk. Then he returned to

Daisy and asked who he could call for her. Tears had started to leak from her eyes. Shakily, she pulled up Charles's number on her phone and handed it over.

The cab driver walked off as he pressed the call button and soon began murmuring into the handset. He returned within a few minutes and stayed by Daisy's side until Charles arrived.

Rose was still asleep when he entered the waiting area, looking around frantically until he spotted his daughter and granddaughter. He rushed to Daisy and gathered her into his arms. Quietly, she began to sob.

"Oh, my darling, my darling. Don't worry, everything's going to be okay," he said soothingly as he stroked her hair.

The kind cab driver stayed until Daisy was called through by a doctor, and Charles thanked him profusely for his help. I stayed with Daisy throughout the difficult consultation, and then as they waited for a bed on a psychiatric ward to become available.

When it was ready, Charles had tears in his eyes as he kissed his daughter goodbye and promised to visit every day. We watched as she was led away, the doors swinging shut behind her.

Finally, Charles broke down. He sat himself down and wiped at his face with a tissue. *What must it do to a parent,* I wondered, *to know that their child had gone into such a dark place that they didn't care if they lived anymore?* I thought of my own parents' grief at my death then, and I sat down beside my brother wiping the tears from my own eyes.

When Charles had composed himself, he returned to the

apartment with a now-wide-awake Rose. I watched as he broke the news to Beth, who had been asleep when the call came through. They sat on the bed and wept together, until Rose interrupted with a cry for attention.

## Chapter Fifty-One

Daisy was in the hospital for over three weeks, during which time she was placed back on an anti-depressant, which she swallowed every morning under the supervision of a nurse. Anton had flown back immediately, and he and Charles, and then Beth when she'd recovered from her illness, would visit daily. Teddy called regularly and offered to fly over, but Charles told him to stay put – there was nothing that he could do. The whole family were in shock, and all felt inconsolably guilty for not realising the extent of Daisy's depression.

*

Life on the psychiatric ward was calm and orderly, for the most part. Many of the patients had been admitted because of suicide attempts, several had a personality disorder, a couple were experiencing psychosis, lost in the confusing thoughts of their mind. "It was like a transparency of sights, sounds and sensation had been placed over the real world, so that I could see and hear things that other people couldn't," one woman, who was on the road to recovery, later told Daisy in a shaky voice. "I was seeing patterns everywhere, and believed wild conspiracy theories. It was terrifying."

As I listened, I ruminated on the frailty of the human mind, and speculated about its capacity for self-deception. Both depression and psychosis could be described as an altered state of perception, a change in the thought process caused by chemical imbalances.

I was glad that the woman, who was called Anna, was safe, and receiving treatment.

For a week, Daisy mostly stayed in her room. She slept a lot, and only ventured out to collect her meals before returning to the comforting isolation of her small hideaway. In the second week, however, she started to gradually spend more time in the homely lounge. She would sit nursing a warm drink, listening as some of the other patients chatted quietly, and as some, like Anna, shared their personal stories. She watched television. She started to read a novel – a gentle family saga. Several times, she spoke to a counsellor, and she had regular sessions with her consultant.

Over the weeks, Daisy's mental strength returned and she came more and more out of her shell. She became on friendly terms with two of the other patients, one of whom had fresh cuts along her forearms, covering old, criss-crossed scars, and they would chat and play board games together. By the time she was ready to leave, she was much more the Daisy of old.

On the day that she was discharged, she exchanged tearful farewells with her new friends and promised to stay in touch, to form their own support group, always available on the phone to listen and empathise. Anton arrived on the ward to collect her and they shared a long embrace. When they pulled apart, Anton's eyes were moist.

On the journey home, he kept up a steady flow of light conversation, and Daisy listened and answered quietly. She seemed lost in thought. I wondered what she was thinking of. Suddenly, she spoke.

"I understand my auntie Daisy better now," she said softly, and Anton's expression saddened. He reached across the gap between the seats and placed his hand over hers. I waited to see if she would continue, but she lapsed back into silence. I blinked away the tears that burned in my eyes.

Her greeting of Rose was everything that I'd hoped for; for the first time in months, Daisy beamed as she spotted her daughter and rushed to lift her into her arms. Rose babbled and grabbed her face, and everyone laughed.

Anton took some time off work, and Charles and Beth stayed for another month, supporting Daisy as she gradually gained confidence and took over the role of main caregiver once again. Rose was sleeping and eating well, and the new routines meant that Daisy got plenty of rest at night and woke refreshed for the day.

Her bond with her daughter grew, and for the first time, it was clear that she was enjoying motherhood. She took her medication religiously, and each week that passed saw her relax more and more into her role. By the time Charles and Beth prepared to leave, she was ready to manage alone.

The farewell scene at the airport was filled with emotion. It was clear that Beth wished she could stay longer, but she knew that it was important for Daisy to be independent, to embrace her role fully. Daisy hugged her parents tightly, and thanked them quietly, but fervently, for their support.

"Call us if you need us and we'll drop everything and come right back," Beth told her, and Daisy promised that she would.

\*

Daisy never returned to that dark place. Over the next few years, she blossomed in her role, and even when Rose underwent difficult stages, like teething, sleep regressions, and the terrible twos, Daisy coped and got them both through. Was it always easy? No. But did she ever come close to giving up again? Never.

*Bad times never last,* I thought as I watched them playing happily on the swings one day. *They always pass, and sometimes we come out the other side strengthened, like steel forged out of fire. If only I had accepted help, perhaps I too would have re-emerged stronger.*

But it wasn't meant to be.

\*

During this time, Ben retired and filled his time with more community and charity work. He mentored others through the AA and raised more money for his charities. He was tireless in his efforts to help others.

Ben worked so hard in his endeavours that he was unexpectedly awarded a British Empire Medal. He blushed when he accepted it from an official in the church hall one evening during a meeting, and I whistled and applauded with everyone else, my heart full. I couldn't have been prouder. *Good things CAN come out of bad* I thought, remembering the days of his illness and how I'd despaired of him ever recovering. *Patrick was right – difficult phases pass. The big picture is what's important.*

Ben was invited to a Royal Garden Party at Buckingham Palace, and, at Vicky's persuasion, he reluctantly attended with her as his plus one. The weather was glorious that day, the gardens showcased to their best in the sunshine. Flowers burst out of the beds, well-tended and colourful. The Palace loomed majestically in the back drop, its grandeur breath-takingly imposing.

When the King arrived and the military band commenced the national anthem, tears swam in my eyes as I realised just how far Ben had come since those dark days of his addiction. And when the King circulated among the guests, and he briefly got to meet him, standing tall and proud in his new suit, my heart swelled so much I thought it would burst out of my chest.

## Chapter Fifty-Two

A few years later, I was sat with Patrick on the Moon one night, telling him with enthusiasm about Rose's wonderful progress in ballet class, when it became apparent that he wasn't listening.

"And then an alien landed and beamed her off into Space," I finished. Absently, he nodded. "Patrick!"

"What?"

"You haven't been listening to a word I've said!"

He opened his mouth as if to protest, then shut it, a sheepish expression appearing on his face. "Sorry."

"What have you been thinking about?"

"Puna."

"Is anything wrong?" I frowned.

"No...well, it's just, I wonder whether she's lonely sometimes."

"The tribe are very close-knit."

"Yes, but I mean, lonely for a *companion*, you know, someone *special*."

I thought about this. "If she'd wanted one, she could have got one easily. The men used to flock around her."

"Yes, but she's older now. I wonder if she ever regrets not settling for one of them."

"She's not the type to 'settle'," I told him, and it was true; Puna was fiercely independent.

"But she could have had children. You've seen how she is with those in the tribe – she's a natural."

"She's always seemed content to me," I shrugged.

"But the way she stops sometimes and looks up at the sky – the way she was when I first saw her. It's very…wistful."

"Have you ever thought that she could be thinking of you?"

He frowned. "But she didn't know of me back then."

"No, but maybe she was thinking of the *idea* of you in those days."

Patrick was quiet for a few moments, then a soft smile broke out on his face. Contented, he wrapped his arm across my shoulder and squeezed gently. "You always say the right thing, Beautiful Nosy Girl."

I laughed. "It's been a while since you called me that. And anyway, it's been a long time since I could get away with being called a 'girl'. I'm nearly seventy, for Heaven's sake!"

"You don't look a day over twenty-six," he responded, and I rolled my eyes.

*

Later that year, I lost my Grumpy Irishman. Puna was foraging in the rainforest one day when she tripped and cut her leg on a rock. Unconcerned, she washed it in the river and then continued on with her day, her long, silver hair shining as she moved in and out of the dappled light of the lush forest.

However, what started as a seemingly innocent gash soon became a festering, pus-filled wound. Back in the settlement, her leg became red and swollen, blisters formed around the site and she developed a fever. Her niece tried to treat her with medicinal plants, but there was no improvement.

"I think she's got sepsis," I told Patrick quietly, as we stood next to the pallet where she lay in her hut.

"She pulled through the other fever; she can pull through this one," he answered firmly.

I shook my head slightly, but said no more. It was clear that Patrick was trying to stay positive.

Puna's breathing soon became erratic. She became confused and eventually lost consciousness, her eyelids fluttering sporadically. For a while, only the sound of her fast breaths filled the hut.

I sat against the wall, cross-legged, and watched as Patrick paced. I thought of all the times we'd talked together, laughed together, cried together. I thought of the adventures we'd had, through time and Space. I remembered the sense of companionship, back when Dean and Kate were still around, and how there had never been any room for loneliness, not when there were such good friends to talk with. I thought of the years to come, and braced myself.

"She's getting worse," Patrick frowned after several hours had passed without us speaking.

"She needs antibiotics," I told him gently.

He raked his hand through his hair. "I always worried about something like this happening." His shoulders slumped, and he came and sank down next to me.

"How do you feel?" I asked, gazing at him.

He thought for a few seconds. "To be honest, I feel completely mixed. I'm sad and anxious, of course. I don't want her to suffer and I don't want her to go before her time. But then, at the same time, I'm also nervous and excited about meeting her, and about what will happen next."

I nodded, but didn't reply for fear of my voice betraying me, however his thoughts seemed to lead him in the same direction as mine.

"And I'm worried about leaving *you*, Beautiful Nosy Girl," he said, nudging me with his elbow, and I couldn't prevent a small sob from escaping. He wrapped his arm around me and I leaned against him, our heads touching.

"We've had some good times, haven't we?" he asked softly.

I nodded, swallowing. "The best."

"I can't imagine what all those years would have been like without you."

"I like to think we'll meet again."

"Me too."

\*

Puna passed the next day. When her ghost appeared in front of Patrick, she gazed at him, her eyes shining, and he tenderly reached out and cupped her face. He leaned in and kissed her lips softly, the way he'd always dreamed of, and she sighed with contentment.

And then they were gone.

\*

The loss of my Grumpy Irishman was like a gaping hole appearing in my life. For the first time since my death, I truly felt isolated. I still hung around Daisy and Ben, but for a while, I felt no joy in watching them live their lives. There was no one to talk to, no one to share good – or bad – news with, no one to sit next to on the Moon, as we watched the Earth slowly rotate below us. I also missed the physical contact – a hand held, a hug received. I became a lone traveller again, only this time, the journey was through life, or rather, existence, and it wasn't through choice.

Loneliness, I realised, is like a form of torture. You can see people all around you, going about their lives, laughing, interacting, but you're not a part of it, but rather, you're on the outside looking in. Of course, being a ghost, this was inevitable, but when my friends had been around, voyeurism had seemed more like a hobby, a study in human nature between interactions. Now it was more like a prison sentence.

Over time, I did get used to being alone, and I would look back fondly on the days when Kate, Dean, Patrick and I would share our thoughts, feelings and experiences with each other. I took to talking to Ben more. Even knowing that he couldn't hear me, it brought solace to be able to express myself aloud, and imagine what he'd say in return.

He was well into his seventies by this time. I'd watch him going about his life: his daily walks with Alfie, the rescue dog who'd taken the place of Barney a few months after he'd passed; his weekly attendance at AA meetings and church; his tireless efforts to support community projects.

    He still visited the rose garden annually, with Charles, Beth and Vicky. They would stand in a circle around my eroded memorial, grey heads bowed, each saying their own private prayers. And then they'd go for a meal and a catch-up, which inevitably became a session of wistful reminiscence of the days of their youth.

## Chapter Fifty-Three

Time seemed to slow down. Days felt like weeks; weeks felt like months; months felt like years. I tried to appreciate what a privilege it was to be able to watch over my loved ones, but without anyone to share it with, it was difficult to feel anything other than my loneliness. I spoke to Ben about it one day.

"I think I miss having someone to laugh with the most," I told him as I sat next to him while he relaxed, drinking a cup of tea in the sun-trap of a garden. Since he'd retired, he'd spent a lot of time working in it and it was now an oasis of explosive colour. Little rockeries were dotted here and there, and he'd added a small pond which contributed to the tranquillity of the scene. The trickle of a small fountain sounded in the background.

"You used to make me laugh so much," I continued. "People thought that you were quiet, but you never were with me." And then, "I always liked the fact that Anton could make Daisy laugh. It was a good sign."

We were quiet then, and I studied Ben's hands. They were the same strong hands that had held me, all those years ago, in joy or sorrow. Now age spots bloomed across the wizened skin. I looked down at my own hands; the skin was smooth and blemish free. The pink nail varnish looked as fresh as the day I'd applied it. I lay my left hand next to where his right rested on the table. The contrast was striking.

"And yet, in my head, I'm an old lady, with the experience and perspective that comes with age," I told him. "I wouldn't fit in with the twenty-somethings of today. I'm of a completely different time." I thought of the modern music that I sometimes heard; the way that technology had moved on; the new language that young people used, and felt all of my seventy-six years.

I remembered watching Daisy grow up, as I was now watching fourteen-year-old Rose, and realised that I had related much more to the former, simply due to there being only a single generation between us. I was two steps ahead of Rose, the equivalent of a grandparent, and I felt the difference.

I sighed and watched as Ben drained the last of his tea and placed the cup down with a clank. He stood and slowly began making his way around the garden, pulling up the odd weed that had snuck into the beds seemingly overnight.

*They're so tenacious,* I thought. *Stronger than the more-showy plants that seem to cry out for attention, their large colourful heads almost begging to be noticed. No, weeds are the survivors, the ones that dig in and refuse to yield, returning again and again. It's like people. Some shine brightly but fail to take deep root; some go unnoticed but quietly persevere.*

"It's like you and me," I said to Ben. "I'm the flower that soon wilted under pressure, and you're the plant that survived, no matter what."

\*

It was soon after that conversation that I first noticed a change in Ben. It started with small moments of forgetfulness, which I initially put down to the normal aging process. He would forget where he'd put his keys, for example, and at times, he couldn't remember the names of familiar items. He also began to struggle to retain new information from conversations with others.

After a few months, Frank, who was still fit and sprightly at the age of eighty, began to look concerned whenever he spoke to him. Vicky, too, realised that something was wrong when he forgot to meet her for a coffee for the second time in a row.

At first, Ben dismissed their concerned questions, insisting that he was fine. However, when he nearly burned the house down when he forgot that he'd left something cooking on the stove, he got a fright. Vicky turned up just in time and spotted the situation.

"That's it," she said firmly. "You're going to the doctor."

Reluctantly, Ben complied.

After questioning him about his symptoms, the doctor referred Ben to a specialist. I waited anxiously as the weeks passed, growing more and more concerned for my soulmate. On the day of his appointment, Vicky accompanied him as he underwent an assessment which tested his memory, orientation, language and visuo-spatial skills; had a blood test; and then when he was sent for a brain scan. A few weeks later, they attended a consultation to receive the results.

Vicky held Ben's hand as they walked back to her car. It was a blustery day, reminiscent of the weather on the day of my funeral, but they didn't seem to notice. I had a hollow feeling in my chest as I followed them through the busy car park and thought myself onto the backseat.

The twenty-minute drive back to the house was completed in near silence. Vicky made a couple of attempts to start a conversation but gave up when she received only one-word responses in return.

When they pulled up on the driveway and Vicky undid her seatbelt, Ben abruptly told her that he wanted to be alone.

"But thank you," he added more softly. "For everything."

She nodded. "I'll be here whenever you need me."

Then she watched as he headed into the house, waiting for him to enter before pulling away, her shoulders slumped, her face saddened.

In the house, Ben made straight for the kettle. His hand shook as he pulled out the box of teabags and began the process of making some tea. Soon the bubbling sound of the water boiling filled in the silence. The final click signalling that it was ready seemed strangely loud, creating a sense of finality. The water was poured into the cup, the rattle of the teaspoon sounded, and then Ben was removing and squeezing the teabag before adding milk. I watched this procedure as if hypnotised, then followed him into the back garden, robot-like.

Ben sat down at the patio table, sipping at the hot liquid for a few minutes while he stared into space. I walked around, looking at the multitude of plants that he'd painstakingly nurtured without really seeing them.

*So much life,* I thought. *So much freshness and colour and vitality. But it was all destined to fade away, to make room for the next generation in the cycle of life.*

When I heard the rustling of paper, I returned to Ben's side.

He placed the leaflet that the doctor had given him on the table before him, and spent time smoothing it out as I stared at the words printed on the front: *Living with Alzheimer's Disease.*

Tears pooled in my eyes as I thought of the future that faced my love. Slowly, he would lose more and more of his memory. Slowly, he would lose his independence. Slowly, he would lose his identity.

And he would do this alone, without a partner to care for him.

The tears spilled over as I watched him read the information. He must have been struggling to concentrate though, because he started over more than once, running his finger back to the start of the line several times as he frowned.

*Will he remember me?* I wondered as I watched him, my aching heart full of love for the man I had spent fifty years waiting patiently for. *Will he look at my photo in the frame and recognise the girl that he'd loved from the age of seventeen? The girl that he'd intended to marry? Or will I become as a stranger on the street, a nameless face, just one of a crowd of unfamiliar people who mean nothing to him?*

"What are you thinking about, sweetheart?" I asked as he finished reading and sat staring into the distance. Was he frightened? Anxious? Frustrated? I had never wished that he could hear me more, that I could talk to him gently, reassuringly, telling him that I was here for him, that he would never be alone. I would hold him, and tell him how precious he was to me, how death was not the end, but a new beginning, a beginning without illness or grief, a beginning filled with hope, and love. The beginning of forever.

## Chapter Fifty-Four

Nothing much changed over the next few months. Ben managed to continue to live independently, with the support of his friends and the introduction of a care plan. Charles and Beth checked on him regularly. Daisy phoned often from New York and Teddy came to visit him one Sunday and they spent the day working in the garden together and discussing Formula One. Teddy's relative youth and energy was refreshing, however the contrast with Ben's slow, stooped figure was unsettling to observe. He had aged so much in the preceding few years.

I was touched when they hugged as Teddy was leaving and he promised to help him in any way that he needed him to.

"I mean it, Uncle Ben," he said, looking earnestly into his eyes, and Ben nodded, his eyes filling at the title that had been bestowed on him for the first time ever.

Frank and the rest of Ben's church friends were invaluable, often helping him with routine tasks like shopping, and Vicky assisted him with managing his finances. The gratitude that I felt for our friends and family was indescribable. Nothing would have been worse than seeing him struggle and there being no one to help him. It made me feel less anxious about my own inability to support him.

*

Inevitably though, there came a time when Ben deteriorated enough that it became clear that he needed more professional help. Another year had passed. One day, Ben was in the supermarket, alone, when he arrived at the checkout and couldn't remember how to pay. He looked confused, and stared blankly at the middle-aged cashier as she repeated the total to him. A young man huffed behind him in the queue. Unseen, I glared daggers at him.

Fortunately, the cashier was a kind woman who seemed to have experienced something similar before. Ignoring the impatient customer, she talked Ben slowly through what he needed to do and then asked if he needed her to phone anyone for him. He shook his head stubbornly and collected his bag, then headed off towards the signposted exit.

Concerned, I stayed by his side as he stepped out into the car park and paused to look left and right, frowning. When he headed right, my anxiety level spiked. Home was in the opposite direction.

Ben walked the streets for the best part of an hour, becoming more and more confused and agitated. He had wandered into a less than salubrious neighbourhood. The houses looked tired and grey, graffiti adorned walls, litter scuttled along in the gutters, a group of hard-eyed teenagers hung out on a street corner.

"Ask someone for help, darling," I begged more than once, wringing my hands and starting to panic, but of course, he couldn't hear me.

Then, all of a sudden, he was crossing a road more than a mile away from the house, when he tripped up the kerb. He landed hard, the sound of his head smacking off the pavement loud on the quiet road. I cried out in alarm.

A man who reminded me of Dean in appearance had been waiting at a nearby bus stop, and he rushed over to help, as did a middle-aged lady who was passing by on the opposite side of the street, her worn face concerned. Together, they got him sat up and leaned him against a garden wall. Blood was pouring from a nasty cut in Ben's head, and when they spoke to him he didn't reply.

The lady who lived in the nearest house must have seen the commotion, and she bustled out with some fresh tissues and they got Ben to hold them against his head. She was an older lady wearing a floral dress beneath an apron, her manner gentle and motherly. When it became clear that Ben couldn't talk or stand, they agreed to call for an ambulance.

My heart was in my throat as I rode in the back with him, seeing his bewilderment and pain. He looked like a lost little boy, completely vulnerable, and I silently thanked God for the kindness of strangers.

In the hospital, he started talking, but he was clearly very confused. He kept asking about Barney, who had been dead these many years. They stitched up his head and gave him pain relief, and kept him in for observation and assessment. He stayed in for over a week, while his care plan was revised and a package of professional support was arranged so that he could continue living at home.

From then on, Ben received twice daily support from

professional carers, who ensured that he bathed and dressed, took his medication and ate well. Again, his friends rallied around and made sure that he had help and company at other times of the day. Rarely a day went by without Vicky, Frank or another member of the church popping by to chat or fetch him some shopping.

Gradually, however, he began to forget who some of them were. When this happened, they would patiently remind him of their name and that they were there to help, and Ben would relax and let them into the house, although he'd have to repeatedly ask their name throughout the conversation.

"It's Frank, Ben," or "I'm Vicky, remember?" they would say, attempting to hide their concern.

I worried that rogue traders could take advantage of him, and every time there was a knock at the door, I would rush to see who was there, only relaxing again when I recognised the visitor.

However, there were still times when Ben was alone, and his gradual deterioration became more evident. Once, he got up in the middle of the night and got dressed, then sat in the living room looking lost and confused. I sat beside him, my hand on his, and talked soothingly to him. It was all I could do.

"I'm here, my darling. I'm always here," I repeated softly, achingly.

Another time, he became paranoid that someone was stealing from him when he couldn't find his wallet. He grew agitated and wouldn't settle until a frazzled Vicky found it in the refrigerator.

Soon, inevitably, his team were discussing residential care.

\*

Ben had stayed in the house that we had lived in together for all of those years. Even though the décor and furnishings had changed, to see everything boxed up and carried away, leaving only an empty shell behind, was heart-breaking. When the last box was carried out, I took a few minutes to walk around, paying a final visit to each room, remembering events and conversations which had taken place in them from decades before.

Here was where Ben had proposed to me after preparing a candlelit dinner, his hand shaking as he held out the ring but his eyes shining brightly with love.

This was where he used to sit while I took a bath so that we could talk about our plans for the future.

That was where our bed was, where we would make love past midnight before falling asleep entangled in each other's arms.

Endings are always so difficult; they signal the passing of time, of a phase in our lives, never to be repeated. I wondered how long it would be before Ben forgot his long life in the house that we'd shared.

The last thing Ben did before leaving was to hand Alfie over to Frank, and a tear slipped down his cheek.

He took only a few possessions into his new home, which was called Clearview, including the photograph of me. It was the first thing that he unpacked, placing it in prime position on his bedside table.

Ben was in his eighties by now, but I could still see the boy

I knew in his watery green eyes as he gazed down at my smiling face, his expression soft.

I explored Clearview thoroughly on that first day. I checked that the staff were professional and caring, even when no one was around to witness. I examined for cleanliness and hygiene practices. It was a relatively modern home, no signs of wear and tear, and I finished my tour feeling satisfied.

\*

Although I was saddened that Ben had reached the stage of needing full-time support, it was a relief to know that he was safe, that he would be cared for, that he would eat three good meals a day, that he couldn't wander off or get himself into dangerous situations. Of course, he was often confused about where he was and who the people around him were. At times, he was restless and would walk up and down the corridor in agitation, until a member of staff gently redirected him to the lounge, or to his room.

Friends visited, and it was hit or miss as to whether or not he would remember them. He started 'time-shifting', believing that it was a different decade, talking about people and events long gone.

When Daisy, Anton and Rose, flew over to visit Charles and Beth, who were also well into their eighties by this time, I was touched that they made the time to travel to see Ben too. His eyes lit up when Rose entered the room, and when he called her 'Daisy' there was some confusion. Daisy thought that he was mixing Rose up with herself, but it soon became apparent that he thought that Rose was me. She was in her early twenties, and although she had her parents' blue eyes and lighter skin than me, the resemblance was enough.

"Oh, my darling…" I said quietly, as he held Rose's hand and smiled at her. Daisy had tears in her eyes, and Anton was also clearly moved. Rose, who had followed in her parents' footsteps and was now a principal dancer in New York, simply smiled back at him, letting her hand rest in his and allowing him to talk to her about people and places that she knew nothing about. About his parents, about friends from college, about holidays that we'd taken and concerts that we'd attended.

We all blinked back tears when he asked her why she'd left him. "I've missed you," he told her, and I closed my eyes against the pain.

I worried about how he'd react when it was time for them to leave, but I needn't have. Ben eventually tired himself out and his head dropped as he fell asleep in the armchair, breathing heavily. Daisy and Rose took turns to kiss his withered cheek, and then they were gone.

## Chapter Fifty-Five

I had stayed close to Ben since his symptoms had developed – the urge to travel non-existent – but once he had settled into his new life as well as could be expected, I debated whether or not to leave him for short periods. Life in the home was not the most exciting, although I discovered another ghost living there and would sometimes chat with her, but something kept me close-by.

Perhaps it was fear that I wouldn't be there when he eventually passed.

The other ghost was a shy lady called Harpreet, who had died in her late seventies. Having grown up in the same era, we would reminisce about the days of our youth. It was a relief to have someone to talk to again.

Harpreet's husband was called Deepinder, and like Ben, he was living with a form of dementia. I liked the way that Harpreet would sit by his side in the lounge, not talking, just waiting, patiently, for the day when they would be reunited.

She told me that they had met in India, when Deepinder had returned home to visit his family. It was love at first sight, though nineteen-year-old Harpreet's shyness was an initial barrier which he had worked patiently to overcome, and they soon married. She described the wedding to me, the memory as fresh as if it had happened only yesterday: Deepinder's arrival on horseback; the *Anand Karaj*, or ceremony of joy, where marriage prayers were sung; the joyful celebration which followed.

Harpreet recounted the trepidation she felt in moving to England with him, how long it had taken her to settle in to this new, coldly-grey country. The loneliness she had felt when Deepinder was out at work all day. How long it had taken her to build the confidence to start making friends. I thought of my gran then, and what it must have been like for her to leave Jamaica behind and settle, alone, in a foreign land, and my respect for the strong woman who had raised my father and uncle increased even further.

Deepinder's dementia was more advanced than Ben's. He was less mobile than Ben, who still paced up and down the corridor restlessly, especially at sundown. I walked with him at these times, hoping that he could sense my presence on some level, and find comfort in it.

Eventually though, the pacing became a shuffling gait. Unsteady on his feet, he fell on two occasions, and inevitably, like Deepinder, he began to spend much of his time in an armchair in the lounge. Ben's speech also deteriorated, and to all effects he became non-verbal.

Although he no longer responded to verbal input, however, I noticed that he did react to music, and texture. He would smile softly when the staff played songs from our era, and often held a piece of fabric which he'd rub between his fingers as he sat there, hour after hour. It was one of my old bandanas.

\*

Those years in the home with Ben were amongst the saddest and the most poignant. Seeing the man you love reduced in such a way, helpless and completely reliant on those around him, deepens your tenderness.

I had seen Ben strong; I had seen him weak; and I loved him all the more for it.

Alzheimer's Disease is a thief. It steals not only your memories, your independence and your identity, but also your ability to truly *live*, to *experience* the world beyond simple sensory input, to interact with it, to feel joy and the whole tumult of emotions that life offers.

I was strengthened by the knowledge that Ben hadn't truly gone, that he would return to me, whole and well when he finally passed. I knew it, for I had seen it happen to others so many times before – to Kim's husband, Ray, to Susie, to John, to Puna. Kate's ghost had displayed none of the ravages of cancer or chemotherapy; my dad's spirit showed no sign of the weakness caused by his heart attack; my own depression had vanished without a trace, forgotten until I was confronted by it. No, my Ben would return to me. I was certain.

\*

One day, in a rare excursion from the home, I re-visited Patrick's Park. I sat on the bench which had long ago replaced that first one on which we had met, and watched the latest generation of ducks and geese as they fed and squabbled. It was spring, my favourite time of year. I wondered if this was to be my final season of re-birth. Ben had deteriorated so much in the previous few years.

I spent time absorbing the sight of purple and white crocuses blossoming neatly amongst the blades of fresh green grass; the cheerful yellow of the daffodils as they bloomed with health; the pale blue sky dotted with candy-floss clouds.

Dog walkers passed by, whistling happily and tossing balls to their eager canines; children threw crumbs to the birds and squealed with delight.

*All this life,* I thought. *All this energy and pleasure and hope.*

The children held my attention the most. Their unblemished, fresh-faced eagerness for the future was like the anticipation of summer arriving after the spring of their youth. The possibilities that they faced were endless; they could become anyone they wanted to, be anything they desired – they just had to reach out, and grasp it.

Then their autumn would follow, hopefully one of comfort and familial warmth, before their winter finally arrived. But this season was not the end, no, it would cycle back again, to a new generation of grandchildren, raising their faces to the pale sun and carving their own path through the seasons of their lives.

And what of the grandparents? After the winter passed, what was waiting for them? For me? For Ben? I knew that it would not be long until I discovered the answers.

I returned to Clearview then; I'd been away for nearly an hour, but the change of scene had done me good. However, I discovered some news which both saddened me and filled my heart with warmth: Deepinder had passed and he and Harpreet had gone to that special place that awaited us all.

Once again, I was without a companion to interact with.

The following months crawled by, and Ben gradually became more and more bed-ridden. He became incontinent, struggled to swallow the food that was fed to him, and lost weight. He was completely reliant on his carers. Much of his time was spent sleeping, and, as I watched his eyelids fluttering, I wondered if he dreamed, and if so, of what. If he did dream, were they flashes of memory, confused and fragmented, to be forgotten as soon as he awoke? Or were they clear and vivid, stories of another life, another world from which he was reluctantly pulled upon awakening?

I never left his side in these final months of his life. I would sit with my hand on his, chatting about events from our lives, from his life – the good times, the happy times. I told him over and over again how proud I was of him, for everything he'd achieved, and how he'd pulled himself out of the darkest times of his life. I shared my love and promised that we would be reunited, soon.

*

It was winter when Ben finally passed. A light blanket of snow covered the ground that was visible from the bedroom window, its stark whiteness brightening the small room. It was the sort of light that always made me imagine Heaven.

Vicky and Frank had visited earlier that day, themselves becoming increasingly infirm. They had sat at his bedside for over an hour, talking quietly about their families and the church's activities. When it was time for them to leave, Frank patted Ben's shoulder, and Vicky leaned over him and kissed him on his sunken cheek. The tender gesture brought tears to my eyes.

I watched them leave, and then settled back into my silent vigil. After some time, the doctor arrived and, after examining Ben, she spoke sombrely to the staff in the corner. It was nearly time.

I sat on, watching his chest rise and fall, rise and fall, until it rose no more. I stood up, my heart in my throat, and my beautiful Ben appeared in front of me. His pale green eyes were clear. Standing tall, he looked at me in shock before an expression of the utmost joy lit up his face. He trembled, and reached out to touch me but withdrew his hand, uncertain. I took it back and placed it on my cheek, where I held it with my own. He smiled and raised his other hand so that he was cupping my face tenderly and we were gazing into each other's eyes.

"Daisy," he murmured, and in that one word he managed to express the whole entirety of his love for me.

"My Ben," I breathed.

And then, we vanished.

By the same author also available on Amazon:

*The Strange Imagination of Pippa Clayton*

Printed in Great Britain
by Amazon